The Paris Rental

Rachel Keerey

Icasm Press

Published in the United States by Icasm Press

First printing edition 2026.

ISBN: 978-1-942318-58-3

For David

Since content warnings can be spoilers for twists that take place in the book, they can be found at the bottom of this page.

I will tell you that no animals will ever be harmed in any of my books. I can't say the same for humans.

The Paris Rental is a work of fiction but was inspired by real-life events, and I'll give you a hint here.

It's all in the family name.

Content advisory: This book includes descriptions of assault, and non-explicit references to sexual assault, death of a child, and child sexual abuse.

My Hotel Peculiar

Today, Father told me a family secret.

The secret is very old and very special. That's why I'm going to start keeping a journal.

I'm writing everything down, because I want to remember this time in my life. I'm writing in English, because it is good practice. Also, because everyone in my family must speak and write perfect English. We are French, but Father demands we master this second language. He says English can be useful.

I'm calling my journal "My Hotel Peculiar," because a British woman called it that. She was from Wales, I think. They have a lot of castles there.

The woman meant to say Hôtel Particulier, but she said it wrong.

She wasn't very smart.

When I asked Mother why she said it that way, she told me the lady was in her cups. I didn't understand, so she told me it meant she had too much Champagne which made her silly and confused. As I wrote above, not very smart.

And Maison Marteau is a bad place to be if you're not smart.

Many things have happened here, in my family home. Special things most people would never understand.

But this is another reason I want to keep a record of our story. My story. So, I'll start over, from the beginning. The beginning for me, at least.

I'll start with the party.

1

The mansion stands in darkness by the time we arrive. Pulling to the curb, the cab stops outside of a wrought-iron gate—tall, solid, and topped by sharp spikes. The kind intended not only to protect, but to intimidate.

White mist floats over cobblestone streets, the weather wet, chilly, and moody, despite the fact it's early April. This time of year, I expected love-and-flowers-springtime Paris, not dark-and-gloomy-raindrops Paris. But I'm not in a position to be choosy, just grateful I have a place to stay. Somewhere quiet and private. Somewhere secret.

Because I'm here to disappear.

It's only for a few weeks. That's what my agent Lin assured me when she made the plans. *The apartment is private, secure, and no one will look for you there. You can lie low until the drama dies down.*

Not any kind of everyday drama, either, but the kind that taints anyone it touches.

Two days ago, I was living out my lifelong dream, having finally landed a major role in a movie of substance. After years of minor parts and character bits, I felt accomplished. Worthy of admiration. Gaining notice and respect from people in the business.

Now those same people are asking questions. Wary. Suspicious. And looking sideways at anyone involved with the project.

Closing my eyes, I fight off the nausea, the sick sense of ruin sitting heavy in my gut.

Only twenty-seven, and my career could be over.

At least I've got Lin on my side. As soon as the story broke, she flew into action. She used her Hollywood connections to find me a place to stay and handle my travel, then insisted I come to Paris.

All to protect me from what's exploding back home—a nasty, finger-pointing, career-killing scandal.

And she doesn't know the half of it.

"This is where you're staying?" The cab driver's words jar me. Beneath his accent, something sharpens his tone. I can't be sure, but it sounds like concern.

He turns to me, his brow wrinkled, as if instead of a mansion, he's brought me to the morgue.

"Maison Marteau?" I ask. Maybe I'm at the wrong address.

"*Oui*," he says and frowns, gaze lingering on me a moment too long before sweeping back to the grand mansion. After a moment, his shoulders drop and he sighs. "Thirty-five euro."

I have the fare and his tip ready, so I hand the money over.

"*Merci*." With a shake of his head, he gets out and opens the trunk, mumbling in French the entire time.

I don't understand his words or his reaction, and I'm too beat down to care. After traveling for over twenty hours, jet lag weighs heavy. My back aches and my clothes pinch, somehow tighter than when I put them on.

Outside, the air is a quick, cold slap, and I wish for a coat, but there was no time to go home for clothes. I flew straight from the movie set in Savannah, like the rest of the cast and crew. All of us scurrying away before the press showed up.

Ducking from the drizzle, I rub my arms and scan the area. Beside the mansion sits a dark open space, only leafy trees and lights in the fog. Maybe a park? A place to sit with coffee and read a book? A Parisian dream.

I imagine the photos I could take for social media—the Eiffel Tower, walks along the Seine, world-famous museums.

But no. There will be none of that. No identifying landmarks. No tagging a location. No hints to the world that I even exist.

Because no one can find out where I am.

Black bars impede my view of the mansion, but lights glow inside the massive building. Stunned by its size, I count one, two, three—no, *four* stories altogether, a row of dormer windows gracing the top.

The windows look tiny compared to the gargoyles, hunched and glaring on every corner. The stone sculptures squat along the roof—gaping jaws, curling tongues, demonic horns.

Their sinister faces raise bumps on my skin.

The cabbie brings my bags and sets them at my feet. "*Merci*," I say, the French strange on my tongue.

He gives one sharp nod and climbs into the car.

As he drives away, I move to a keypad by the gate. Lin sent me the code in a text, so I check my phone and punch in the numbers. Four beeps, followed by a click and a soft slide of metal.

Easing the gate open, I enter, shut it just as gently, and inspect the place I'll be living. The mansion stands strong, like a stone goliath. Making me feel especially small.

Subtle lamps highlight beige stone, ornate masonry on every surface. More scowling faces grace terraces and doors, mostly raptors, lions, and wolves.

All of them baring fangs.

In front of the main entrance, two sets of steps curve up like wings, leading to a set of heavy, wooden doors. And on one side a portico, the arched doorway framing darkness and the glistening spray of a fountain.

I can't help staring. Luxury like this isn't in my budget, and I only got this place through Lin's connections. I don't know who owed her a favor, but it must have been a big one.

The residence isn't typical, even by Parisian standards. A *hôtel particulier*. Not a hotel, as the term suggests, but a private home and historic urban mansion, occupied by a single family.

Despite the opulence, there's an emptiness about the place. A desolation.

A soft, rhythmic sound carries from somewhere nearby, coming from inside the gates. The light tapping of footsteps.

Tensing, I stand still and listen.

Maybe it's the late hour or the foggy night, but a shiver of apprehension prickles my back.

I glance around but don't see anyone, only covered walkways and entrances, all made of stone. An echo chamber.

The sound could have come from anywhere, so I listen again. Nothing but the murmur of distant cars.

A shudder shakes my body—from cold, exhaustion, my finely frayed nerves. The fog and stillness don't help, reminding me of an old black-and-white movie. The kind with evil creatures lurking in shadow.

Or on the roof.

I ignore the looming gargoyles, chastising myself for being so jumpy. Sleep deprivation. That's all. I just need to crawl into a nice, comfy bed.

Two wings extend from the main building, housing apartments at each end. Both are identical and have their own entrances. The one to my left glows softly, as if a lamp is burning in the interior.

But the one opposite—the one that's mine—waits in darkness.

Around the corner, I should find the door and a key under the topiary. Their word. Not mine. No ordinary potted plant for these folks.

I don't know who owns the apartment, and any communication with them must go through Lin. Including the basic information she passed on to me, details about where to go and how to get in. And a single rule.

Don't disturb the family.

Which is why the clatter and clunk of my luggage makes me cringe, the sound echoing off the high walls. I slow down, trying to be quiet as I follow a paved walkway from the courtyard. I round the corner and pass under a giant tree, branches rattling in the wind overhead, clacking together like dried bones.

No light burns above the door, so I deposit my luggage on the stoop and turn on my phone's flashlight. Kneeling, I tip the planter to one side and shine the light underneath. Nothing's there. I tip it the other way.

Still no key.

No way to get inside.

Dread drags its teeth up my spine, then takes a cold bite between my shoulder blades. *No, no, no.*

Desperate, I pick up the pot, ignoring the sharp leaves jabbing my cheek. I set the topiary aside and scan the grainy stone with my light.

Nothing.

The key's not here.

"This can't be happening." My arms fall to my sides, and I stare at the locked door. What am I supposed to do?

The thought of knocking on the main house's door sends my system spiraling.

Don't disturb the family.

I'll call Lin. She'll be able to—

Footsteps again, echoing through the night.

The same rhythmic sound as before, rising from the cobblestones.

Only this time it's loud.

This time it's close.

"Hello?"

No one answers.

But someone is here.

Panic ratchets, rising in my chest.

Whoever it is, they're coming this way.

And all I can do is stand frozen as a dark shape rounds the corner.

2

Light from the courtyard hits at a new angle, casting the person in silhouette. A woman. She stops when she notices me, lifting her hand to one side of her head, then the other. Removing earbuds.

I release my breath in a rush, my heart kicking three times before it slows. She didn't answer because she didn't hear me.

"You must be Brooke," she says, her French accent light and smooth. She hurries down the walk—petite, thin, angel-blonde hair. "Sorry, I forgot to put the key out. I hope you haven't been waiting."

"No," I say, the last dregs of tension draining from my body. "Perfect timing, actually."

"Oh, good." She puts a hand to her chest as if she's as relieved as I am. "My aunt called from California earlier and asked me to leave it for you. It's her place," she adds, jutting her chin toward the building.

Closing a hand around her earbuds, she shoves them into a pocket and lifts her other hand. A key dangles. "Since I'm here, why don't I give you a tour?"

Before I can answer, she grabs one of my bags, steps around me, and unlocks the door. She leans in and lights flicker on around us.

In the light, I can tell she's young, maybe late teens or early twenties. She wears a short ivory dress with boots—stylish and chic but with a waifish vulnerability. Young, friendly, energetic.

And not at all what I expected from *the family*.

"So, you are here on vacation?" she asks, stepping back to let me in.

"Yes." I press my lips together, hoping this is the last of her questions.

The last time I'll need to lie.

The thought of being recognized used to thrill me. It was a goal, a daydream, to have someone stop me on the street or come over at a restaurant, tell me they saw me in a movie. And *remembered* me.

But since the movie fell apart, I keep my head down and wear sunglasses.

Either the young woman doesn't know who I am, or she's too polite to bring it up. "You've come to the perfect city for a vacation, so *bienvenue*. Welcome," she clarifies in English. "I'm Luci." She spreads her arms and spins. "And this is Maison Marteau."

Her game-show exuberance lifts my mood. More at ease, I pull my suitcase through the small foyer to an entrance hall.

I cross the parquet floors, my head spinning with wonder. Reds and wood tones dominate the décor, heavier and more old-world than the pristine white of so many Parisian homes.

A grandfather clock ticks away time in one corner. In another, an antique globe rests on a stand. A lavish staircase, a grand piano. Every corner holds proof of wealth. The air even smells rich—clean but with the slightest hint of something floral.

Mom would love this place.

Mom.

The thought of her is a bubble that fills my chest.

Then bursts.

Grief seeps into the space left behind. I can't call my mother and tell her about the mansion. I can't send her pictures of the opulent rooms. Not anymore.

Not since November.

I squeeze the suitcase handle until my fingers sting. "The apartment is bigger than I expected." My voice comes out as a whisper, strained by the punch of emotion and bittersweet memories.

But Luci doesn't notice my distraction as she points to a doorway. "The kitchen and dining area are through there. And over here..." Switching directions, she passes me and walks toward the curving staircase.

I'm right behind her when she stops by the wainscoted walls and puts her hand on the dark wood. "This used to open into a main hallway, but my grandfather closed off the ends of each wing. He wanted separate living spaces for more distant relations. The hallway in back is the same."

Now I can make out two floor-to-ceiling panels that blend with the walls, and I spot the handles. "Oh, doors?" I push down on the brass levers.

A small wrinkle forms between Luci's brows. "Don't worry. They lock on both sides."

"Sorry," I say, my default method for handling conflict. Smile and apologize, filling my voice with a people-pleasing tone. An instinct hard-wired at an early age.

Followed by a compliment to smooth things over. "Your English is perfect, by the way."

"*Merci.*" She beams, pleased by the praise. "English is a Marteau family requirement. We're practically taught from birth."

She studies me from head to toe. "And I love your brown hair and blue eyes. Such an American combination." She winks and tugs lightly on my hair, making her seem younger than I'd thought.

She picks up my bag again and points up the steps. "We'll go this way. The hidden stairs are too narrow."

"Hidden stairs?" I already feel unbalanced by the connecting doors—vulnerable and exposed—despite the assurance of locks.

"An old servant stairwell," Luci says.

The staircase we're on now is the opposite of narrow, and certainly not built for servants. Wide steps and ornate railing, with oil paintings adorning the walls. Grim-faced portraits of people who must be Marteau ancestors.

The clothing and style of the paintings suggest the 1900s, but the colors are deep and moody. Midnight blue, blood red, funeral black. The faces glower down at me, stares piercing and full of disdain.

We reach the second floor, and Luci points out another set of the tall, connecting doors. "My quarters are on the other side, so if you need anything, come here to knock." She whirls with her arm extended. "In front we have a bedroom and *un petit salon*—sorry, I mean a small salon facing the courtyard."

"Don't worry," I say. "I love hearing the French. I only know some basic words, how to thank someone and how to ask for the toilet."

She rewards me with a light laugh. "You'll never have to go far for one of those. You'll find en suite bathrooms in every chamber. One here, one in back, and two on the top floor."

"Four bedrooms to choose from?" I stare up at the plaster ceiling, imagining yet another level. This place is as big as a New York brownstone.

"Yes, but only three are available. One is being used for storage."

She leads me toward the back, stopping to tap on a smaller door. "The hidden stairs are here, a shortcut to the other floors."

She pushes on a wall panel, and a door springs open to reveal a stairway—dim and musty, a cobweb string hanging in the air. "The steps also lead down to the basement, but the door at the bottom is double-locked. I doubt you'll want to go down there, anyway. It's cold and damp and smells funny." She curls her nose. "Gives me a headache."

I imagine a basement the size of this mansion, the endless dark. "That's not a problem."

After peeking into the first bedroom, I move to the one in the back corner. Ambient light outside reveals two windows, one facing the street and one with a view of the park, lampposts glowing through the trees.

"That one is my favorite." Luci watches from a distance.

Flipping on the light reveals a space that's much brighter than the rest of the apartment, with embossed wallpaper the color of ivory. The light shade gentles the space, a feminine quality to balance the heavy furniture.

"I'll take this one," I say.

"Good choice." Luci hovers near the balustrade as if she's ready to go back downstairs. "You must be tired, so I'll leave you to get settled."

She can't know what an understatement that is. I'm more than ready to be done with this day. Actually, the last *two days*. They've been one long, continuous blur, filled with shock and sadness and running and hiding.

But I stifle a yawn and join her for the walk downstairs. Following her to the door, I listen as she reels off local cafés. I try to grasp one or two, but the French names sift right through my weary head.

"Oh, and this is yours." She hands me the key. "I almost forgot."

"Thanks again for letting me in."

"*Bien sûr.*" With a whirl, she turns on her heels and opens the door.

Then she jerks to a stop.

"Ric." She almost spits the name, her jaw clenching. "Why are you here?"

A man stands outside smoking a cigarette—casually facing the door as if he's been waiting. His slicked-back hair is dark, almost black. Like his eyes. In the low light, they're deep as pitch. Lifeless and empty.

Luci hurries down the steps. "Let's go," she tells him, looping her arm through his.

With his unnerving stare locked on me, he responds to Luci in French. I might not understand what he's saying, but the look he gives me exists in every language.

A dirty smirk.

One that rakes over me from head to toe and leaves an invisible trail of slime.

I keep a mask of calm in place, refusing to give him any reaction as Luci pulls on his arm.

He doesn't move. Only stares.

Luci jerks harder, finally dragging him away. She talks to him in a low mumble that sounds scolding. But she's all smiles again when she tosses a glance over her shoulder. "Good night, Brooke."

"Good night." As I watch them walk away, I imagine the doors dividing my apartment from the rest of the house. I imagine Ric standing on the other side.

Testing the lock.

As if he heard my thoughts, he pulls free of Luci's grip.

Facing me, he walks slowly backward, giving me that slimy smirk again. "Sleep well, *jolie fille.*"

A cringe skitters over my shoulders. Because those words I understand.

Pretty girl.

He gives me a wink, and my stomach twists.

Easing back inside, I shut the door. And turn the deadbolt with a solid *thunk.*

3

The jarring sound of my cell phone jolts me from sleep.

Dim, barely light outside. A ceiling looming high above me.

Where am I?

My vision clears, and the room sharpens. Lavish bed, large room, armoire by the wall. The pieces coalesce into a memory.

I'm in Paris. Maison Marteau.

Still groggy, I roll over in the fresh-smelling sheets. I reach out, slapping my hand on the night table until I find it. I don't bother to check the screen. "Hello?"

"Brooke, morning." Lin sounds too alert and awake for . . . what time is it, anyway?

I hold the phone away from my ear to check. Eight in the morning, which means in LA it's . . . I have no idea.

I sit up and rub my eyes. My brain is buried in sand and I'm sifting for clarity.

"I wanted to call," Lin says. "Make sure you got there, got inside all right."

"I did."

"And," she pauses, "no trouble?"

I snap awake. Trouble could mean anything—planes, trains, emotional baggage. But I know what she's really asking. "Nope." I release a breath. "No one recognized me."

"Good. Good." A low hiss comes from her end, and I wonder if she's vaping again. "So, you're settled into the apartment, got all you need."

"Yep."

"How are you doing?"

"You know, staying positive." I try to sound lighthearted, try to convince her of an optimism I don't feel.

"Listen, I know the producers canceling the movie is a kick in the gut. I get it. But with filming on hold, you have time to devote to other things."

"I hope it's not too much time." I don't want to languish until I'm forgotten, waste energy and momentum until I'm written off. Like so many once-promising actors that studios now overlook.

I dread the idea of people saying, *Whatever happened to her?*

The Last Wave was the role I'd been waiting for, working toward for years. A respectable role in a meaningful film, and my supposed big break.

But I've lost it all.

Maybe for a few months. Maybe forever.

"Do you really think I need to stay here for two weeks?"

Lin's low chuckle rasps from the phone. "What, you're not enjoying that swanky Parisian apartment?"

"It's amazing," I say, glancing around. Morning sunlight streams into the bedroom, shining on creamy silk wallpaper and expensive antiques. I couldn't ask for a better hideout.

"Maison Marteau is one step below a palace. And in *Paris*. I mean, I'm living the dream. Right?" More of that fake enthusiasm seeps into my voice.

"But?" Lin says. She knows me too well.

I nibble on my thumbnail. "With everything falling apart back home, being here . . . I don't know. It just feels *wrong*."

Lin sighs. "You aren't the only one who's lying low. Everyone else is doing their best to pick up and move on with their lives."

Except those whose lives *can't* move on. Not in the way they had before. I itch to know what's happening in Los Angeles, but I don't ask about rumors. I don't ask what she's heard.

I don't ask about Mackenzie.

"Lin, do you think . . ." Clouds cover the sun, and the room dims. I pull the duvet up to cover myself. I'm by myself, all alone, yet I feel naked before a thousand eyes. Exposed, vulnerable, powerless. But most of all, I feel judged.

Because that's what guilt does to you.

"Am I doing the right thing?"

A weighted pause falls between us.

After a moment, Lin answers, her tone flat. "You're not asking about being in Paris."

"No."

"Brooke," she sighs, "don't waste time beating yourself up. These things happen."

"Not *these* things," I say. Although they always have.

My mother's words whisper through my head. *Hollywood makes its own rules, Brookie. If you want to get ahead, you have to get along*. An actress since childhood, she raised me to follow her lead, giving guidance and tips I didn't always understand.

Now that I understand, I don't always agree.

Lin's tone is moderated, steady and unyielding. "I've worked with a lot of actors. Talented actors. But you and I both know talent isn't the only thing that counts in this business."

I nod as if she can see me.

"You also need to be smart and play the game. It's not my job to tell you what's right or wrong, but I can tell you the risks."

I murmur a sound of agreement. Even today, Hollywood

masters hold the careers of many in their tight, iron fists. The last thing I need is to put myself in the spotlight, drawing the attention of the silver-screen elite. Wealthy and connected people. Powerful people.

The kind that could crush me like a bothersome bug.

I lean on the quilted headboard and sigh. "You're right. And I appreciate all you've done for me. Honestly, this place is so nice I expect someone to show up any minute and kick me out."

"Nah, don't worry about that. The apartment is almost always unoccupied."

"How does anyone own a home like this and leave it sitting empty?"

"Who knows why the super-rich do what they do?" Lin sucks in hard and blows out. Definitely vaping. "I arranged the lease with the owner's husband. He said his wife likes her privacy, so I didn't ask questions. The important thing is that you have a place to lie low for a while."

"A place with coffee, croissants, and charming cafés."

"Right, well, don't get too used to the good life." An edge of something I can't name lifts her voice. "There's a chance you'll soon be roughing it again."

"Roughing it?" A fluttery sensation builds in my chest before traveling down my arms. "What do you mean?"

She chuckles again. "You should check your suitcase."

The luggage Lin had packed for me before I left. Last night, I only pulled out a few toiletries.

"Hold on." I scramble from the bed and to the suitcase open on the floor. Setting down my phone, I dig through the contents.

My clothes cover two items at the bottom. A thick brown envelope and a large black box. I pick up the envelope, recognizing the weight and feel. A stack of pages that can only be one thing.

A screenplay.

My heart goes weightless, floating higher in my chest. And I'm fully awake now, buzzing from a shot of excitement-fueled adrenaline.

I pick up my phone again. "Lin?" Hope and anticipation lift my voice as I climb back into bed. One leg folded beneath me, I tear open the envelope and pull out a manuscript.

I read the first page. *The Whisper House.*

The title gives me my first clue. Then I notice the screenwriter's name.

My heart drops back down like a lead ball. "What is this?"

"It's a working title."

"It's a *horror* movie."

"Hear me out," she says, using the tone I know better than to argue with. "This film is a great opportunity. Well-written, well-produced, and rumor is, they're talking to Joyce Sandman about directing."

"Joyce Sandman?" The thrill I felt before tries to flutter back to life. A relatively new voice in the movie world, she's quickly become known for films that are both socially relevant and entertaining.

But still.

"I've never done horror. Even in the early days." A time when so many actors take what they can get.

I try to swallow but my throat is dry. "Is this a step back for me?"

"Did Toni Colette take a step back?"

"No, but—"

"John Krasinski and Emily Blunt?"

"Of course not, but those were standout horror films."

Lin's silence is her only reply.

The script sits in my lap, suddenly as heavy as my pending decision. "You think this movie is on par?"

"I absolutely do, and if they get Sandman, this could be as

good, if not better than, *The Last Wave*. And with a wider audience."

Which means more eyes on my face. More people learning my name.

"And it's based on a true story, which always sells better," she says. "Remember all the trouble in Maryland? A supposedly haunted estate?"

"Hmm." I make an affirmative sound as I scan the pages of the script.

"Anyway, it's not an open call. They're only auditioning a select pool of candidates, and you made the list. The black box contains your tripod, ring light, microphone, and an external lens for your phone."

"They want a video audition?"

"In three days."

"Three days?" I sit up straight, mentally running through a checklist. I can do it. I *have* to do it. Because if Lin is right, this could be a lifesaving jolt for my dying career.

"Do you know who else is on the list?"

"I feel good about this, Brooke."

"That's not an answer."

"You've got a blank calendar and a private place to work," she says, still avoiding the question. "A place I made sure you got into, because I thought the environment would be... *inspiring*."

"You mean creepy?"

"Whatever it takes. So while you're in that big old, empty place—like your character is going to be—you need to dig into the script, learn the character, and decide how you can make her yours. This movie has scare factor, but it also has heart. I think it could be big."

"Okay. I hear you." I sigh into the phone and melt into the soft headboard. "A horror movie."

Lin makes a noise in her throat. "Joyce Sandman."

"Right." I remember Sandman's Oscar nomination two years ago, and excitement starts to trickle back in. "Thank you, Lin."

"Thank me by getting the part." She chuckles again and hangs up.

I drop my phone on the bed and flip through the pages, hardly able to believe what's landed in my lap. Literally.

A new script.

Another chance.

Tucking myself in, I turn to the first page and trace my hand over the paper.

My finger stops on the main character's name. "All right, Claudia, tell me your story."

4

Warm light splashes on the bedroom wall. Did I fall back to sleep? If so, good. I needed it. I stretch my arms and legs—relaxed, languorous, and more rested than I've felt in days.

Then memory surges, and my eyes go wide.

The script.

I bolt upright as the early-morning call with Lin rushes back.

My phone sits on top of the manuscript. Both lie beside me in the bed, where I left them when I fell asleep.

Grabbing the bound pages, I run my hand over the title. I recall some of what I read this morning, mostly the opening scenes—good dialogue and intriguing setup—the first hallmarks of an elevated horror story.

I flip to the first page again to refresh my memory, but I only read a few lines before my stomach gurgles. Now that I'm awake, I'm hungry all the way to my bones.

When did I last eat? The cold sandwich on the train? The German salami on rye I barely picked at?

I need a good breakfast. And coffee. So much coffee.

According to Lin, the apartment has been unoccupied for

months, so I doubt there's anything to eat downstairs. But Paris is the land of street cafés. I'll go grab a bite, get my bearings, and then stock up on groceries.

Once I have necessities, I can dive deep into the script.

After one more glance at the title page, I set aside the screenplay. Earlier, I couldn't stop myself from reading, but I need to wait and start over fresh. I should be clear-headed and focused for the initial pass, because I only have a few days to prepare for the audition.

And I need to nail this role.

I make a quick, mental list of all I need to do—read the script, research my character, analyze scenes, choose an outfit, pick a place to film. And that's only the prep work.

Grabbing my phone, I type the list in a note-taking app. Organization and efficiency are key, because I've got no time to waste. This audition could turn everything around for me, and I'm thrilled by the possibility of working with Joyce Sandman.

And yet . . . worry niggles at the base of my brain.

I think of my previous role and the lost opportunity. How could a horror movie measure up to *The Last Wave?* The director once characterized the film as "a meditation on the nature of truth and history."

A description my mother would have loved.

Long after the money dwindled and her fame faded, she maintained religiously high standards. She turned down roles for a variety of reasons—location conflict, required nudity, amateur production, bad script.

I can imagine what she'd say about a slasher movie.

My shoulders tighten in an involuntary cringe. It's true more highbrow scary films have gone mainstream, but the old Hollywood adage remains: horror movies can be where careers are born.

Or where they go to die.

But Joyce Sandman as director? No matter the genre, working with her would be a dream.

Curious, I pick up my phone and type *The Whisper House* into the search bar. I find scant information online, other than a short article listing writers and producers. Not surprising, since production hasn't started yet.

But studios usually make social media accounts for movies. I open Instagram and search the title. Nothing yet. Then I try the screenwriter, but his last post is two months old.

Out of habit, I click the icon for my home feed, scrolling through videos and photos from accounts I follow. A few pictures make me miss sunny California, and one of my cousin's pugs brings a smile to my face.

I scroll a little further and stop, my finger hovering.

A picture from *The Last Wave* fills the screen, a few of the crew gathered on the last day of shooting. Over two hundred likes and forty comments. I waver with indecision.

I want to read what people are saying.

But I'm afraid to look.

Knowing I shouldn't, knowing I'm torturing myself, I click on the post and go to the page. The crew photo is the last one shared. No one has posted since the movie shut down.

It's like the whole experience is frozen in time, all the previous shots of actors on set, the camaraderie and smiling faces. A dream come true for so many.

For others, a nightmare.

My gaze lands on another picture, and I suck in a breath.

Mackenzie and me, arms around each other's shoulders, grinning like fools for the camera.

She's radiant with joy and hope. Unlike the last time I saw her—jaw clenched, eyes haunted, hope ruined.

Regret coils in my belly like a newborn snake.

Where is Mackenzie now? How is she doing? If I texted her, would she respond?

Lin warned me to stay off the grid, explicitly ordering me not to contact anyone in the business. But especially anyone who worked on *The Last Wave*.

Tossing down my phone, I slide from the covers, blocking out any thoughts of Mackenzie.

And the guilt that follows like a shadow.

I take a quick shower before pulling on comfy jeans and a T-shirt. No need to "glam up," since I'm trying to be incognito.

With a frown, I dig in my bag for the ball cap and glasses Lin insisted I bring. Just a precaution. A quick and easy disguise employed by celebrities.

I'm not a celebrity, not on magazine covers, and probably the last person paparazzi would try to track down. There are far more famous people embroiled in the scandal, but it's smarter not to take chances.

Sun brightens the world outside and pulls me to the window. The street in front of the mansion ends at a permanent blockade, metal bollards blocking cars from the park. Only a small section of the park is visible, but I can tell people are out in droves—children playing, a woman reading on a green metal bench, and busy pedestrians on the walking paths.

Everyone's moving. Except for one person. A blonde woman beside a lamppost across the street. Her stiff posture stands out in the buzzing activity. She's rigid, intense, and staring at Maison Marteau.

There's nothing remarkable about her clothes. A black ball cap and jacket with a red and gold patch emblazoned on the sleeve.

But there's something about her body language, the tension and unwavering stare.

She doesn't move. Doesn't glance around. Doesn't check her

phone. She leans casually against the pole, as if she's exactly where she wants to be. Waiting. Watching.

Like paparazzi.

I whirl from the window and press close to the wall. Is she a photographer? A reporter? How did she find me? Lin said she'd handled everything discreetly.

I risk another peek out the window. The woman is still there, still leaning against the lamppost, but her head is turned the other way. No longer fixated on Maison Marteau.

And probably not stalking the B-list actress no one even knows is here.

The quick shot of panic drains to my bare feet. Humility returns, and I rub my face. I need to get a grip on myself. Paranoia's not helpful.

As I grab my shoes, phone, and purse, I shake my head. Paparazzi aren't searching for me. Reporters don't want an interview.

Why would they?

They don't realize how much I know.

5

I slip on my shoes and take the stairs at a jog. On the main level, I walk through the kitchen to the dining room, where the French doors open to the private grounds.

Paranoid or not, I won't risk exiting through the front.

In the sheltered garden, I hurry to the pebbled path, winding through evergreens and budding blooms. When I round a corner, I find a woman standing in silence.

Shiny blonde hair styled to perfection, she wears a navy jacket over a silk blouse. When she sees me, she goes rigid, her gaze narrowing with sharp accusation.

"Hello," I say, frozen in place.

She scowls. "What are you doing here? How did you get in?"

Her scathing eyes travel over me, and I shrink inside my T-shirt, feeling every stray thread of my frayed blue jeans. It doesn't matter if that's how they're designed. Beneath her withering stare, I don't feel fashionable. Only disheveled and inferior.

"I'm...I'm Brooke," I stutter, pulling off the hat and glasses. "I'm staying in the end unit."

My explanation changes nothing. She continues to level me

with a glare. "The gardens are for family." She punctuates every word, each knocking me down an inch.

"I'm sorry." Flustered, I step back, the one and only rule sounding in my brain like a siren.

Don't disturb the family. Don't disturb the family.

Face flaming, I retreat another step, hands up in apology. "I didn't realize."

"Please," a second voice breaks in, "you are welcome to use the gardens." The words carry from behind the shrubbery, and a woman in a wheelchair rolls forward to reveal herself. Much older than the blonde, but equally elegant. Even sitting, her stature is regal, gray hair twisted in a classy chignon.

She darts her sharp gaze to the other woman. "Please, excuse my daughter-in-law. I'm sure Chantal is only surprised." Her voice is smooth as silk, barely catching on the pointed barb.

The blonde stands taller but stares at the ground. I get the sense of an established hierarchy. And Chantal is not on top.

The woman in the chair rolls closer. "My name is Musidora Marteau." Everything about her shouts authority, and I'm certain I've met the mistress of the house.

"Luci said you'd arrived late."

"I did. My flight was rerouted." The heat recedes from my cheeks, but then I remember my suitcase clattering in the courtyard. "I hope I didn't wake anyone."

"Not at all." She lifts her chin and studies me, friendly but appraising. "Will you be with us for a while?"

"A couple of weeks."

At this, Chantal makes a sound in her throat and stalks away, as if sharing a roof with a commoner is too much to bear.

Musidora continues to hold her smile, ignoring the other woman's behavior. "We want you to be welcome and at home." Crossing her hands in her lap, she nods once, as if she's made a decision. "You should join us for dinner. Tomorrow night." Her words offer invitation, but her voice issues command.

I feel like I can't refuse, but the idea jangles my nerves. Dinner means conversation, conversation means questions, questions mean evasion.

Which is a nice word for lying.

"Thank you, but I'd hate to be a bother."

"Nonsense. You'll have a chance to meet the rest of the family." She wiggles her brows. "So no one will accost you if you dare wander in the garden."

I can't keep my lips from turning up at the corners. The older woman and I have a silent exchange, acknowledging Chantal's rudeness without saying a word.

I move closer, holding the hat to my chest like a shield. "Your home is beautiful, and it's nice that you all live here together."

"Oh, yes. Chantal and my son Vincent, their two boys. And Luci, of course."

She doesn't mention Luci's parents, and I don't ask. Instead, I work up a cheery grin. "I'm on my way out for groceries, but I'm glad I got to meet you. And dinner tomorrow, what time should I—"

"Eight o'clock. You'll be welcomed at the front."

"I'm looking forward to it," I say, telling the lie smoothly, like the actress I am. But this family speaks English as if born to the language, and I get the sense nothing slips past Musidora Marteau.

She inclines her head. "Enjoy the city."

As she rolls back to whatever she'd been doing before, I continue on the path, my muscles melting with relief, as if I've passed a test I didn't know to study for.

Dinner wasn't on my schedule for tomorrow, and I hate to give up the time I could be working instead. But I also don't want to offend Musidora. Clearly, she's the family matriarch.

At least I know how to mingle with the privileged few, a skill required to navigate Hollywood. Whether Los Angeles or Paris, one thing holds true.

The rich and powerful are a different species.

The gardens span half the length of the park, but eventually I reach the back gate. More black metal bars but older, the door opening with a creak to a shaded alley.

Stone walls enclose the walkway like a labyrinth, three paths curving in different directions. Children's voices carry on the air, so I let them guide me toward the park.

As I round the outer wall of the mansion gardens, I find a mismatched patch of cobblestones, the stones slightly off-color and more worn than the rest. Ivy trails over most of the wall, but the exposed lower section looks like a metal door.

Where does it go? Does it lead to the gardens? Maybe an old entrance no longer in use?

Curiosity overrides my good sense, and I glance in both directions before easing closer to search the ivy. Pieces of the vines pull away in chunks, leaving roots clinging to the iron.

Instead of damaging the plant, I switch tactics, gently spreading leaves, searching for a doorknob. Instead, I find a metal plate and a heavy padlock. My fingers brush over metal, climbing higher and higher until they bump over a hard rim.

I move aside more ivy, revealing a long, narrow window in the door. I close one eye and peek through.

But there's no garden on the other side, only darkness and the stink of mold filtering from the hole.

The door leads underground.

Stepping back, I rub my nose and exhale, trying to rid myself of the musty smell. Nothing but an old door to an old set of stairs. Probably leading to the basement of the mansion.

Nowhere I'd want to go.

Suddenly chilled, I turn and walk down the path, happy to leave the alley and the mysterious door.

6

Two hours later and the sun has sunk, casting pockets of shade on every street. As I cross the park and head back to the mansion, a cool wind whips through the trees. Two re-usable bags weigh down my arms, bulging with enough groceries for several days.

Along with pens, notepads, sticky notes, and highlighters. Probably more than I need, but office supplies are my secret kink. Other women get excited about jewelry, but I'll take color-coding over karats any day.

Now that I've got supplies, all I need is to find a designated workspace in the apartment. A room with a desk or table, and a comfortable spot to read the script.

As I round the winding trail, I spy the metal bollards rising from the ground. The short poles are my landmark to make a turn, which will take me to the sidewalk in front of the mansion.

Because I am *not* cutting through the gardens again.

Walking with my head down, I don't see the young couple until I'm close. Too close to turn around.

They're loitering near the gates of Maison Marteau. The guy

pivots slowly, repositioning in measured turns. He's holding up his phone. Taking pictures.

When he notices me, he swings the phone in my direction.

Ducking my head, I whip up my hand to shield my face. "Please, don't."

"What?" He lowers the phone, looking bewildered. "Don't what?"

The girl with him moves in closer. "Sorry about him. He gets excited about the tourist spots."

My hand falls to my side. Tourists. Of course.

My bunched-up muscles relax, and I glance at the grandeur of Maison Marteau. A gorgeous and historic building, one probably photographed a thousand times each year.

"I get it," I say, risking a return smile as I shift the bags and tug down my ball cap. I forgot to put the sunglasses back on.

But it's clear they don't know me, and I doubt they're paparazzi. Judging by their age, backpacks, and neon-green skull on the guy's black T-shirt.

That's the second time today I've let suspicion rule my mind. And as my paranoia fades, embarrassment rushes in.

Worrying I'll be recognized is stressful.

Never being recognized is humbling.

The girl clocks my grocery bags. "Oh, do you live here?"

"Just visiting." Without thinking, I nod toward the mansion.

"No way." The guy's mouth drops open. "This is where you're staying?"

Wishing I could pull the words back in, I snap my lips shut and give a non-committal shrug.

But he's latched on to what I've already confirmed. "Oh, how cool. Maison Marteau." The way he draws out the name reminds me of Bill and Ted and their excellent adventure.

"So have you been down to the catacombs? They run under this part of the city." He edges closer, the neon skull staring straight at me. "The tunnels stretch for miles and miles. We've got tickets for the official tour but are trying to hook up with some catophiles."

"I'm not sure—"

"You know," he says, "people who explore and hangout down there. They make maps of the tunnels."

"Illegally," the girl chimes in, crossing her arms. Maybe not as eager as her boyfriend to explore the deep, dark underground.

"Listen, I know we just met," the guy says, "but could you get us inside?"

"Inside?" I shake my head, confused. "The catacombs?"

"No. Here." He thrusts a hand toward Maison Marteau.

"Oh, no. I'm sorry. I can't." I start to edge around him.

He blocks me, his voice getting higher and faster as he tries to persuade. "Just for a few minutes. To take pictures."

"I don't think—"

"Jaden, back off." The girl steps up and puts a calming hand on her boyfriend's shoulder. "Sorry," she says to me. "Dark tourism is kind of his thing." She sends him an exasperated glance. "Sometimes he gets a little crazy."

"No worries." My laugh sounds fake and fluttery. "Sorry I can't help, but I'm only a guest myself." I step toward the gate.

Then her words register.

"Wait." I face them again. "Dark tourism?"

"Yeah." She shrugs. "You know, visiting places like Chernobyl, Bodie ghost town, Lizzie Borden's house."

"The catacombs," the guy says, shifting his gaze to the mansion. "And here."

"Here? Maison Marteau?" An eerie sensation whispers on my neck.

The guy drags his gaze back to me. "You mean you don't know?"

"Know what?"

He leans closer with a ghoulish grin. "You're living in a murder house."

7

Unease spreads through me, crawling down my back like a hundred baby spiders. I swallow and my voice comes out sounding ragged. "Murder house?"

"Yeah." The guy's face lights up with wicked glee. "More than one person has met a bad end in this place. And the woman who was killed here?" His eyes gleam, morbid excitement oozing through his voice. "Not just killed, but what was done to her body—"

"Okay." The girl interrupts him by grabbing his elbow and giving him a hard stare. "We should go if we're going to make our ticket time for the catacombs."

My nod is automatic, politeness taking over despite the unease reeling in my head and roiling in my gut.

What murder is he talking about? What woman? When? I have so many questions. Questions I'm not sure I want answered.

At least, not by him.

The way he smiled when talking about a woman's dead body. . . The neon skull leers at me, and I shudder with disgust.

Oblivious to my reaction, the guy tosses me a wave and lifts his phone, taking a few more pictures as he leaves.

Trance-like, I punch in the code, push through the black bars, and enter the apartment on autopilot. I cross gleaming parquet floors, pass the grand piano, and enter the spacious kitchen.

I should be thrilled to stay in this luxurious place, but questions plague me as I set my bags on the counter and put away the groceries.

What happened here? Who died? Was it really a murder?

Though not yet sunset, darkness creeps into every room. Craving more light, I flip on the overheads and notice a business card on the kitchen island. Plain white paper with a typed font, listing basic information for the apartment. Including a WiFi code.

WiFi. Internet.

Maybe there's more information online. I can research the history of Maison Marteau. A quick search and—

"No," I say in a stern voice, refocusing on what's important. The screenplay. My career. My life.

If my mother were here, I know what she would say.

You can have distraction or you can have your passion. But you can't have both.

One of her favorite adages. And she'd be right. I can't afford to be distracted right now, especially by tales of murder.

Murder committed in this house.

But I still need WiFi access, so I slip the card in my pocket. Ready to get to work, I boil water and make a cup of mint tea. The pretty packaging caught my eye in the store and promised the aroma would be an "uplifting experience."

I'm in dire need of a mood-lift right now, so I take the mug in one hand and the bag with office supplies in the other. With bright papers, pens, and highlighters purchased, the next step is finding a temporary office.

The first floor is laid out for entertaining—kitchen, dining room, main salon, and entry hall. None of the rooms here will do, so I hurry upstairs to the next level, to what I think of as my area. And a familiar space.

On the front side, expensive furniture fills *le petit salon*, too stiff and decorative for me to relax. And neither of the corner bedrooms will work. That leaves the unexplored back corridor and whatever waits for me on the top floor.

Rounding the banister, I pass my room and end up facing a long hallway. A door stands ajar halfway down. Creeping closer, I go in and flip on the light. One look and I know I've found my spot.

A desk sits near the windows, an antique piece flanked by bookshelves. The rest of the room holds a sitting area, a sofa and two chairs facing a fireplace. Dark wood makes up the mantle and surround, carved with intricate designs. The room is masculine with somber colors but has a rainy-day kind of charm.

Perfect.

Leaving the bag of supplies on the desk, I retrieve my laptop, its charger, and the script from my room. I intend to investigate the third level, but exploration will have to wait. I'm too eager to get back to the screenplay.

Back in the room I now think of as *the study*, I turn on a lamp to beat back shadows and check my laptop battery. Sixty percent. I take it and the script to the sofa, tucking my legs beneath me on the plush cushion.

I read the opening scenes again and reacquaint myself with the setup. The heroine is reliving a trauma from childhood. Slivers of backstory introduce her character, while atmosphere and tension keep me turning pages.

A scary old house with a tortured past.

And present-day characters paying the price.

When a line of dialogue mentions a local legend, I glance up from the pages. Didn't Lin say this was based on a true story? And if so, is the character based on a real person?

Curiosity has me sliding a glance to my laptop. Taking the card from my pocket, I join the WiFi network and open my browser. A French version of my usual search engine greets me with a color photo. Crowds gathered in the streets of Paris, fists raised, mouths open, faces furious.

I don't need to understand French to know this is a protest. Maybe the transportation strikes that re-routed my flight.

Whatever the problem, I hope the trouble is over by the time I leave. I ignore the article, but as I type the name of the screenplay in the search bar, I keep thinking of the real-life mystery I find myself in.

Not just killed

I freeze, fingers resting on the keyboard.

A neon-green skull flashes in my head.

but what was done to her body

A shriek shatters the silence, and my muscles clench, barbwire wrapping my spine in a tight, tingling squeeze.

Pulse fluttering in my throat, I glance at the windows overlooking the gardens. I set aside the laptop and cross the room. Shades of night create shapes outside: an expanse of grass, shrubbery, and winding paths. But nothing else.

Thinking on the sound, I'm not sure it was human. But it was terrifying—so sudden and sharp.

Instinctive fear still chills my blood as I scan the dark garden again. Then shadows shift near the base of the tree, and a small creature emerges. A little black cat, slinking along the hedge.

Relief deflates my lungs, and I rub my calming heart. "Please don't make that awful sound again. You scared me to death."

Although, dark-tourism-guy is really more to blame. Talking

about murder and dead bodies. His gruesome teaser is like an unfinished puzzle, and I'm itching to get it done. To close it up in a box once and for all.

What was done to this poor, unknown woman from the past? The not-knowing is what keeps me unsettled, allows my imagination to paint the picture.

And the picture I see is grisly.

Better if I just find out for myself, then I can focus on my work.

Huffing, I delete the film's title in the search bar. One letter at a time.

In its place, I type *Maison Marteau Paris murder.* Articles about the mansion fill the first page. Out of curiosity, I follow a few links to society pages and other sites discussing the influential family.

From what I can tell, the Marteaus have been in the chocolate business since the 1800s, which explains the excessive wealth.

Everyone loves chocolate.

A few more clicks and I land on a website with history and obscure trivia about Parisian mansions. The page shows an old newspaper article with a grainy black-and-white photo. The paper is from 1922. A line through the middle marks the fold, the original scanned to create an electronic copy.

ATROCITÉ À LA MAISON MARTEAU

In the photo below the headline, a couple poses with two children. The mansion stands in the background. As I scan the text, a few words leap out at me—*Marteau, chocolat, suicide.*

Suicide?

The article is in a photo, so I can't copy and paste. Typing in words makes translation more difficult and time consuming. I check the spelling and accent marks, and write the first paragraph into my language app.

Luckily, one paragraph is all I need. A murder-suicide and suspected love triangle. A man named Mathieu Marteau killed his wife and himself, leaving one child behind. A son.

Tragic. Sad. Needless.

But not the horrid murder dark-tourist guy made it out to be. And I still don't understand why he mentioned the woman's body.

Working backward, I type in "body" and get the French word *corps*. Methodically, I scan every line, searching. I find no mention of the word.

Maybe the details were too graphic? Too scandalous for the times?

Or maybe the powerful Marteau family kept the newspaper in check.

Shocking or not, it happened over a hundred years ago. Their tragedy has nothing to do with the here and now. Nothing to do with me.

Outside, lampposts glow in the park, disembodied white orbs floating in the night.

A sudden chill overcomes me. I pick up my tea, but it's gone cold. So has the room, lit only by the lamp on the desk. Shadows encroach from every corner, making me wish for a fire.

Murder house. Such a ghoulish description.

So what if the mansion has a dark history? Centuries-old buildings often do. Still, my mind plays a reel of death scenarios. If I could take snapshots of this building's past, what would I see? Would I see a woman being attacked?

Would I see her strangled on the floor, fighting for air?

Pushed down the stairs, landing with a *crack*?

Or stabbed in the kitchen, dress turning red?

Pressing my hands to my temples, I shake my head and will the images away. In the absence of knowledge, imagination takes over, and that's all I'm seeing. Figments of my overactive—*over-morbid*—imagination.

Pulling my hair back in my hands, I clear my thoughts and refocus on the script. It's not a sappy romcom or feel-good film, but a movie that touches on other emotions. Self-doubt and discovery, betrayal and pain, and all with an underlying vein of fear.

A fear I can almost taste.

The best actors use their own experience, bringing memories and trauma into their work. If I'm smart, I'll do the same. Using this place to my advantage, I'll channel everything this building is making me feel—isolation, loneliness, paranoia.

I'm by myself in a new and unfamiliar world, just like the heroine in the screenplay. It seems Claudia and I already have some things in common.

The Whisper House is fiction. Maison Marteau is my reality.

And both are horror stories.

My Hotel Peculiar

I leaned as far over the railing as I could, the tips of my toes barely scraping the wood floor.

I was trying to peek at the people below. My parents were having a dinner party. Not the big party they have every year, the one with dancing and games, but still a lot of guests.

When I heard my mother's voice, I pulled back over the bar. Peering through the balusters, I saw her walk by below. She was with a woman.

"This house is amazing," the woman said. "How do I get a hotel peculiar of my own?" She laughed then, a funny sound, like she had a potato stuck in her mouth. And when she stumbled, my mother grabbed her arm.

Keeping the woman steady, my mother led her down the hallway, whispering to her with words I couldn't hear.

Once they left, I sat on the floor and thought about it.

What was wrong with that woman? Why did she call our home a hotel peculiar? Was she making a joke?

I didn't understand and decided to ask Mother the next time I got the chance. She'd know I was spying on the party and up past my bedtime. She might be angry. But not too much. Not as long as I stayed upstairs.

Which is why I had to be careful.

I waited a few more minutes, until I could no longer hear the clack-clack-clack of their shoes. Then I crept down the stairs, hurried down the hallway, and headed toward the blue salon. But I didn't go inside.

Peeking around the corner, I saw all the people had finished dinner and moved to the salon. A quartet had set up their instruments in one corner, and an area of the floor was cleared for dancing.

Keeping my head close to the wall, I looked around the room. A flash of silver caught my eye. The woman again.

Her sparkly dress was hard to miss. Only my mother was gone, and the woman was leaning into my father.

He smiled in a way that made me uncomfortable, and he pulled her into his arms to dance. I kept looking until I found my mother. She was watching my father and the woman. She didn't look happy, but she didn't look angry, either.

Until she turned her head and spotted me.

I raced back down the hall, but my mother's sharp voice stopped me before I could get away. "I thought I told you to go to bed."

I turned back to her, afraid of how much trouble I was going to be in. I'm not supposed to be downstairs when guests are here.

She walked up to me and crossed her arms. "You know the rules."

"Yes, Mother."

Instead of chastising me, she put a hand on my shoulder. She sighed and stared at me, running her hand over my hair.

"Are you tired?" I asked her.

"Yes." She took another heavy breath. "Very tired. And this party is for adults."

"Yes, Mother." Lowering my eyes, I pretended to be sorry and let her lead me back to the stairs.

I walked up three steps and turned around. "Why did that woman call our house a hotel peculiar?"

"What?" My mother pulled her attention back to me. She seemed distracted. "Oh, her. Don't mind her. She's deep in her cups."

"What does that mean?" I asked.

"It means she's had too much Champagne."

I nodded. I've seen my mother drink too much Champagne before.

She waved her fingers at me, shooing me upstairs, but I didn't go. Not yet. I had another question before being pushed up to my boring bedroom.

"Why does Father smile at her that way?"

My mother jerked her head back to me and frowned. "That's enough now. Don't concern yourself with adult matters, or with that woman. She's not important."

My mother gave me a light push on my back, and I could tell she was out of patience.

Frowning, I dragged my feet and took one step at a time. But halfway up the stairs, I heard my mother mumble, "She's not important at all."

8

The apartment isn't as scary in the daytime.

I stand in the *petit salon* on the second floor. Spring sun filters through the windows, falling on antique tables, gilded frames, and an elaborate crimson rug. The room has excellent morning light.

Which is why I'm here.

I need three things to film my audition. Enough wall space, a clean background, and natural light.

The windows face east, which means they also face the courtyard, but the higher floor provides privacy. No one walking by and peering in while I work.

As if to assure myself, I move to the windows and stare down at the cobblestones. No activity. No one in sight. The mansion may feel forsaken and covered with gargoyles, but at least it's quiet.

I spent the morning reading the script for a second time, taking notes on the narrative and the character arc. To nail the audition, I need to understand Claudia—her past, her hopes, her fears.

Once I understand her, I ask the questions that will bring her to life. How will I approach her character? Will I be believable in the role? What scene should I choose?

I can't afford to play it safe.

The choice I make needs to be strong. Bold. So even if I take things in the wrong direction, a risky scene choice will show the directors I've studied my craft. I've done the work.

If only I had someone to help me run lines.

The thought is like a blade to my heart.

Mackenzie used to run lines with me. She and I shared a living space on location for *The Last Wave*. Neither of us were top-tier stars, but we ended up loving our roommate situation.

Mackenzie isn't a nepo-baby like me, but a girl who grew up on a farm in Virginia. Bright, funny, and so very talented. She won me over the moment we met, asking if my soy milk would be offended by hers from a cow.

The memory makes me laugh.

Then I feel the sting of tears.

Please, let her be okay.

Emotion tightens my throat, so I march from the room. Despite what my mother might say, I need a distraction. And I need it now, while I'm on the verge of a good crying jag.

The wide stairs loom before me, their gleaming steps an invitation. This is a good time to explore the top level.

Moving up, I find the same wide steps and ornate railing. The paintings on the wall are different, though. Landscapes and buildings instead of portraits, but with the same moody colors as the ones below.

As soon as I reach the top floor, I sense the change. The air is heavy, the shadows longer, and the space oozes with a sense of neglect.

I hug myself and look around. Every door is closed, blocking natural light from the surrounding rooms. I move to the nearest door and open it, allowing sunlight to brighten the landing. The layout is the same as downstairs, so I work my way around—small salon, bedroom, another bedroom, media room with a large TV. Nothing too out of the ordinary.

Until I have only one place left to search. A closed door on the back side, cloaked in shadows at the end of the hall.

Running my hand along the wallpaper, I edge up to the door, turn the brass knob, and step inside. The smell of dust hits me.

This must be the storage room Luci mentioned.

Furniture crams against every wall, even blocking out the windows. Stacked boxes and paraphernalia litter the floor, all of it creating a musty maze of shadows.

Fighting off a sneeze, I quickly back out and shut the door. "No, thank you."

With all the other doors open, sunlight floods the space, and as I round the landing, a panel in the wall leaps out at me. My brain is picking up on an inconsistency, but I can't make sense of it yet.

Then I do. One section stands out, slightly misaligned.

I walk over, place my palms on the wood, and push. The panel gives slightly and pops open.

Old hinges protest the movement, groaning as the door opens to reveal the servants' staircase. I almost forgot it existed. Steep, cramped, dark. No frills or flourishes here. Only plain wooden steps and bare walls.

I fumble for the light switch, flip it up and down.

Nothing happens.

I pull my phone from my back pocket and turn on the flashlight. Dust motes and cobwebs glisten in the glow.

Cobwebs mean spiders. And I'm not good with spiders.

But the webs drag and stretch, telling me they're old, not recently inhabited by little eight-legged biters. And I'm already inside, just a short trip to the floor below.

I pull the door behind me, turning the stairwell into a tomb. My first step is slow and cautious, but the boards are sturdy. As I continue, I slide my hand along the wall, only pulling back when my fingers touch grime.

A few more steps, and I stop on the next floor. The door is outlined by thin lines of light.

I've made it this far, might as well keep going.

Moving with more confidence, I make it to the main level. The piano should be right on the other side.

Below me, the stairs disappear into darkness, descending into what must be the basement.

I shine my light down and take a step. And one more. Cool air moves past me, and I taste must and mildew. I feel a wisp of a cobweb.

Then tiny legs tickle along my cheek.

With a shout, I swat at my face and hair, turning to rush back upstairs. I burst through the door and into the entry hall, wiping at my clothes as I dance in place.

I'm still shuddering all over when I hear a knock. Someone is at the door.

I pause, my hands mid-swipe. Who's here? Luci?

Sidestepping, I peek through the glass from a distance. A man I don't recognize stands outside.

One more pat for my hair, and I open the door. He stands on the steps, chocolate-brown hair, casually handsome. He wears blue jeans with a button-down, and something about his stance tells me he's American, even before he speaks.

"Hi," he says, both the greeting and accent confirming my guess. "Sorry to bother you." He angles toward the courtyard. "I live in the other apartment and thought I'd introduce myself."

"Hello," I say, and wait.

He grins at me. "Oh." With a shrug, he sticks out his hand. "I'm Noah. That's the introduction part."

I'm not sure if it's his charm or the fact he's from the States, but my shoulders relax. No pressure to impress or apologize for my presence. He's just another tenant, and not part of *the family*.

"Noah Marteau," he says, and my muscles bunch again. An American Marteau, approachable and attractive. But still one of them.

Shaking his hand, I force a pleasant expression. "Brooke." I leave off my last name. It's certainly not a *household* name, but I can't risk recognition.

He shifts on his feet, as if I'm making him nervous instead of the other way around. "I won't keep you. Thought I'd come over, in case you ever need anything. I've been here a couple of years and know my way around. And I speak French."

"I appreciate the offer," I say. "All of you have been so welcoming."

"Really?" Something I can't read flickers on his face, but he covers it with a grin. "Good."

I remember Chantal's cold reception. "Well, most everyone."

He laughs, and I relax even more, sensing a we-don't-fit-in fellowship with the stranger on my steps.

He edges back, signaling his exit. "Like I said, if you need anything I'm right next door."

"Great, thanks. And I guess I'll see you at dinner tonight?"

"Sorry?"

"At the main house. Family dinner?" It's a safe assumption he'll be there.

"No." He drags out the word, smiling oddly as he diverts his gaze. "I wasn't invited."

"Oh." Discomfort ties my tongue, and I'm not sure what else to say. There's a story underneath his tone, one he's not willing to share.

However, since he's here. . . "Any tips on what I should expect tonight? And what I should wear?"

Noah chuckles. "As long as it's not jeans or shorts, you should be fine."

"So, business casual or Sunday clothes?" I join in the joke, feeling the camaraderie again. Two outsiders from another world.

Or maybe he is from this world, just slightly removed.

"Exactly," he says. "Don't worry. You'll be fine. And the food is always excellent, so enjoy yourself." He walks down the steps. Pauses.

When he faces me again, the friendly smile is gone, replaced by a wary expression. "One thing, though."

He grits his teeth, like he's chewing over what he wants to say.

"Be careful with Ric."

9

Light pours from the windows of the main house, clear and golden, like fine Champagne. Glancing down, I smooth a hand over my ivory pantsuit. It's simple yet classic, something I'd wear to any dinner party hosted in LA.

But standing on the doorstep of Maison Marteau, I can't help feeling underdressed. Or that the wine in my hand isn't good enough. Not expensive enough. Not *vintage* enough.

Keep calm. Play the part. Keep up appearances for a couple of hours.

I blow out a long, controlled, calming breath and ring the bell. Before I lose my nerve.

Almost instantly, one door swings open. A man steps aside to let me in, wearing a steel-gray uniform with gold buttons. More Parisian flair than the standard English butler.

I step inside, my heels clicking softly on the parquet floor. The woodwork extends to a massive staircase, spiraling up to a mezzanine. Red carpet runs from top to bottom, spilling down the steps like a river of blood.

"Brooke!" Luci's voice breaks into my morbid thoughts, her

smile bright and welcoming. "I'm so glad you're here." She hurries over and leans in close to one side of my face. She makes a kissing sound and repeats the gesture on the other cheek.

The French greeting known as *la bise*. This afternoon, I looked up French etiquette, wanting to be as prepared as possible. But at this point my head is buzzing, and I only remember three things: don't choose my own seat, don't switch the fork between hands, and don't ask for butter.

"Your grandmother was so kind to invite me," I say, hearing the stiffness in my tone. My body feels just as rigid, filled with the dread of dealing with Ric and Chantal again. Both for different reasons.

"You brought wine." Luci takes the bottles, studies the labels, and nods. "Come. The others are in the grand salon."

I walk with her down a corridor, stealing glimpses inside rooms as we pass. So much opulence, I can't take it all in. Gilded mirrors and paintings, porcelain and crystal, antiques and velvet. Luxury fit for a palace.

A palace built by chocolate.

The hall makes a sudden turn, and Luci breezes through a case opening wide enough for six people to stand shoulder to shoulder.

Inside, the family is gathered near a stone fireplace. Chantal sits on one of two sapphire-colored sofas, speaking to a young man on the opposite couch. His brown hair is a shade lighter than Ric's, but a resemblance tells me they're closely related.

Musidora sits in her wheelchair, positioned near the young man, with her hand on his arm.

"Our guest has arrived," Luci announces, and three heads swivel.

"Ah, Brooke." With impressive agility, Musidora maneuvers around the furniture and rolls herself to me. "So lovely to see you."

"Thank you for having me, Mrs. Marteau."

She tuts and waves a hand. "Please, call me Dora."

I tilt my head in acknowledgement. "Your home is stunning," I say, syrup running sweet and thick in my voice.

I inherited more than my love of acting from my mother. I also learned how to play the game. The Hollywood game—how to fit in with the wealthy and socially elite.

Though it never sits well on my shoulders.

"You remember Chantal." Dora flicks a hand to her daughter-in-law. Chantal lifts her chin to acknowledge me, but she doesn't speak.

"And my grandson, Lyam."

"It's a pleasure," Lyam says, charming with a dimpled grin and puppy-dog eyes. He stands from the couch and walks to join Luci. "And you've brought us some wine." He studies a label as Luci did. "This will pair nicely with dinner."

Still holding the wine, Lyam angles toward his grandmother, making it clear who has final approval.

"Of course," Dora says, lifting one brow to someone across the room. A woman in a black uniform stands near the wall, so motionless I hadn't noticed her before.

Now she jumps to Dora's unspoken command, moving like a wraith, swift and silent as she comes to take the bottles.

"I had planned to have the Pommard François," Chantal says with a purse of her lips.

"Nonsense." Dora speaks over her shoulder to her daughter-in-law. "Not when Brooke has been so considerate."

Chantal shoots me a look so full of loathing it could burn my skin.

Unsettled by her open hostility, I focus on Dora again. "You have a beautiful home."

"Thank you, but I'm afraid I can't take credit." As she speaks, she turns and points to the fireplace. Two lions roar from each corner of the mantle, their forms carved from gray marble.

"Much has remained unchanged since my grandfather's time." She points to a framed photo resting next to a vase of flowers. From across the room, I can make out shapes of people, but the background is indistinct.

I do a half spin to take in the décor. "Your artwork is remarkable."

"We practically live in a museum," Luci jokes. She takes my hand and leads me closer to a wall lined with paintings. "This is my favorite." She taps the frame of a piece even I recognize.

"Is this..."

She laughs when amazement steals my ability to speak. "Monet."

Together, we stare at the iconic bridge arching over water lilies.

"Take your time," Luci tells me, a light touch on my elbow as she leaves to take her seat with Chantal.

A glance back at the others tells me they are engaged in conversation. I don't want to be rude, but another minute appreciating the art should be acceptable.

Slowly, I ease along the wall, taking in the collection of pictures and sculptures. I come to a large painting in a carved wooden frame. Black is the primary color, offset only by moody browns and beiges and a touch of deep green.

The hues as dire and gloomy as the subject matter.

A woman stands in a dark room, the space littered with items —candles, books, knives, and a lute without strings. All amid a chaos of human bones. A single table stands in the center, holding an hourglass and a skull, whose empty sockets somehow appear terrified.

I lean closer to study the skull.

An object juts from its mouth, but I'm not sure what it is. Brown and thick, another book? Some sort of pouch?

"Remember that you have to die." A deep voice rumbles behind me.

I whirl around. "Excuse me?"

An older man is standing close, eyes like simmering coals and black hair going silver at the temples. He waves a tumbler of brown liquid toward the painting, and I can smell the alcohol. "*Memento mori.*"

He continues to stand too close. "An artistic reminder of the inevitability of death."

A faint memory surfaces, one from my introductory art class in college. "*Memento mori.*" I scan the image again, pausing on the skull. "Translation, remember that you have to die."

So, he wasn't threatening to kill me.

"Very good," he says, giving me a once-over. I assume he's referring to my correct answer, but his direct gaze makes me squirm inside. Maybe the perverted apple doesn't fall far.

"Uncle Vincent," Luci says, easing up to us, her usual happy energy subdued.

I do the math and put the family together. Vincent is married to Chantal, so Ric and Lyam are his sons.

Vincent reaches past me, but I shift before he brushes my bare arm. Unwilling to budge an inch, he holds two fingers near the thick swirls of ancient paint. "The skeletons represent death." He edges closer. "And the hourglass is time running out."

I nod and swallow, wishing for an interruption, for Luci to drag me away or for Dora to call to her son. I'd even take a snarky comment from Chantal if it would create some space between me and Vincent's hot, whiskey breath.

"Sorry I'm late." Ric strolls into the room, his swagger anything but apologetic.

Not the rescue I'd hoped for, but at least Vincent backs up.

"Finally." Chantal rises from the sofa and makes a beeline for the door.

"Dinner," Luci chimes out, her expression strained as she goes to Dora, gripping the handles to push her chair.

"Brooke, can I escort you?" Lyam offers his arm, walking to meet me at the door.

But Ric intercepts him and angles himself between us. "Don't overstep yourself. You can't have *everything,* little brother."

I can almost taste the bitterness as Ric glares at Lyam, then slides his hand to my lower back.

My spine stiffens, but he only digs his fingers into my waist.

Resentful energy sparks between the brothers, but I stop paying attention. All I can focus on is the hand on my back.

Suddenly, I'm no longer in the opulence of Maison Marteau but in another grand house.

I'm back there, two years ago, to that night in Beverly Hills. When another man touched me without invitation, his foul words slithering into my ear.

I've been watching you.

10

"Brooke? Are you all right?"

I blink away the past to find Lyam staring at me with concern.

"Fine," I say, pulling myself back to the here and now.

Ric's hand still rests on my waist, and I fight the urge to reach back and twist a finger. Sudden fury is not like me, and violence is not in my nature, but a wildfire of rage heats up my chest.

Holding myself together, I rein in the emotion. I clench my teeth and reorder my features into a pleasant mask. A handy skill. I am an actress after all, and this isn't the first social event I've faked my way through.

"Ready?" This time I take the initiative, looping my arms through both Lyam's and Ric's, one brother on each side. "Such gallantry," I add with a smile, trying to keep the peace between us all.

Warmth from Ric's skin radiates through his shirt. Touching him turns my stomach and sours my mouth, but I don't let my revulsion show.

There's a point when people-pleasing crosses a line, to a place where you're giving away a part of yourself. But I haven't crossed it with Ric. Not yet. And I can't risk upsetting anyone in the family.

I need to stay in Maison Marteau until I've submitted my audition. Time spent relocating would be time taken away from preparation.

So I'll handle Ric and his groping hands. I'll navigate this evening with all the grace I possess, cloaked in manners and shielded by lies.

Not so different from Hollywood and its sordid games. Games my mother taught me to play, for my own protection.

The brothers guide me down another hallway, Ric stiff and silent on my left, while Lyam sends me the occasional grin and points out interesting aspects of the mansion.

The dining room boasts as much elegance as the rest of the home, with enough glitz and glamor to host royal guests. And it probably has. A crystal chandelier glistens above the table, and the chair Ric pulls out for me is an intricate marriage of gold and velvet.

As I sit, he touches me again under the guise of chivalry, trailing his fingers down my back. He moves low enough to make me flinch.

I instantly regret my reaction. He's toying with me, and I don't want to give him the satisfaction of seeing me rattled. I recognize the performance for what it is, an assertion of dominance. Ric's the kind of man who feels entitled—to wealth, deference, pleasure, women.

And now I understand Noah's warning.

Dora sits regally at the head of the table, catching Ric's eye for a split second. Just a flash, but the message is clear. Ric huffs through his nose and glowers as he takes a seat across from me.

Luci sits in the chair next to mine, and I relax with warm relief. At least I won't have to worry about Ric's stray hands under the table.

Soon the butler begins the dinner service. He and the uniformed woman who took my wine pour drinks and bring the first course, mushroom bisque in a delicate bowl. Once the female servant leaves, the butler takes up position near the door.

Spoon poised over her bowl, Dora fixes me with a look. "Brooke, I hope you're finding your way around the city and the apartment suits your needs."

Caught off-guard, I quick-swallow the soup. "I am, and the apartment is perfect."

"Noah lives in the other one," Luci says before adding in a dreamy voice, "our handsome American cousin."

Across from her, Lyam rolls his eyes.

"My brother's grandson." Dora presses her lips together, but the ghost of a frown remains.

Lyam glances at his grandmother before steering the small talk in another direction. "I saw you with some people outside the gate yesterday. I hope they didn't bother you, but with the park trails so close, we tend to get a lot of tourists."

I swallow and clear my throat. "They were taking pictures of your home, actually, and had tickets to see part of the catacombs."

Chantal scoffs. "Naturally. Americans and their love for the macabre." She sips her wine and makes a face, silently giving her opinion of my gift.

"You're right," I tell her, getting a look of surprise in response, as if she'd expected me to ignore her sly insult. "They called themselves dark tourists."

At this, Luci laughs, the sound high-pitched and strangled at the same time. "Of course they were. And of course they had

Maison Marteau on their list. We're mentioned on a lot of those websites."

I glance around the table, and no one seems surprised their home and history are internet fodder.

"*Memento mori*," Vincent mutters from the other end of the table. Somewhere along the way, his tumbler has been refilled, and he tosses back half of the brown liquor.

Dora angles her head to him. She wears a smile sharp enough to slice, but her tone is carefree as she offers a vague explanation. "What Luci and my son are referring to is an unfortunate accident from years ago. Sadly, when you combine a building like Maison Marteau and any hint of mystery, well, you know how people are. And it always fuels the fire if it involves families in our position."

"Rich families." Luci turns to me, wiggling her blonde brows. "Especially those who live in *Maison de la Morte*."

With my wine glass halfway to my mouth, I pause and do a quick translation. Did she just call this place the house of the dead?

Dora shakes her head at Luci but doesn't scold. She apparently has a soft spot for her granddaughter, letting her get away with more than her male cousins.

Lifting a shoulder in a careless shrug, Luci sits back in her chair as the servants remove the soup bowls and bring the main course. "Anytime someone dies in our *arrondissement*, the rumors start up again."

Chantal glares at Luci before transferring her baleful expression to me, as if I'm somehow to blame for her chatty niece.

"That must be difficult," I say, "having a family tragedy turned into gossip and entertainment."

"Oh, it wasn't family." Luci shifts toward me. "It was a little girl."

Chantal slams her hand on the table and speaks angrily to Luci in French.

"*Maman.*" Lyam puts a hand on his mother's arm to calm her.

Tension crackles around the table. Even Ric wiggles in his seat.

I'm not sure what to say, so I play it safe and stay silent. This is not what I read about online, not a marriage gone wrong and a husband turned murderer.

Luci's talking about the death of a child. But why would that stir up rumors about the family?

Dora sighs. "Such a terrible accident." She nods slowly, shadows of sadness on her face. "A young girl who lived in the neighborhood. Missing for weeks."

"How awful." I grip my utensils but keep my attention on the people at the table.

"They eventually found her in the catacombs." Lyam delivers the news in a matter-of-fact tone.

"Yes, in the catacombs." Ric huffs. "She wasn't found *here*."

I can't tell if he's bored by the topic. Or agitated.

The morose conversation weighs heavy in the air, and I'm grateful when Luci asks if I've tried the family chocolate yet. I tell her I haven't had the chance, and she promises to bring me some tomorrow.

The topic of chocolate turns to chit-chat about the history of the company and seventeenth-century Paris. The lighter subject matter carries us through the rest of the meal, but an air of tension remains.

When dessert is finished, Vincent stands abruptly and leaves. Dora ignores his rude behavior as she rolls back from the table. "Care for a nightcap, Brooke?"

"Thank you, but I should probably go. Jetlag isn't quite done with me yet." The others stand, so I follow suit, speaking directly to Dora. "Thank you for a lovely evening."

Dora glances to her granddaughter. "Luci, please, see our guest out."

Luci nods and meets me in the doorway. Only Ric and Lyam walk with us to the foyer, Chantal disappearing without saying a word.

Luci opens the front doors to a damp wind and the sound of pouring rain. "Uh-oh."

Ric grabs my hand and tugs. "I'll take care of you, Brooke. We'll go through the house, so you won't get wet." He licks his lips and rubs his thumb in the center of my palm.

My skin tightens, and I feel dirty all over.

Thankfully, Lyam intercedes. Frowning at his brother, he points to the courtyard. "The covered walk will keep you dry for the most part. And you can take this with you." He opens the door to a huge wardrobe and retrieves a black umbrella.

Pulling free of Ric, I accept the umbrella, resisting the urge to wipe my palm on my thigh.

Suddenly stone-faced, Luci gives me air kisses on both cheeks again. "Good night."

She puts an arm around my shoulders and guides me out the door. I say my last goodbyes and leave.

Rain batters the cobblestones, drops splattering the legs of my pantsuit. But the cool breeze cleanses the last *ickiness* of Ric.

Careful in my heels, I hurry to the covered walk, my mind already on my laptop and my next internet search. The uncomfortable dinner and Ric's handsy behavior have already taken a backseat to Luci's announcement.

If the missing girl was found in the catacombs, why did Dora instantly link her to the dark tourists' interest in Maison Marteau? And why is the mansion called the house of death?

At the end of the walkway, I lift the umbrella again and

make another short dash around the corner of the building. With the umbrella up and my head down, I don't notice the visitor at my door until the last minute.

Stopping short, I stare at my unexpected guest. "What are you doing here?"

11

The little black cat huddles beside my door, her fur shiny with wet streaks. Crouched down, she stares at me, eyes bright green in the porch light.

"Hi, sweet girl." I'm only guessing she's female, because of her size. And something in the sweetness of her heart-shaped face.

After a moment, I squat and hold out my hand. Keeping a safe distance, she sniffs the air but makes no attempt to run.

With slow, easy movements, I stand, lean over her to unlock the door, and give it a little push.

She rises and turns in one liquid motion before taking a cautious step inside. Now that she's on her feet, I see how painfully thin she is and take a mental inventory of what I have in the fridge.

When she's over the threshold, she pauses to sniff again. Finding no apparent threat, she wanders in, her paws leaving tiny wet spots on the floor.

I don't second-guess my decision to let her into the apartment. Not for a minute. I'm only a renter, and the family might object—might even kick me out—but I can't turn her away.

As she sniffs along the walls and furniture, I make a large arc around her and head to the kitchen. Taking a small plate from the cabinets, I load it up with cold cuts and set it in the middle of the floor.

I find a small bowl for water, but by the time I fill it up, I catch a black flash from the corner of my eye.

She's found the meat on the plate, and it's almost gone.

"Poor thing." I watch as she finishes the cold cuts, licking the plate for every morsel.

When the dish is clean, she glances up at me. Back to the plate. Up to me again. *That's all you've got?*

"Okay, but only a little more." Smiling as I open the fridge, I take another slice of turkey and drop it on her plate. "I'll get you something better in the morning."

Leaving the kitchen, I make my way through the dim apartment. The space seems bigger at night. Cavernous. Abysmal. As if the mansion has swallowed me whole.

As I head upstairs, I'm aware of the oil portraits looming above me. Their facial details are lost in the dark, but I feel their eyes tracking my steps, their scorn slicking my skin.

I'm halfway up when a sound rises.

Barely a shift of air, soft and muted. Like someone in a corner whispering . . . *Hush.*

I freeze in place, listening.

Silence thickens, and a sensation crawls on the back of my neck. An indescribable feeling of *other*. A feeling that I'm not alone.

Ric's name surfaces, greasy and unwelcome. His voice curls around the edges of my mind, whispering, *I'll take care of you.*

Lightning illuminates the apartment, pulsing like a strobe on the creepy portraits.

Slowly, cautiously, I lean over the railing and peer down. The grand piano gleams in the corner, a sliver of light on its shiny black lid.

Logic tells me I'm overreacting, but logic is fragile in the face of fear.

And instinct always rules in the dark.

Seconds pass. Still, I hear nothing. No sigh or rustle or bump in the night.

"Because it's fine." My whisper sounds loud in the heavy silence. "There's nothing downstairs."

Nothing but cavernous rooms with ancient Gothic vibes. Enough to give anyone the chills.

Plus, all the talk of death is getting to me.

Suicide.

Murder.

Little girls lost in dark tunnels.

Not to mention the creepy screenplay I'm reading.

More and more, I'm becoming Claudia. When she feels paranoid, so do I. When she feels terror, chills race down my arms.

Which is exactly why Lin sent me here. In this big, empty place, I can relate to Claudia. I've never been much of a method actor, but the atmosphere of the apartment is a lesson in realism.

Because I understand what it means to be alone and afraid.

No matter how I rationalize, my mind won't settle. Won't let it go. I need to check all the doors, or I'll never fall asleep.

Annoyed with my reaction, I grip the banister and hurry back down, as if speed will ward off any unseen threats.

It's a straight shot to the front door, so I can see through the glass from where I stand.

Spindly tree limbs. Evergreen shrubs. Black fence.

I creep to the door, stopping inches from the glass, and slide my hand to the doorknob. Locked.

Taking the short corridor to the kitchen, I stop to look out the windows. From there, I cut through the butler's pantry to the dining room. Ambient light filters in from the park, coming through a set of French doors. I check the locks here, too.

Exiting from a different door, I find myself in the back hallway, with the second set of connecting doors at the far end. Could the sound have come from there?

As I stand, staring, something touches my leg. The dainty cat walks a figure eight on the floor. Turning to make a second pass, she bumps my leg again as if claiming me for her own.

"Sorry, no more food tonight."

She stops in her tracks as if she understood me.

But her tail lowers, her body tenses. She stands fixated, only the tip of her tail twitching as she stares at the doors.

I follow her line of sight, bumps prickling on my arms. "What do you hear, kitty?"

She ignores me, focused on the end of the hallway.

But as quickly as she clenched up, she relaxes again. Calm and unbothered, she lets out a feminine *mew*.

Still, I hurry to the doors to test the handle. Locked tight. No one getting in through here.

The cat races ahead of me to the main hall and zooms around the corner. Maybe her sensitive ears picked up on the Marteaus moving around next door.

Or maybe she's only chasing shadows.

Like me.

Either way, her presence makes me feel less lonely, and the giant stone mansion a little less daunting.

When we reach the stairs, she bounds up to the second floor, her black tail raised like a flag. Smiling, I follow.

Until I reach the portraits.

Pausing at the halfway point, I think of the strange sound. That barely audible *hush*.

Probably nothing. Just an old house, full of settling beams and cool drafts.

But as I grip the railing and continue the climb, I send one last glance over my shoulder.

12

The next morning, the rain is gone, and sun greets me when I step out of the market. After a sleepless night reacting to every strange sound, I find myself craving a change of scenery, some fresh air, and the presence of people.

The spring air lightens my mood, and my fear from last night feels like a strange and distant dream. It's easier to console myself in the light of day, easier to think clearly about Maison Marteau.

The murder happened a long time ago.

Children go missing in every city.

No one was in the apartment last night.

No one but a silly cat who ended up sleeping next to me, her steady purr a comfort throughout the night.

And the reason I stopped at the market, to load up on food, treats, and toys for my new little friend. The sweet girl cat I've named Clairee.

Being surrounded by French words and names led my mind down a linguistic path, one that ended at *Steel Magnolias*. The female-led drama was my mother's favorite movie, and a running soundtrack to most of my childhood.

I grew to love the movie too, but for different reasons. It was one of the few films we could simply watch—no running commentary, no teaching points. Just my mom and me on a lazy afternoon, laughing, crying, snacking.

And making memories.

There's a sassiness in the cat that reminds me of my mother, a can't-keep-me-down spirit of survival. And I think she'd approve of the name.

I believe she'd also approve of the horror script.

A tote bag hangs on my other arm, large enough to hold the bulky pages. By now, the paper is worn from being handled, a coffee stain blemishes the title page, and a yellow tab marks a particular scene.

All signs of deep-reading and preparation, so I know the story as if I wrote it myself. The screenplay is good. Really good. And as usual, Lin is on point.

Typical for most horror movies, the fear and tension are there. But it also has heart. An undercurrent of emotion threading through the drama. I find myself attached to my character. I root for her. I worry for her. One moment my heart is hammering in my chest, the next it's pinching with empathy.

A film like this is a rare find, and I want the part more than ever. I don't simply want it, I *need* it. The desire to play Claudia lights a fire in my veins, sparking a fast and furious whirl of ideas.

I've chosen a scene, so the next task is to make notes on the scene's rhythm, paying attention to where I need extra emphasis. How does the dialogue affect my breathing? What are the dominant sounds? Where are the words that relay emotion and nouns that paint a picture?

This is where I'll focus, the most compelling section. The

lines that will show casting directors what I want them to see. My skill as an actor.

Not the nasty scandal nipping at my heels.

Coming to a stop at the corner, I check my phone to verify my location. The café I want to try sits on the next block. The perfect place for a working breakfast, with round wooden tables and minty-green walls.

Quintessential Parisian charm. Bright and cheery.

Unlike the apartment.

Picturing dark paneling and hidden stairs has me lifting my face to the brisk, clean wind. And that's when I spot a familiar form.

My feet stutter to a halt. *Why is she here?*

Slipping behind a rack of postcards, I hunker down and peek out to the street.

It's the woman who was watching Maison Marteau. I'm sure of it. She's wearing her blonde hair down and without the ball cap, but the patch on her jacket gives her away.

She stands on the sidewalk, her head swinging back and forth, like she's searching for something.

Did she follow me? Maybe lost me when I popped into the market?

She bounds into the street, crossing to this side, scanning the sidewalk as she walks. Then her eyes lock with mine. Recognition tightens her face, and she makes a beeline in my direction.

Dammit, dammit. Paparazzo. She has to be. It's the only thing that makes sense.

Did she get a good look at me? Or worse...did she get a picture?

The story in Hollywood is blowing up, and the press is hunting cast and crew who worked on *The Last Wave.* Gaffer, key grip, makeup artist. Even non-principal actors like me. Overnight, we all became tickets to fast cash.

But if my name is linked to a salacious scandal, my odds of landing the new role will plummet.

A tall man passes by, so I slide in front of him, rushing back the way I came and cutting down an alley.

The woman is nowhere in sight, but she'll be rounding the corner any second. I need to get off the street.

A restaurant comes up on my left, so I slip inside. The door closes behind me, shutting out the din of the city.

The storefront is nothing but glass, so I move close to a partition and try to blend with shadows.

I don't see the woman. Did I lose her?

"*Voudriez-vous une table?*" A mustached man is beside me. He holds a menu, brows raised in question.

"Sorry?"

He clears his throat and nods. "Would you like a table?"

"Uh..." Another glance out the window and I make up my mind. "Yes, please."

It's not the place I'd planned on, but it will have to do. After enough time has passed, I'll head straight back to the apartment and lock myself inside.

He starts toward a table with a clear view of the sidewalk. If I can see out, someone else can see in.

"Do you have a table in the back?"

Another nod before he leads me to a far corner.

"Perfect," I say. "*Merci beaucoup.*"

He sets down the menu and sweeps out an arm. "Someone will be with you soon."

When he leaves, I pull out my phone. My first instinct is to text Lin and tell her about the woman.

But maybe I shouldn't bother her with this. I'm sure she's in bed. Besides, what could she do to help? I'm halfway around the globe in a sticky situation of my own making. She did all the work of getting me to Paris and booking a swanky apartment, giving me only two directives.

Keep your head down. And don't disturb the family.

Only three days here and I've failed at both.

An older woman comes over and takes my order. I ask for a croque madame and a coffee with milk.

Minutes pass and my anxiety fades, so I lean back in the booth. I'm safe for now. The restaurant is almost empty, only a few people at other tables. Peaceful and quiet.

Which is why I hear sound rush in when the front door opens.

The man who greeted me speaks to someone in French, before coming back to where I'm seated. He brings the blonde woman with him.

Smiling, he speaks to her again and gestures to me, as if we're two friends meeting for coffee.

I shrink down, but there's nowhere to go. I've trapped myself in the back corner, and she's blocking the only way out.

She walks over to my booth, no apology, no explanation. No pretending she didn't chase me down the street.

At least she doesn't sit, only stares at me. "My name is Alice Hughes, and I'd like to speak with you."

Her tone of voice surprises me, somewhat stern and with a British accent. "No comment."

A line of confusion settles in her brow. But then her expression flashes to one of understanding and she shakes her head. "You think I'm a reporter?"

I do a quick scan of her clothing. No camera in her hand or hanging from her shoulders.

"I still can't talk to you." Lowering my head, I slip on my sunglasses. "Please, go."

"It's about my sister," she says.

This catches me off guard, but I don't understand what she means. "I'm sorry, but I don't know your sister."

"I still need to talk to you." She slides into the opposite seat. "Because she used to live in your apartment."

13

"My apartment?" Her words stun me into stillness, and I take off the glasses.

"Yes, the unit on the end that's always empty. I've been watching the place." She pauses, shadows passing behind her eyes. "Because my sister discovered something while she was there."

Her somber tone sends a chill down my spine. "What do you mean? What did your sister tell you?"

"Nothing. She didn't get a chance." Alice stares at me for a moment and leans forward. "Rose is missing, and the last place anyone saw her was the mansion." She curls her hands into fists. "With *those people*."

Those people.

The Marteaus.

Words tangle in my mind and lodge in my throat, but I finally break some free. "How long has your sister been missing?"

"Five months." Alice sits straight as a board, but then she collapses, slumping forward to rest her elbows on the table.

The server returns with my drink, her expression neutral but strained. I'm sure she's picking up on the tension. It fills the air around us, thick as molasses.

She asks Alice if she'd like something, but Alice shakes her head.

After the waitress leaves, I sip the hot coffee and study the woman across from me. I can't imagine what she wants from me.

"What did the police say?" I ask.

"The police." She barks out a harsh laugh and shakes her head, her features hardening again. "The police didn't follow up. They didn't do anything at all. The Marteaus made sure of it. One word from them and the police shut me down. They accepted whatever those people said."

"Which was what?"

Even her shrug reeks of anger. "That my sister left the mansion. Nothing else. And I have no proof of anything different." Her jaw clenches, and she levels me with her stare. "But I know something happened to her."

Brow furrowed, she starts twisting a ring on her finger. "The truth is, Rose and I weren't speaking at the time. When she was living here in Paris. So I knew something was wrong when she called me from the apartment. It was a video chat, and I could tell she was freaked out. Scared."

I squeeze the warm cup in my hand, thinking of the mansion's disturbing reputation.

Maison de la Morte.

Alice leans in, lowering her voice as if she's afraid we'll be overheard. "Rose said she'd found a book in the apartment. Some kind of journal. She was waving it around the whole time she talked."

Alice exhales, her breath shaky. "She wanted to tell me about something she'd read in it."

"What?" I lean forward, mirroring her body language.

"I don't know." She jerks her face up, her wild eyes meeting mine. "She only said, 'It's so horrible. You won't believe it.' All of a sudden, she stopped and looked over her shoulder. Like she'd heard something. Maybe someone knocking at her door?" Another shrug. "She said she had to go but would call me back."

Alice swallows, like she's choking on emotion. "She never did."

Needing to process what she's saying, I take another drink of my coffee. Ten minutes ago, she was following me, stalking me. Now she sounds like the first episode of a true-crime podcast.

I need to parse out the details. "So you have no idea what she read in the journal?"

"No."

"Then you can't be sure it had anything to do with the Marteaus."

"It must have. They wouldn't let me into her apartment after she went missing. They wouldn't even talk to me. Why wouldn't they talk to me?" She reaches over and grabs my arm. "I'm telling you, they know something."

"Okay, okay." I shoot a glance at the waitress, longing for a third-party presence. Keeping my voice steady, I ask Alice, "Are you sure you don't want something to drink?"

"I'm fine," she says, though she's clearly not. She releases me and folds her arms into a tight knot. "The Marteaus told the police Rose left on her own, and it's not their job to keep track of renters."

It sounds exactly like something Chantal or Vincent would say, conceit dripping from every word. I doubt they concern themselves with anyone else's problems, especially people they deem inferior. But that doesn't mean they would hide information about a missing woman.

"I don't know the family well," I say, "so I'm not sure what I can do to help you."

She goes still, her features tense as she holds my gaze. "There is something you can do. You're on the inside. You're in her apartment."

She holds out her hand but stops just short of grabbing me again. "You can try to find the journal." She's talking faster now, excited at the prospect. "It's dark blue, a navy color."

My hesitation must show on my face, because she presses on. "Please, do this for me. A small favor. One look around the apartment. It's all I'm asking."

"I guess I could look, but it's possible Rose took the journal with her."

"No, Rose didn't—" She breaks off and presses her fingers to her temple, frustration sharpening her words. "Rose is *missing*. And the police won't listen to me unless I give them a reason. I'm certain this journal is the proof I need."

Her tears form as she stares at me. "Please, I have to find her. The police won't help. The Marteaus won't help. Rose has stopped using social media and her phone always goes to voicemail. Like it's turned off or . . . dead."

At the word *dead,* she shudders.

And I don't think she's imagining the phone.

Alice is clearly suffering. Her pain is a physical presence, vibrating around her like a force field. But by her own admission, she and Rose were having personal problems. They weren't speaking to each other.

Maybe Rose still isn't speaking to her, and Alice doesn't know it.

Whatever the truth, I can't turn her away, the way everyone else has. I can try to help, even if I'm searching for a book that will never be found. It's the least I can do.

"No promises," I say, "but I'll try to find the journal."

"Thank you." Alice releases a heavy sigh, relaxing all over like someone pulled a plug. She rubs both hands up her face before pressing her palms to the table. "Okay, when Rose was younger, she kept her secret things hidden. Under loose floorboards, window seats, or in her stuffed animals."

I picture the many nooks and crannies in the apartment. The journal could be anywhere. If it's on the property at all. But I offer her an encouraging grin and wait for her to finish.

"Here's my username on Instagram. You can message me there." She pulls a scrap of paper from her pocket and slides it across the table, already prepared in case I agreed. "Please, contact me as soon as you can."

"I will." I put the paper in my purse.

She rubs her hands together and licks her lips. "Sorry, I didn't get your name."

"Brooke." I don't add my last name, because it's the same as my stage name.

She nods slowly, studying me like she's trying to puzzle something out. "You look familiar. Have I seen you on a reality show?"

Panic flutters in my chest and warbles in my voice. "No."

"I swear." She squints. "Your face . . ."

My mouth goes dry. "I get that a lot."

"Are you an influencer or something?" For the first time, she smiles. "I know I've seen you somewhere before."

The waitress brings my food, and I use the sandwich as an excuse to keep my face lowered, hoping she'll move on from asking who I am.

Alice taps her fingernails on the table. "Why did you think I was a reporter?"

I stare into the depths of my coffee, feeling cornered and uncomfortable. "A friend of mine is going through something at the moment, and tabloids have no boundaries."

It's not a complete lie.

"Hmm," she murmurs, unsatisfied with my answer.

But when I glance up, her expression is flat. "Listen, all I care about is finding Rose. If you'll do this one thing for me, it could be a big help."

"I'll do what I can and be in touch." Picking up my knife, I slice my croque madame.

"Thank you." Alice sits there for another moment, but finally she stands and walks away. Before she turns the corner, she gives me a wave.

I smile but don't wave back.

After she's gone, I stare a few seconds longer, the smile slipping from my face.

Alice says her sister is missing, and I don't see the harm in searching for the journal. But if I'm honest, I have my own reasons to find the book.

Rose was afraid of someone in the family.

She lived at Maison Marteau.

And my apartment was the last place she was seen alive.

My Hotel Peculiar

It was much later that night, but I still couldn't fall asleep. I was hungry and too excited. I wanted to go back downstairs to see the decorations and what was left of the food.

Finally, I heard my mother's voice. She was upstairs, calling down to a servant with instructions. Then I heard her heels clacking down the hall toward her bedroom.

When the house fell quiet, I knew it was time.

I sneaked out my door and hurried toward the stairs, my bare feet slapping on the parquet floor. I passed the horloge de parquet. *No. I mean the grandfather clock. (I looked up the word, and it's always best to write both the English and the French. For better memory.)*

The grandfather clock told me it was after one in the morning. I began to tiptoe down the main stairs, but I changed my mind. That would be too obvious, and if I got caught again, I was really going to be in trouble.

So instead, I took the secret stairs. If I passed a servant on the way, they would never tell, because I could make them lose their job. And they all knew it.

I made it downstairs without any problem and pushed out of the secret panel. I stepped out into the blue parlor. The sound of clattering dishes came from the kitchen, so I crept over and looked out into the hall.

Seeing none of the caterers, I ran to the room where the food had been served. Most of it was still on display.

My eyes grew wide, and my stomach growled. The desserts had been picked over, but there were plenty left. And all so pretty with their blue-and-white icing or chocolate swirls.

I tried a macaron, and a mendiant, and a strawberry truffle. I had a vanilla square in my hand when I heard a voice. My father's voice, answered by a woman's laugh.

I recognized the potato-in-the-mouth sound from before.

Their voices grew louder, headed my way.

Throwing down the sweet square, I dove under the nearest table, letting the long white cloth hide me from view.

The laugh came again, growing louder, until two sets of feet walked by in the hallway. My father's black dress shoes, and the woman's thin ankles in sparkly high heels.

The same woman my father had been dancing with. The one who my mother said was in her cups.

But why were they walking in that direction? Toward the back? She should be going out the front doors like everyone else.

Dropping my treat, I slid out on my belly and sneaked to the door. They weren't in the hallway anymore.

I padded quietly down the hall in the direction they'd walked. I peeked around the next corner, and there they were.

My father was walking beside her with one hand on her back. The way he touched her made me feel hot and itchy. Not right.

When they got close to the kitchen, my father hurried ahead and shut the door. Maybe he didn't want her to see the mess?

They kept going and turned the corner.

Careful not to make too much noise, I ran down the hall but stopped short at the corner.

When I looked around, I saw them in front of a small door. It slid open, and they stepped inside.

This time, I didn't follow. Because the door only led to one place.

A place I'm not allowed to go. Not by myself.

I turned to go back the way I came. I was disappointed, so I decided to make a plate and take some food up to my room.

But even as I piled fancy sweets on a plate, I couldn't stop wondering about the woman with my father. Why was she still here? Why did he touch her like that?

And why did he take her to his special place?

14

I begin my search in the most obvious place. The grand salon is on the first floor, the largest room in the apartment, filled with couches, chairs, tables . . . and a full wall of bookshelves.

After eating at the café, I came straight back to the mansion. I haven't studied my scene from the script like I'd planned, too intrigued by the journal to focus on anything else.

As I cut through the entry hall, my mother's voice whispers to me, reminding me about distractions and how they steal your dreams.

Lifting my gaze, I say, "Mom, as soon as I search the apartment, I'll get back to work. Promise."

Because I gave my word to Alice.

And I'm dying to know what Rose read in the journal.

In the salon, I peruse the shelves, taking time with any book in the family of blue. When I find one, I check the first pages. So far everything is history or a work of fiction. Nothing in the format of a journal or diary.

After half an hour of scouring the shelves and other potential hiding spots, it's clear the journal isn't hidden in the grand salon.

Covering the rest of this floor doesn't take long, most of my time spent in the kitchen and butler's pantry. I check every drawer, cubby, and cabinet, even running my hand beneath a sideboard in the dining room.

All the while, curiosity scratches at the base of my skull. The same morbid question echoing again and again.

What did Rose read that was so horrible? The mansion's nickname floats to mind—house of death—and I roll my shoulder to dislodge the chill.

First floor completed, I go upstairs, pausing to study the grim portraits. When did the dour-faced people live here? What atrocities have they seen?

What secrets have they kept all these years?

When I reach the landing, I put my hands on my hips and survey the area. Then I start the hunt. Like most of the apartment, the second floor is museum-clean. Every closet or cabinet uncluttered and organized. It makes for a swift search.

But still no journal.

By the time I finish with the third-floor bedrooms, I'm drafting a message to Alice in my head. Regret and disappointment tangle inside me. Alice is worried about her sister and suspects the worst. She needs answers.

But so do I.

If Alice's suspicions are correct and Rose discovered something about the Marteau family, something that scared her, I need to know what she found.

Because I'm living under their roof.

With a sigh of defeat, I return to the landing. I don't have the journal, after looking every possible place. Every drawer, nook, pillow, and every loose floorboard. In every single room.

Except one.

The storage room.

My stomach clenches, a sense of dread building as I walk down the corridor, creeping into darkness.

The door opens with a low, moaning creak. A sound worthy of any haunted house.

I flip the switch, but the light barely reaches the floor, blocked by taller furniture draped in sheets. The stale scent of neglect fills my nose, and I almost change my mind.

I take a step back, then I remember Alice's eyes, wide and desolate. Begging for help.

I'll want a shower afterward, but I need to go in. Boxes and furniture pack the space, leaving narrow, crooked paths to walk the room. Dustsheets cover only a few pieces, as if wrapping the items required too much effort.

This space isn't as organized as the rest of the apartment, creating hundreds of hidden spots to stash a book.

I doubt I'll finish this room today, but I can make a cursory check. I start with the furniture, larger pieces built for the purpose of storage. It's not long before my skin is crawling with filth. Dust in my eyes, my hair, my mouth.

I'm already grungy, so I might as well finish with the furniture, leaving boxes and crates until tomorrow.

Antiques cram against the walls—a porcelain bowl and pitcher set, a violin with no strings, a box of silverware with missing pieces. Even the junk here is expensive.

I'm near the windows facing the park when a bulky shape in the corner draws my attention.

An old steamer trunk, the navy leather turned gray by dust.

Kneeling, I open the locks on each end. But the middle lock doesn't budge. I grip the ancient latch and give it a shake. The metal holds firm.

"Damn." A missing journal. An old steamer trunk. An attic in an old mansion. The Nancy Drew of it all has my fingers itching. Should I pry the lock?

No. It doesn't belong to me, and if I can't get in, then Rose couldn't have, either.

I give the trunk a smack of frustration. A black spider scurries from beneath and heads straight toward my foot.

Leaping up, I stutter-step backwards, bumping into a stack of boxes. Dust motes explode in the air and crawl up my nose. Three sneezes and I raise both hands. "That's it. I'm done."

I twist and turn my way through the clutter, making a new path to the door. Grudgingly, I turn to the side, squeezing between two tall, heavy pieces. My foot kicks something, and it clatters across the floor.

A silver picture frame, backside facing up. I pick it up and flip it over.

The scene in the photo feels familiar, so I wipe away dust to see it better. An old picture of Maison Marteau. If the sepia tones didn't give away the photo's age, the barren land around the mansion would. No trees or shrubbery planted yet, only the residence and cobblestoned courtyard.

A man and woman stand in the foreground, two young boys in front of them. Their expressions are serious, typical of the early 1900s. But what is the man wearing? A type of shawl hangs around his neck, like a graduation stole with a picture or markings on one side.

I peer closer. No use. I can't make out the details. I pull my phone from my back pocket and turn on the flashlight.

The design is too small. Maybe the letter V combined with other shapes or letters? Finally, I give up and set the frame on top of a box.

The storage room is full of castoffs and abandoned rubbish, yet the photo and frame show no damage. A photo of ancestors, a record of the family legacy.

So why is it in here?

15

I've lost the morning light but think I have what I need.

"I should," I mumble to myself, stripping the camera from the tripod. "I've only done a hundred takes." The number is probably closer to thirty, but still excessive.

Yesterday is a blur in my mind—meeting Alice, searching for the journal, breaking down the scene, filming rehearsal clips. And watching them over and over until I couldn't see straight. Micro-expressions. Word emphasis. Timing. Obsessively fine-tuning every detail.

Then this morning, I let it all go, allowing practice and emotion to blend, to create something new. Raw and authentic. Hoping to capture Claudia's character the way I'd planned.

And I think I got it. I feel good.

If casting directors walked in right now, I'd be ready. If they asked me to read like I were auditioning for Stephen Spielberg? I can do that.

For M. Night Shyamalan? Of course.

For Joyce Sandman? No fucking problem.

Even if I don't get the part, I know I did good work. I understand the material. I'm fully prepared.

And my mother would be proud.

A sound rises from the floor, interrupting my dreams of success. Clairee stares at me from the doorway, her meow full-throated and insistent.

"Ready to go out?" She's getting a little too comfortable, but I don't mind. I'm growing attached to her little face and her gentle purrs. And honestly, I feel less alone in this giant apartment.

I fold the tripod and follow her to the door. I need a break. Some food. Time to recharge before I review the videos, a grueling process of elimination that might take hours.

She trails behind me down the stairs to the front door. We've developed something of a routine, and she rubs my calf as she passes. "See you later."

I grin after her, pleased with my productive morning and the sunny day.

"Good morning." Noah stands on the walkway, watching me.

And the cat scampering down my steps.

"I . . . hey," I say, fumbling my words. I'm sure pets are forbidden, especially with velvet sofas and teak tables, all begging to become scratching posts. I gesture to the bushes where Clairee disappeared. "She just showed up the other night. And it was so rainy and cold and..."

Embarrassed, I falter, tugging on the hem of my shirt.

His chuckle surprises me. "Don't worry. Your secret is safe with me."

He slides his hands in the front pockets of his jeans. "All of your secrets. Brooke *Summers*."

My face goes slack. "How did you find out my name?"

"I talked to my aunt last night." He indicates the building.

"This is her place. She told me not to bother the actress staying here, because she wanted to keep a low profile."

He gives me a sheepish grin. "After that, I couldn't help searching for actresses named Brooke."

I lick my lips. "Does anyone else know?"

"I haven't told them. And I won't," he says, giving me a look of camaraderie and shared secrets.

"Okay. Thank you." I relax in a way I didn't expect. His knowing my secret should be upsetting, but it's not. Maybe because he's American. Or maybe it's all the ways he's different from the other Marteaus. And the fact they exclude him.

"I thought you might like to join me for coffee," he says. "I also have croissants," he adds, before I can reply. "Fresh from the bakery." His voice lifts, teasing, as if he's offering something I can't refuse.

And he's right, because I'm starving.

"You picked the perfect morning, because I haven't eaten yet." My shoes sit by the door, so I slip them on and grab the keys to lock up.

I join him on the walk, and we make small talk as we cross the courtyard. Safe subjects only, like the cat and the weather and if I take coffee or tea.

The layout of his apartment is different from mine, a less conspicuous set of stairs climbing one wall. The décor is stylish but more modern, dark-gray walls and sleek furniture. We pass a sitting room on one side, and an office on the other, windows framing a view of the courtyard.

"I've set up in the kitchen," he says, walking slightly ahead of me, not leading as much as guiding.

In the kitchen, Noah points to a high stool at the island. "Have a seat, and I'll pour your coffee." The granite is covered with dishes—meats, cheeses, fruits, jams, and of course, the famous croissants.

Did he lay this out for himself? Or did he go to all this trouble on the chance I'd join him? The effort strikes me as more than a neighborly gesture, and a strange warmth settles in my chest.

I'm suddenly glad I filmed this morning, that I put on makeup and wore real clothes. Not my usual yoga pants and T-shirt.

He sets a cup in front of me, along with cream and sugar. "How did it go the other night?"

I blink. "Sorry?"

"Dinner with Dora." His voice is casual as he fills a plate, but I detect an underlying strain.

"Fine," I say, but my face must tell a different story.

"That bad?" Judging by his tone, I'd guess he understands exactly what dining with the family is like.

I use the tiny fork to take some cheese. "There were some strange moments." I avoid eye contact as I gloss over the truth, but when I look up, Noah is studying me.

"Okay." I sigh. "Let's just say I understand your warning about Ric."

He tenses, a glower tightening his face. "What did he do?"

"Nothing." I shake my head. "Nothing too bad. But I can tell he's used to getting what he wants." A diplomatic answer. Better than saying Ric's a leering, hand-wandering perv.

Noah's expression remains dark. "I'm sorry. He's a real . . . piece of work." Switching to a more polite description, he nods. But I can tell another word was on his tongue.

"Ric always thought a lot of himself, even when we were kids. He wants to be next in line to rule Maison Marteau, even before Victor."

"His own father?"

Noah shrugs and shakes his head.

Smearing butter on my croissant, I paste a pleasant expression on my face and shift the conversation away from Ric. "Did you visit here much when you were younger?"

He takes a moment, then finally says, "My mother and I stayed away for a long time. She's from the States, so after my father died, we didn't have much reason to return."

"I'm sorry. I shouldn't have—"

"No, it's fine." He waves away my concern. "My aunt and uncle live in California. They're good people, and we stayed close."

Good people. The phrase sits oddly. As if he needs to separate them from the rest of the Marteaus.

"I can't imagine living somewhere else when you've got a literal mansion in Paris." I try to make my tone light and playful, but Noah remains pensive.

"Family life here can be complicated, especially if you're like me." He meets my eyes. "Not the right *bloodline*."

He puts emphasis on the word, as if he's heard it from someone else. My bet would be Dora.

He angles his head toward my apartment. "My aunt and uncle in California are the ones who own your unit."

"Do they rent it out often?" I keep trying to avoid negative topics, but as soon as I ask the question, I think of Rose.

I didn't mean to open this particular door, wasn't planning to interrogate Noah.

But now I'm on edge, waiting to hear what he says.

Staring over my head, he sips his coffee and squints in thought. "They used to rent it more, but it's been a while."

I stir the scrambled eggs on my plate and scoop some up. "Such a beautiful place to sit empty. I'm lucky my agent could get me in. She has connections and, apparently, one of them led to your aunt." I hold my fork but don't take a bite.

I'm too busy phrasing my next question, following the

natural path of the conversation. "Was the last person who stayed in the apartment family, or a family friend?"

The eggs wobble on my fork as I hold my breath.

"I'm not sure. I was away on business a lot during that time, but I did speak to the last tenant once. I remember she was a Brit."

My skin prickles.

Rose.

Should I ask when he last saw her? Was he here when she left? Was she alone or with someone else?

I'm close, much closer to answers than Alice has ever been. No one in the family will talk to her.

They probably wouldn't tell me much, either.

But Noah's not like the others. He grew up somewhere else, somewhere sheltered from the lifestyle of Maison Marteau. Protected from the privilege that created a creep like Ric.

He has different values, his own moral code, unsullied by the corrupting influence of wealth.

Can I trust him?

Rubbing my hands on my thighs, I sit up straight. "Were you here when she—"

Laughter cuts through the moment.

We both turn our heads.

Noah crosses to the window and shoves the curtain aside. "We've got company."

16

The taste of coffee lingers on my tongue as I look over Noah's shoulder. Luci is in the courtyard, holding the hand of a man I don't recognize.

She leans into him, smiling up into his face.

He takes a step back.

Noah sighs and turns to me. "Guess we'd better go save him."

Together, we go out and follow the walkway around the corner. "André," Noah calls, lifting a hand in greeting.

Luci has her fingers curled around the man's bicep, practically swooning, but her face lights up even more when she sees me. "Brooke, hi." She stands on her tiptoes and waves.

Noah introduces me to André and says, "You didn't tell me you were coming by."

André lifts a shoulder. "I was in the neighborhood." His French accent is thick—smooth, lyrical, charming. He nods at me with an affable grin, and I can see why Luci has a crush.

"André lives across the park," Noah explains to me. "He's always in the neighborhood."

"And aren't you glad?" André soft-punches Noah's arm.

Luci beams at the tall Frenchman. "Well, I'm happy he's here. But I'll be even happier if he agrees to come with me." She presses against André, mouth pouting and eyes pleading. "Please?"

André tilts his head back. "*Oh là là.*"

"What's going on?" Noah furrows his brow, glancing between the two.

Luci practically vibrates with excitement. "I invited André to *La Danse des Monstres*."

"She's trying to convince me," André says, "but I don't think it's a good idea." He looks down at Luci, expression serious. "You are too young for me."

Luci waves off his concern. "We won't be alone. All of my family will be there. Noah included."

André's brows shoot up. "You were actually invited?"

"Yeah, yeah." Noah laughs, clearly unfazed.

"Sorry," I finally break in. "Can someone explain?"

"*La Danse des Monstres*," André says. "The monsters' dance. The Marteaus have a party every year, and only the most important people are invited. Very chic," he says. "Very, how do you say? *Swanky*." He flutters his fingers in mock excitement. "A gathering of the beautiful and the wealthy."

Luci gives him a friendly punch on a shoulder. "You're rich, too."

"Not that kind of rich."

I'm still missing something. "Sorry, why monsters?"

Luci steps closer, as interested in convincing me as much as André. "Remember those rumors we talked about? *Maison de la Morte*? A party for monsters was my grandmother's idea. It's a way of snubbing our noses at the gossip."

"Thumbing our noses," Noah corrects.

"Yes." Luci frowns, and I remember how important speaking English is to her family.

Noah's gaze flicks to me. "Why don't we all go? Luci and I have to attend, but we'll have a better time with people we know."

"You mean people we like," Luci says.

I'm still puzzling over the monster theme when Noah's question registers. "You want me to go?"

"It's Saturday," he says, preempting my next question.

Caught off guard, I can only blink at Noah while my mind races. Saturday. By then, I'll have sent in my audition. I'll have the time. Plus, being with Noah isn't exactly a hardship.

But another night surrounded by *the family*?

I shoot him a look of apology. "Not sure it sounds like my kind of thing."

"No, no. You'll love it." Luci bounces and shakes André's arm. "Tell her."

"You'll love it," he says, voice flat and dry.

"You will," Luci insists. "Dancing, decadence, high society. So many glamorous people."

I feign enthusiasm. "Sounds amazing."

Sounds awful.

Just hearing her description makes my nerves twist and sting. High-class events might be fun for other people. But not me. I've attended enough glitzy parties with distinguished guests, and I have different associations.

Different memories.

A distant hallway, a quiet bedroom. The sound of his heavy breathing as he follows me in.

And locks the door behind him.

Nausea works its slimy way through my gut, but I don't let it show. Instead, I clear my throat and offer an excuse. "I don't have anything to wear."

"Don't worry. I can tell you a place." Luci has an answer for everything.

"Well," I hedge, racking my brain for another plausible reason to refuse.

"Oh, come on." André gives me a mischievous wink. "If you go, I'll go. We can back each other up." He jerks his head to Luci. "And you can help me keep an eye on this one."

"*Oui*!" Luci squeals, standing on her tiptoes to kiss André's cheek. "Thank you. Thank you. Thank you."

"Luci!" A shout echoes across the courtyard, and we all turn. Lyam strides from the main doors, his expression thunderous.

For a moment, I can only stare, shocked by his anger. He was so friendly at dinner; he and Dora were the most normal and down-to-earth people at the table.

But a different personality is on display now. He stops walking and makes a jerking motion for Luci to join him. Why is he so upset?

Luci quickly puts distance between herself and André, her face falling. "I must go," she says before whispering to André, "but I'm holding you to your promise." With a huff, she hurries over to Lyam.

He speaks in a low voice, so we can't hear what he says, but he glowers at Luci, jaw clenching as he speaks. As if he's scolding her.

Noah watches me watching them. "He's very protective of Luci. Since her parents died, he's been like an older brother."

André lifts both hands. "Hey, don't look at me. I didn't do anything."

"Don't worry about it." Noah's tone tells me he's used to the drama.

"So, Brooke," André says, drawling my name. "Which way are you going to go?"

"Sorry," I say, pulling my gaze back to him.

"Your costume? What will you wear?"

"Costume?" I turn to Noah. "A detail you failed to mention."

He clears his throat. "Ah . . . it's part of the theme."

"Oh. Can I think about it?"

"Of course."

André fixes me with a stare. "Think fast," he says. "You only have two days to choose your costume, and you must make an important decision. Will you be a monster?"

He leans closer, his voice a whisper of something dangerous. "Or a victim?"

17

"Too strong. My voice needs to be softer." In the study, I sit hunched over at the desk, critiquing the videos I filmed this morning. Are my expressions nuanced? Does my voice carry undertones?

I tap the space bar to pause the video and jot down a note. With the recording silent, I hear a tapping sound. Unlike random noises I sometimes hear in the apartment, this knock is firm and intentional.

Rolling back the office chair, I hurry out and am halfway to the stairs when the knock comes again, but from down the hall. From inside the mansion.

When Luci gave me a tour the first night, she told me her living quarters were right on the other side. But I check to make sure the door is locked before I answer. "Hello?"

"It's me." The voice is dulled by the thick wood, but I can tell it's Luci. I turn the knob with a *clunk* and swing open one large panel.

Luci balls her hands together, like a child who's got a secret they're bursting to share. "Hi, are you busy?"

My head turns slightly, and I itch to get back to the videos. "Not really."

Luci whispers as if we're engaging in spy craft. "I thought you might like to tour the rest of the house. Everyone is gone to a board meeting. Well, except for Aunt Chantal, but she's locked away in her room."

"Why are you whispering?" I whisper. Then I clear my throat to speak in a normal voice. "If I'm not supposed to come inside without—"

"No, no." Luci laughs and shakes her head. "I thought you'd be more comfortable without everyone around." She rolls her eyes. "I definitely will."

"You said Chantal is home, and she's not my biggest fan."

"Please?" She reaches out with both hands to grab one of mine. She's acting the way she did earlier with André, cheerful, but almost childlike in her manner. Where is the poised and mature young woman I met on my first night?

But if a simple tour will make her happy, I can spare a few minutes. "Okay, let me get my shoes." I'm not walking through the lavish mansion in my *Kim Possible* crew socks.

When I'm ready, she tugs me by the hand, an actual bounce in her step as she guides me down the hall. We take a turn into a room with silk-papered walls, and she points out the view of the gardens.

Moving and speaking with heightened energy, she takes me through room after room until they become a blur of lush fabrics and gold-framed paintings. Like my apartment, dark paneling runs throughout, the style somber and moody despite the daylight.

Luci gestures with her hands, spouting off names in French —*galerie, logo du concierge, salle à manger*. As we exit a room whose name I've already forgotten, I spot a blue book on a coffee table. I come to a stop. It's not dark, but it gives me an idea.

If Rose did leave the journal in the apartment, maybe the cleaning staff picked it up. And if those people also clean the mansion, it's possible they brought the book to the main house.

And put it in the most logical place.

I spin around to Luci. "Do you have a library?"

Something flickers behind her eyes. "*Oui*," she says, breaking from her usual English. "Straight ahead." She lifts her hand, pointing down the corridor, to another set of doors standing open at the end.

Instead of taking the lead, Luci drags a half-step behind and lets me enter the library first.

"It's huge," I say, my voice breathy with awe. Floor-to-ceiling shelves line every wall, with rolling ladders to help reach the books on top.

"Amazing, right?" Luci's hollow tone doesn't match her words, but I'm focused on the grandeur of the room.

"Amazing is one word for it." Turning in a slow circle, I take it all in. The library of every book lover's dreams.

And far too many books for me to investigate. Not by myself. And I can't ask for Luci's help.

I sweep my gaze around the room, trying to home in on any blue books. My eyes land on the fireplace, and the prominent portrait hanging above the mantle. The man from the photo in the storage room. He's older, with more wrinkles and hair turned white, but I recognize his face, the sharp nose and brooding gaze.

And he's wearing the same shawl.

I approach the painting, studying the wrap hanging around his neck. The painting is in color, red lettering popping against the black fabric. I can clearly make out the design. The letter V in a bold, Roman style, with an S within the angle.

No, wait. I step closer.

Not a letter, but a serpent. Rearing its head from inside the V, its long body forming an S-shaped curve.

The portrait commands attention, a picture light casting shadows on the man's stern face. "He must be important."

"Mm-hm." Luci nods. "My great-great grandfather. He built Maison Marteau."

Pretending I'm noticing for the first time, I point to the symbols on his scarf. "Is this some sort of family crest?"

"No." She presses her lips together. "I...I'm not sure. Like a fraternity or something, I think." She folds and unfolds her arms, body wired tight enough to snap. Standing in the doorway, just over the threshold.

Barely a step inside the library.

Even from across the room, I can tell how stiffly she's holding herself, like she's bracing for impact. She tries to smile again, but something makes her mouth twitch and her shoulders cinch tight. Something that tugs on my heart. Sadness. Insecurity.

Or damage.

She almost folds into herself, like an injured bird trying to hide. The look in her eyes takes me back in time, to a certain night. A horrific night.

She reminds me of Mackenzie.

Forgetting the painting, and the journal, and all of the mansion's secrets, I walk over to her. I speak softly, because she looks like she might break. "Luci, what's the matter?"

Her throat bobs with a hard swallow. "Nothing."

Her voice is barely audible, so I inch closer and touch her arm. "Do you want to go somewhere and talk?"

Draping one arm over her stomach, she opens her mouth to respond. Closes it again.

Seconds pass as we stare at each other.

Then she blinks and breaks from the trance, as if somewhere a hypnotist snapped his fingers. She smiles brightly. "No, I'm fine. I'm just not much of a reader."

I drop my hand. "Okay, but—"

She cocks her head, listening. "I think Chantal is up. We should probably go."

By "we," she means me.

Whirling, she retraces our route through the hallways, and I fall into step beside her. This time we take a direct path. No detours into rooms or commentary on the artwork. The tour is over.

A sidelong glance tells me Luci is still wearing a happy mask, but her smile doesn't reach her eyes. Not like it did when she came to my door.

As we move closer to my apartment, I feel an opportunity slipping away. The library was too big to search, and now I've wasted the time I had alone with Luci. Time I could have used to ask about Rose.

"Thank you for showing me your home," I say, figuring out a way to broach the subject. "Am I special, or do you give all of your tenants a tour of the mansion?"

She scratches her cheek as if puzzled. "You mean Noah? He grew up here."

"No, I meant the other people who stayed in my apartment." My breath hitches. "Like Rose."

"Rose?" Her tone leaps to a higher note. "Rose. Oh, the woman who lived here before you?"

"Yes," I say, watching her closely.

"I met her once." Her gaze darts to the side, past my shoulder, down to my chin. "How do you know about her?"

"I talked to her sister, Alice. She's trying to find Rose."

"Alice. Yes, she's been a problem." Luci frowns. "My grandmother and Uncle Victor don't like her. She made them very angry."

She tosses a glance over her shoulder, down the hallway. "Alice is not a good subject to bring up in this house. It's probably best if you don't get involved."

"Of course," I say, feigning indifference. "I was only curious."

Letting that serve as my answer, I open my door and step through. "Thanks for inviting me over."

"Je t'en prie." Luci falls back on her French again, something she seems to do when she's excited. Or when she's distressed.

Shutting the door, I make sure the lock falls firmly into place and listen for the latch on the other side.

But all I can hear are Luci's last words, telling me not to get involved.

She claims she only met Rose one time, but I get the feeling she's keeping secrets. About Rose. And the strange symbol.

Growing up in the mansion, she must have seen the portrait many times, along with the photo on display in the main house. An exact copy of the one I found in the storage room.

The symbol is everywhere around the mansion and clearly held significance for Luci's ancestor. Her entire family. So how could Luci not know its meaning?

And why was she so afraid of the library?

18

My finger hovers over the trackpad, ready to tap and click "send."

I've spent hours reviewing my audition clips, choosing the best one, and finally attaching the video to an email. Now my message to the casting director is ready to go, but I can't bring myself to hit the button.

Did I forget anything? Did I do all I could? Is this my best work?

"It will have to be," I mutter, because the deadline is today. And I'm out of time.

Doubt and anxiety try to creep their way in, so I steel my nerves and press the button. The outgoing message leaves with a *whoosh*, the finality of the sound almost taking my breath.

The empty screen taunts me for a few more seconds, then I sigh and sit back in the chair. A rainbow of emotions filters through me. Doubt, relief, elation. Doubt again.

Swiveling the chair, I face the windows. Nothing to do but wait. Wait and hope for a callback.

Outside the window, the night seems to go on forever. No moonlight or movement, only thick heavy clouds.

After the last few work-filled days, I feel the vastness of my sudden free time. Endless hours rolling out before me. What do I do with myself?

My gaze drifts to the ceiling, my thoughts drifting even farther. To the storage room one level up, sitting in the dusty dark.

I should probably finish looking for the journal, but I can't summon the will to return to the cramped, dirty space. Not tonight.

Then I think about Noah and his invitation to *La Danse des Monstres*. The monsters' dance.

According to André, it's a much sought-after invitation, an exclusive event for the Parisian elite. And great social events often draw the media.

Which could be a problem.

I sit up straight and return to my laptop. The truth is, I have no idea what to expect from the party. High-society events often have photographers present.

Wondering if I should cancel with Noah, I click out of the email server and open a search engine. News of the protests is the top story, and the crowds on the streets have doubled in size.

So many more people than before. Hundreds. Maybe thousands. So far, they seem to be focused on the heart of the city, but I don't think I'll be travelling any time soon.

Putting political unrest out of my mind, I type "*La Danse des Monstres*" in the search bar.

Several links fill the page. None of the sites have photos, so I click on the link for images. Several pictures of the mansion come up, but they're only exterior views.

At last, I hit paydirt. A single photo of people mingling in a lavish ballroom, many wearing masks or costumes.

The picture is uncentered and taken from a lower angle, as if the one holding the camera was sneaking a shot. Is that why I'm having a hard time finding pictures? Are cameras not allowed at the dance?

Visions of golden masks and black robes fill my mind. I shake my head at where my thoughts have led. "I'm not playing a role in *Eyes Wide Shut.*"

At least, I hope not.

I'm sure the privacy is to protect the party guests, or maybe secrecy helps create mystique. If it's one thing Hollywood has taught me, it's the power of illusion. And what people will do for a little taste of fantasy.

The photo doesn't tell me much, other than masks seem to be optional, and I still have questions about the monsters' dance.

Luci said this party was a way of making fun of the local gossip, the family saying they don't care what other people think. But something about the explanation doesn't sit right with me.

The deaths of a husband and wife in the early 1900s isn't recent enough to inspire so much interest. And surely no one—even the haughty Marteaus—would host a yearly party to mock gossip involving a child's death.

There has to be more to the story.

Thirty minutes later, I've searched every combination of words related to Maison Marteau or the monsters' dance. I even searched for *Maison de la Morte,* in its specific arrondissement. Still nothing. No explanation or history of *La Danse des Monstres.*

I remember the enthusiasm of the dark tourist, with his ghoulish attitude and skull T-shirt.

What was done to her body.

The words send chills down my back, but I still have no idea what he meant. How did he know so much? Where did he get his information?

The idea hits me like a lightning bolt. He knew, because he was into dark tourism.

My fingers fly over the keyboard, and this time I search for dark tourist websites. Several pages populate, an overwhelming amount, so I take my time with each link. I sift through a few amateur blogs, links to social media pages, and a site last updated five years ago.

Finally, I land on a forum, the latest entry from only two hours ago. Using the search box embedded in the site, I type in *Paris* and scan through the topics. I find mostly information about the catacombs and graveyards.

I need more about the mansion. Specifics. And I'm betting these are the people to ask.

When I try to post a question, I get a pop-up box with a message. *Access restricted to members only.*

Typing in my junk email and my usual nickname, I apply to open an account.

I wait five minutes. Check my email. Another five. Another check.

"This is ridiculous." I refresh the page one more time.

Thunder rolls outside the window, and those thick, dark clouds release the rain.

My first thought is of little Clairee. The rain will bring her to my front door, ready for supper. And so am I. With the whole day spent working, I've hardly eaten.

Hand on the railing, I jog downstairs, and as soon as I open the door, Clairee dashes in. She doesn't bother to shake the drops from her fur, only beelines for the kitchen.

"Well, I guess I know what I'm good for."

She stops and meows at me.

"Yes, yes. I'm coming."

In the kitchen, she sits in her spot, watching me as I fill her bowl. By the time she's licked it clean, I've got water boiling for pasta.

My food is in the pantry across the kitchen, my few items dwarfed by the huge space. I grab rotini and meat sauce, an easy meal. And the bottle of merlot I forgot I bought. With my audition submitted, a little relaxation—and celebration—sounds like a good idea.

I skirt around the island, pour rotini into the pot, and read the instructions. The pasta needs nine minutes to cook. Enough time for a quick change of clothes.

Rushing through the entry hall, I pass a red velvet chair.

Something pops in my peripheral vision.

I stutter to a stop.

My brain is slow to process what I saw.

I turn and look again. There, in plain sight, rests a small book.

A book that wasn't here before.

A book I've never *seen* before.

Slowly, I stare over my shoulder, to the large connecting doors. The ones I left unlocked when I took a tour with Luci.

Alarm jolts down my spine, the shocking heat of fear. And I'm certain . . .

Someone's been in the apartment.

19

I stare at the book for at least a minute, body numb and mind searching for an explanation.

Most of the book's cover is scarlet, the same color as the velvet chair. Almost camouflaged. I simply overlooked it.

At least, this is the reason I give myself.

I don't see how I could have, because now the book glares like a beacon, pulsing blood-red on the velvet chair.

Fluid black curves create a picture, and as I stare, an image emerges. A woman, the top half of her face cut off by the cover's edge. Black hair slithers down the front of her shoulders.

Carmilla.

The title seems familiar, but I can't place it.

Reaching for the book, I pick it up by the corner, as if it might bite, and take it with me to the kitchen.

As I make my meal, I glance at the book on the countertop, telling myself it was there all along. Sitting on the chair. Probably since before I arrived.

But the other side of the argument pushes back. Yesterday, I searched everywhere, looking *specifically* for a book. How could I possibly have missed one lying out in the open?

But did I check the chair? I can't remember.

The debate continues until my food is gone and my dishes are in the washer. Unable to ignore its presence, I pick up the tattered paperback. The figure on the cover pulls at me, somehow sensuous and ominous all at once.

And despite how unsettled I feel, I'm compelled to read it.

Cover to cover.

Pouring another glass of merlot, I drink it down. And pour another.

Wine glass in one hand and the book in the other, I go upstairs to the study. Rain continues to lash outside, rivulets on the glass casting serpentine shadows.

Because the night calls for it, because my mood calls for it, I light the logs in the hearth and settle on the couch.

The book is short, more novella than full novel, so it shouldn't take me long to read.

Yellowed and worn, the pages crackle in protest as I open the book. The font of the copyright page is old, the text printed slightly off-center. But the story itself dates even farther back. The sentences long, the language formal.

Still, the eerie tone draws me in, filled with Gothic castles and misty nights.

A tragic story set in the heart of the Austrian forest. A young woman named Laura lives with her father. Isolated. Innocent. Untouched.

Until a woman arrives.

A woman called Carmilla.

Despite the intricate writing style, an unnerving sense of danger seeps from the page. Soon, I've forgotten my wine, engrossed in the story as horror unfolds.

Carmilla is more than a new companion. She's a seductress,

using her body and her words to enthrall young Laura. The author employs no crass language or pornographic scenes, yet the images are undeniably erotic.

As the sexual tension builds, I turn another page. And find the first words scribbled in the margins. Handwritten. In red ink.

Comparing the note to the text, I realize someone has rewritten a quote from the chapter.

"You are mine, you shall be mine, and you and I are one forever."

Neither masculine nor feminine, the writing consists of angular letters scratched in cursive.

Who did this book belong to?

In a later chapter, more red ink, though this time the note is underlined. *No sacrifice without blood.*

By this point, the vampiric reference is clear. Carmilla is an evil figure, one disguised by sweetness, glossy lips, and skin pale as the moon. Again and again, she takes Laura's blood, giving her nightmares and torment in exchange.

Riveted by the tale, I read on as Laura weakens daily, and Carmilla grows more volatile, wandering the night in search of what she craves. I read of ethereal hands stroking Laura's cheeks, of warm lips pressed to the pulse in her neck.

Of a figure standing by her bed, bathed from chin to foot in one great stain of blood.

Terrified and with no escape, Laura lies in bed. Waiting for a lethal kiss.

Afraid of what's lurking inside her own home.

I glance around the study and imagine a figure walking the halls, floating through the door, creeping up behind me to trail cold fingers—

"Stop." I chastise myself and scrunch my shoulders, trying to erase the phantom touch. Pulling a throw blanket from the back of the sofa, I wrap it around me like a makeshift shield.

Why am I letting this book get to me?

Or maybe it's the idea of someone entering the apartment. Leaving the book for me to find.

No. Ridiculous. No one's sneaking around here when I'm gone.

Or when I'm still here.

Another red mark catches my eye. This time, it's drawn close to the fold. Pulling the pages wide reveals a symbol, one I recognize.

The letter V below a winding S. The tip of the S is slightly bulbous, meant to represent the snake's head.

The symbol again.

But what does it mean? It must represent something important—at least to the Marteau family.

And here it is again, in the margins of a book. A strange and unsettling book.

Lightning flashes and I startle, my hand reflexively moving to protect my throat. Staring at the windows and the rain streaming down, I breathe deep to steady myself. But my heart is an aching throb, filling my chest and pressing on my ribs.

Calm down. Calm down. Calm down.

I tuck my legs beneath me, firelight flickering on the walls of the study. The hall beyond the doorway stretches long and hollow, as I sit and listen to the apartment breathe.

Reaching for my wine, I take a sip. But all I taste is the bitterness of fear. My nerves prickle, as if sensing an unseen presence nearby. Watching. Waiting. Lingering in the walls.

My gaze flits to every corner, searching the shadows for movement, for an emerging threat. All the doors in the apartment are locked. The place is quiet as a tomb. But I can't shake the uneasy feeling.

That I'm not alone.

My Hotel Peculiar

I went back to the food display, but nothing tasted good anymore. I took some cheese and pretty crackers with the sweets, but I couldn't stop thinking about my father and the woman.

Why did they go through that door? It only led to one place.

And it's not a place for a woman in a shiny dress.

Out in the hallway, I checked the clock again. Almost half an hour since my father disappeared with the British woman.

I needed to go back to bed. I didn't want to get in trouble. But I couldn't stop my wondering, couldn't stop imagining what they might be doing. Would my father touch her again? Would he kiss her?

All while my mother was asleep?

Taking my snacks, I went back to the secret stairs. I started up.

But then I stopped, wrapping the food in the napkin and leaving it on the side of a step. I was curious, but also upset.

Something didn't feel right.

I raced down to the next level. The cellar. My parents stored wine down there, but that's not why I went.

The floor in the cellar was cold and rough. I didn't like the way it felt on my bare feet, but I didn't have time to return to my room for shoes. I didn't know how long my father and the woman would be in his special place, and I wanted to look.

I wanted to see.

Just inside the cellar door, a flashlight hung on the wall. I took it and ran across the room. Halfway down, I turned between a set of wine racks.

A door blended into the dark wall. Another secret passage, one the servants never used. One that would take me to my father without anyone hearing, seeing, or knowing I was there.

The handle was an iron ring, so I grabbed it and pulled. The door opened with a creak, a low, scary sound. It carried down the stairwell on the other side.

I took a hesitant step. Those stairs were old, older than the house and carved from stone. With one hand on the wall to steady myself, I followed the winding stairs down into the earth.

The air grew colder, a damp chill settling on my skin and raising bumps on my arms. But I was determined.

I remembered how my father stared at the woman, the strange expression on his face. The look in his eyes bothered me, though I couldn't say why.

It took me several minutes to get to the bottom. So many steps. Much slower than the little elevator my father and the woman used. But at least that way, I wouldn't be caught.

By the time I reached the last step, the soles of my feet burned from cold. I opened the door there and stepped into a passageway. The ground was dirt and pebbles, wet enough to stick to my feet.

I stood frozen, listening as I looked both ways. I'd never been down here alone before. I wasn't allowed.

The catacombs could be dangerous.

But I had an idea where my father had gone. To his special room.

The lights were on in the tunnels, but I still held the flashlight. Following the curving path, I made my way to a particular tunnel. The room was there, behind a strange door.

A door that was always locked.

After a few turns, I came to the tunnel. I stopped walking and turned off the flashlight.

The door was right in front of me, but I was suddenly too afraid to go any farther.

What if my father caught me? What would he do? I'd broken rules before, but never anything like this.

In the yellow glow from the tunnel lights, I crept a little closer to the door.

A low murmur stopped me in my tracks.

My father's voice.

He sounded stern, the way he talked to my mother when she displeased him.

I held my arms to my stomach, so afraid I thought I would wet my pants.

My father spoke again, louder this time, but his words were muffled by the wooden door.

I took a step back, my heart fluttering in my chest. I didn't want to be there anymore.

Another step. One more. Only a little bit more, and I would turn the corner. Breathing loud, I stared at the door.

And then the woman screamed.

20

Someone hovers at the foot of my bed.

Tall. Silent. Staring.

The room is dark, but I can still make out their shape. Long hair. Male or female?

I try to shift my arms, my legs, but I'm paralyzed.

The shape moves closer, slowly advancing along the side of the bed. Their movements smooth with no sound, as if they're floating.

Moonlight shines through the window, pale blue illuminating the creature above me. Black hair falls forward as they lean down, their mouth wide, plunging fangs into the flesh of my breast.

My scream echoes in my ears as I sit upright in bed.

Something pushes on my thigh. Clairee's small feet as she stumbles off my legs with an irritated *mew*. Finding her footing, she leaps to the floor and scurries out the door.

"Sorry," I call after her, running a hand through my hair. She must have been sleeping on me, maybe nuzzling my face. A sweet, friendly caress.

But that's not what I felt in my dream.

Throwing back the cover, I walk to the bathroom and start the shower. Hot enough to burn away cold prickles and the lingering sensation of teeth in my skin.

I don't need a therapist to tell me the source of the dream. It's the book. *Carmilla.* Filled with gloom and foreboding.

But also the questions behind the book. Was it always in the apartment? Or did someone sneak in and leave it for me?

Its blood-red cover blended perfectly with the velvet.

Easily overlooked, right?

Turning off the water, I step out of the shower, wrap up in a towel, and stare at myself in the mirror.

Right?

With my hair towel-dried, I get dressed, head downstairs, and start a pot of coffee. While the machine spits and hisses, I open my phone.

A notification pops on the screen, from the photo-sharing app. Tapping the icon, I open the app to find a red dot by the little arrow at the top. A message.

A message from Alice.

Have you found the journal yet?

My first reaction is to type a reply, but then I pause. Instead of messaging Alice, I tap her picture. Once I'm on her profile, I click on the list of who she's following.

Hundreds of accounts are listed, but I assume her sister would have been one of her first contacts. Family and friends usually are. I scroll all the way down, almost to the bottom, before I spot Rose's name.

A prickly sensation fills my chest as I stare at her picture. Bright eyes, dimpled smile, hair blonde—but curly where Alice's is straight.

Another moment of hesitation, and I click through to her profile.

I start with her last post, a generic photo of a sunset. It could have been taken from anywhere in the world, but the caption is what gets my attention.

Au revoir, Paris. I'm ready for my next adventure.

Over eighty comments on the picture. Rose was a popular girl.

Expanding the comments, I read various versions of the same thing—well wishes, questions about where she's going, exclamations about how lucky she was to live in Paris.

I scroll down to the next picture. This one is a selfie of Rose, grinning sideways toward the camera.

As I scrutinize the photo, the wall behind her catches my attention. Rather, the painting on the wall. A landscape I've seen here, in the main salon. The selfie was taken in this apartment.

Rose stares directly into the camera, her eyes soft and hooded, as if flirting with her followers. The caption below reads: Paris is an amazing city, but not all riches are made of gold. I will always treasure our time here, ma douce bête.

Ma douce bête.

What does it mean?

Leaving the app, I open the translator and write the French words. Double-checking the spelling, I add the accent mark and read the translation. *My sweet beast.*

Did Rose meet someone while she was in Paris?

I go back to her profile and review the captions. In one post, she wrote about enjoying her time in Paris, as if that time were ending. In another, she says goodbye.

No wonder the police didn't investigate. Rose clearly left of her own free will.

The coffee is finished, so I pour a cup, my mind whirling with everything I've learned. And everything I still don't know.

Why is Alice so certain something happened to Rose? Because of Rose's behavior in the video chat? A chat she never resumed?

Alice admitted she and Rose weren't on speaking terms. Did something in the journal make Rose change her mind, make her want to reach out to her sister?

Even if she did, it's possible Rose needed more time and decided not to tell Alice where she was going next.

At this point, I don't know what to believe.

Alice is a stranger to me. I don't know her any better than I do the Marteaus. Sure, the family's eccentric, the mansion has a history, and Ric is a creep. But is all that reason enough to accept Alice's theory? Her accusations?

Cup in hand, I march to the stairs and up to the study. The book sits where I left it on the sofa. Not nearly as ominous as it felt in my hands last night.

"You were always on the chair, weren't you?" Blowing out a breath, I roll my neck before sipping the coffee.

I have days left in Paris, and I don't want every hour to be tainted by doubt and delusions. No more figures in the dark or blood in my nightmares.

I'm sick of being scared. Sick of questioning myself.

Opening my phone again, I send a text to Noah.

Does that invitation still stand?

In less than a minute, I have my answer.

Absolutely.

I can almost picture his face as he typed his reply, and the thought makes me smile.

> Then I'll see you Saturday.

Little bubbles appear to tell me he's typing.

> I'll pick you up at your place. Don't need directions.

A laugh escapes me. Not only handsome but funny, too.

My mood improved, I walk next door to my bedroom. It won't take long to dry my hair and get ready. Then I can go out.

I need to get a costume.

21

I exit out the front door, then turn the corner to walk through the gardens. After last night's rain, the leaves glisten and the greenery seems fuller—fresh and invigorating, like only a spring garden can be.

I'm not sure what clicked for me this morning. Maybe having my audition done or realizing I'd let trivial things erode my inner peace. But today, I'm full of energy.

Despite the nightmare driving me from sleep.

I weave my way through the shrubbery, until I come across Dora pruning her shrubs. "Good morning," I call out, trying not to startle her.

She spins her wheelchair to face me. "*Bonjour*, Brooke. You're up and about early."

"Yes, I have some shopping to do." I pause, excited but apprehensive. I'm not sure if she knows I've been invited to the dance. "Actually, I'm on my way to buy a costume."

"Ah, yes." Dora nods and rolls closer. "Luci told me you were coming."

"I hope I won't be intruding."

"No, dear. *You* are more than welcome."

Her emphasis implies someone else isn't as welcome. Maybe Noah?

"Luci is bringing that terrible André." Dora gives a faux shudder, and I can't help but grin.

I hold up my phone. "I've found a couple of places with costumes." Shops I found online, because Luci never gave me any recommendations.

"What have you got there?" Dora slips off the gardening gloves she's wearing and holds out her hand.

I pass over my phone.

She squints as she lifts reading glasses to her face. "No." She shakes her head. "These won't do." She starts typing, her fingers moving with surprising dexterity for someone her age. "Here."

I take my phone when she offers it back. She's put in an address.

"Thank you. This helps a lot." I step closer, the scent of roses engulfing me. "Luci was very kind to invite me. I hope she's feeling better."

Dora's pleasant expression falls to a frown. "Luci?"

Should I not have said anything? Am I betraying Luci's confidence?

"I saw her yesterday afternoon, and she seemed . . . down." I'm not going to tell Dora about the covert tour her granddaughter gave me. Luci said it would be fine, but for reasons I can't name, I'm not so sure.

"Oh, she was probably just having one of her days." Dora's gaze slides past me, as if she's staring at the flowers. Or into her own thoughts.

She looks back at me, her smile shaky. "You're sweet to worry, and the truth is, Luci's had some emotional issues. Some of these things can run in families. On her mother's side, of course." She adds the last with a meaningful lift of her eyebrows, as if certain no "emotional issues" could originate from the Marteau bloodline.

"You never can tell," she continues. "Particular personality traits often skip a generation before showing up again. Then losing her parents at such a young age."

I only nod, hoping my expression reads as empathetic and not surprised. This conversation feels too personal for my involvement.

Dora heaves a sigh. "I've raised her since she was twelve years old, but she's never truly recovered. It's hard to lose a parent, at any age."

"I understand."

Dora tilts her head, questioning.

"I lost my own mother last fall."

"Oh." She reaches out and squeezes my hand. "I'm so sorry."

"Thank you," I say, her compassion bringing a surprising burn of tears to my eyes. "Cancer." I squeeze out the word, because it still brings me pain.

She nods and lets go of my hand, both of us silently agreeing to let the moment pass.

"I hope you find something fun to wear," she says, rolling backward as she slips on her gloves.

"I'll do my best. And thanks for the help." Tossing her a wave, I follow the path behind the mansion, a lone tear trailing down my cheek.

As the gate latches behind me, my phone pings in my hand. Shaking off the melancholy, I glance at the screen. A notification from the photo-sharing app again. Opening it, I find another direct message from Alice.

How's the search going?

I don't have anything new to tell her, so I slide the phone into my bag. Guilt pricks at my conscience, but I tell myself I'll reply later.

After looking over Rose's Instagram this morning, I have some questions of my own.

Is Rose missing, like Alice claims?

Or is she avoiding her sister?

22

"You've got to be kidding me." I stand on a cobblestone street, staring at the shop. White stone, dirty and cracked, as if the building knows it's been relocated to a back alley. But it's not the location that surprises me most.

A carved wooden sign rests above the door. My French is amateur level, but one word is unmistakable.

Vampyre.

Scenes from *Carmilla* creep into my head. A delicate young woman masquerading as a friend, as a lover. Slipping through night shadows in search of blood.

Vampires. Murder house. Monsters. My time in Paris is supposed to be a retreat, and the mansion a sanctuary.

Not a house of horrors.

Wind gusts down the alley, making the sign swing back and forth. The chain squeaks in the metal brackets, an ominous sound shivering through my veins.

I roll my shoulders and take a breath. What did I expect? I'm here because I need a costume, one suitable for a monster-themed ball.

But after last night's reading and this morning's nightmare, I prefer a different category. Why not witches, mummies, or Frankenstein?

At this point, I'd even take werewolves.

I push the handle, and the door opens with a sigh, as if the air is welcoming me. When the door closes again, it's like I've stepped into a different world.

LED lanterns flicker on vintage wallpaper, a damask design of red and black. Shelves and tables fill every space, mostly dark wood with old-world carvings.

Each surface displays a collection of oddities—stuffed ravens, silver goblets, miniature skulls. Arranged in no apparent order.

I'm taking it all in, when a framed portrait on the wall piques my interest. I move to study the picture up close. A signed photo of Bram Stoker.

With a price tag to match.

Despite a few mass-produced items, the store holds an air of authenticity. And judging by the cost, many of the items are rare finds.

Stopping at a bookshelf, I tilt my head to read the titles. *French, French, French.* Words I can't translate. But then English jumps out at me.

Essays on the Undead: A Survival Guide.

The dramatic title seems appropriate for the stiff yellow pages and faded blue binding. The book looks ancient, weathered and worn.

Sliding it gently from the shelf, I open the cover, spine cracking like a dry bone. Ghoulish headings fill the table of contents, but the vampire section takes up most of the book.

I flip the pages gently, careful with the old paper. Every so often, black sketches help illustrate the text. A man in a graveyard, plunging a stake into an open casket. In another, a child cowers in a corner, shrinking back from a dark shape.

The next drawing catches my eye, because the scene doesn't make sense. A man in a cloak holds a vampire's arms while another shoves an object in the creature's mouth. Rectangle and thick. I can't tell—

"A brick to stop the bite."

I jump and shut the book with a *whump,* whirling to face the man who crept up on me. He sports a gray ponytail and tiny glasses. *Spectacles.* The word suits them better—small and round and wire-rimmed.

"Hello…uh…*bonjour,*" I stutter, my brain racing for simple phrases as I take a step back.

"You are American?" He smiles and nods, gesturing to the book in my hands. "Which is why you have found one of the few English titles I own."

"It grabbed my attention," I say, folding my arms but holding on to the book. "I was just browsing."

"And you are welcome to continue." He bows slightly, the perfect gesture for his late nineteenth-century attire. In addition to the glasses, he wears a ruffled shirt and shiny vest, as if he's channeling the character Lestat.

"I am Benoît, and this is my boutique. Please, enjoy."

Before he walks away, I step forward. "I was told you have costumes?"

"Yes, madam. This way." He extends his arm in invitation and winds through the furniture to a door in back.

I follow him to a separate area where racks of clothing fill the space. A partial wall divides the room into female and male attire, both equally eclectic in style and color.

He steps to the first rack and pulls out a dress. The lace bodice and capped sleeves remind me of an old-timey milkmaid. A very *sexy* milkmaid.

"I don't think that will work," I say. "I'm attending *La Danse des Monstres.*"

"Ohhh. At Maison Marteau?" He makes a face, but I can't tell if he's shocked or impressed. "Then you are right. This won't work at all."

"I'm staying there. Temporarily," I add. "I'm renting one of the apartments."

"*La Danse des Monstres* is a coveted invitation." He nods and puts the dress away. "I have what you need."

He guides me to another section where the pieces are of better quality fabric and embellishments. I run my hand along rich red silk. "I want to dress as a monster, but do you have anything besides vampires?"

"Yes." He chuckles. "You will see several Draculas and other fanged creatures at the dance, but many avoid those costumes. *Especially* at Maison Marteau."

I let go of the rich fabric. "I don't understand."

"The summer ball was always a tradition, but the name and theme changed some years ago. From what I've heard, it was a way for the family to . . . *poke fun* at some nasty stories being whispered at the time."

His explanation is similar to what Luci said, but I still can't make the connection. Why would dressing like a vampire be a problem?

Feigning interest in a dress, I turn my attention to the rack. "Stories?"

He crosses his arms and leans in, as if preparing to share a juicy secret. "The hearsay is based on old accusations about the Marteaus. It's said they gained their money through wicked means."

My laugh is light, but a weight lands in the bottom of my stomach. "As in what, dark magic or something?"

He moves his head side-to-side. "Or something." He stands back and opens his arms, his eyes tracking me up and down. "You are a size six in the USA?"

I blink at the rapid change of topic. "Yes. Size six."

"And you prefer to be a monster?"

"Sure," I say with a shrug.

He curls the finger resting against his chin. "Excellent."

Tapping his hand along the rack of clothing, he names off options as he goes. "Grim Reaper, demoness, wicked witch." He glances back at me. "Because not all witches are bad."

Finally, he stops, gives me another once-over, and whips out a dress. "How about this?"

As soon as I see the bodice, I know he's found a winner.

He shows me to the dressing room, pulling the curtain closed and leaving me to change. I place my clothes on the small bench provided before gently removing the dress from its hanger.

It slides on easily and fits just right. Black satin and lace, fitted long sleeves, beads trailing up the arms and along the hem. And the bodice of the dress—a mysterious yet regal high neck with an embellished waist.

I admire myself in the mirror, grinning at the ironic choice. Not a vampire. But still a beast.

One that bites.

If I'm going to a party with the wealthy, the elite—*and Ric*—the last thing I want is to appear weak.

Like a victim.

Or prey.

Satisfied I'll be neither, I step out of the dressing room ten minutes later and find the store owner at the checkout counter.

"You liked it?" he asks with a smile, taking the dress and slipping it into a zippered bag.

When I nod, he taps buttons on a brass cash register and tells me the price. "Cash or card?"

"Card." I blink at the number and open my purse. The rental amount would get me three sexy milkmaids, but at least I have a costume worthy of a Parisian chateau.

"And the book?" he asks.

I'm still holding the collection of essays on the undead. A prickle of instinct has me setting it atop the glass counter. "Yes, please."

As I sign the receipt, I say, "You never told me what the stories were. About the Marteaus."

"Couldn't you guess?" His grin is feral. "They're vampires."

Surprise squeezes a breath from my chest. "What?" My laugh sounds weak and watery. "But that's crazy."

He lifts a shoulder. "As I said. Stories." With a serious expression, he holds up the book. "But if you're interested in the family history, you might enjoy a visit to Père Lachaise Cemetery."

"A cemetery?"

"Oh, yes. Parisian cemeteries are world-renowned, and the Marteau enclosure is truly something special." He looks at me intently as he slides the book across the glass. "I think it will interest you."

He takes a business card and writes on the back. "I can hold the dress until you return."

He hands me the card, and I get the feeling he *wants* me to visit the cemetery. I stare at the name and address he wrote down, along with Metro directions.

"You must send a lot of tourists there," I say, trying to make sense of his odd suggestion.

"Only those who need to go." His expression is suddenly grave.

"Surely, you don't believe the rumors," I say. "They're ridiculous." Crossing my arms, I hold the book to my chest. "There's no such thing as vampires."

Placing his hands on the counter, he leans in and whispers, "No. But the question isn't whether or not the Marteaus are vampires."

His gaze flits to the book and then back to me. "But why the rumors started in the first place."

23

By the time I reach the cemetery, the weather has shifted. Roiling clouds cast the world in shade, the air thick and heavy with the threat of rain.

The entrance is not what I expected. Instead of a fence, I find towering stone walls. And instead of green grass, wide cobblestone paths meander through the graves.

I check the business card again, the shop owner's black ink scribbled on the back. Tombs and monuments spread farther than I can see, so I'm grateful to have step-by-step directions to the Marteau family mausoleum.

A gentle roll of thunder carries from a distance, and for a moment, I hesitate. Maybe I should leave. What am I doing here anyway? Searching for a tomb? And I still have to go back for my dress. Protective bag or not, I don't want to expose it to rain.

But even as I consider leaving, curiosity pushes me forward, moving my feet across the uneven stones.

Slipping my hand inside my purse, I touch the cover of the old book, as if to reassure myself it's there.

Père Lachaise is a tourist site, known not only for its size but for the famous people resting inside its walls. It's an interesting contradiction, such grandeur in a graveyard. Beauty and art mixed with reminders of death.

The Memorial to the Dead sits at the end of the main passageway, and the instructions tell me to veer right before reaching the massive stone. As I progress, the side trails grow smaller. They feel more personal and private, tombs and statues closing in on both sides.

I pass a monument surrounded by a wrought-iron fence, bars covered with fresh flowers. The famous tomb of Frédéric Chopin.

A little farther, and I reach the landmark noted on the card. A huge circle of grass with a statue in the center. I walk around to the far side and follow the sign pointing up a slight incline.

The path grows darker the farther I climb, ancient trees looming overhead. Narrow stone steps lead me to a raised plot and a fenced section with a gate. The Marteau enclosure. Secluded and cordoned off, as though they believed themselves superior. Even in death.

Beyond the shrubbery, the mausoleum waits. It's impossible to miss. Twice the size of any others, with stone steps and pillars gracing the entrance. The name MARTEAU embossed above the doors.

Wind races down the corridor, rattling leaves as clouds swirl above. I step closer to the gate, put my fingers on the handle, and pause to scan the grounds.

No one is in this part of the cemetery, only one older man with his back to me, heading downhill with a withered bouquet.

The handle squeaks beneath my hand. I cringe, glancing around again. Is it illegal to enter a mausoleum? Pushing open the gate, I slip in and ease it shut, squaring my shoulders and trying to look natural. Like I belong.

Hurrying to the vault, I climb three stone steps and press on the doors. I'm almost surprised when they open. Surprised and unnerved. An abyss waits beyond the doors, a dark void smelling of must and decay.

Taking a moment, I question the wisdom of trespassing on a sacred site. Especially one of a powerful family.

But I've come this far, so I shove inside and quickly shut the door.

Immediately regretting the loss of light, I fumble in my bag for my phone and its flashlight. One tap and the beam cuts through the black, illuminating carved marble and intricate designs.

But no windows. No light.

"Because vampires can see in the dark." My voice echoes in the chamber, my self-comforting joke falling flat.

I don't believe in vampires.

I don't.

Ignoring my unease, I move around the space. One wall is divided into rectangles with engraved plates. Burial chambers.

Most of them have the Marteau surname, though some of the women have their married names included.

A few small doors have no plaques, still waiting to be filled and marked. The last two are a man and woman, likely the most recently deceased. Pierre Marteau and Lillian Bouchard Marteau.

I trace a finger over the brass plate. Luci's parents?

Swinging my phone to the back reveals several large structures. I'm not sure what to call them. Caskets or tombs or sarcophagi? Effigies top the containers, stone carvings of the deceased person lying within. These family members clearly ranked a higher status.

The heirs, my mind whispers.

Like Dora.

I take soft, quiet steps to the back, as if I might disturb their rest. Several tombs sit in a line, stretching from one side of the space to the other. But one, by far the grandest effigy, stands alone in the back.

It's not until I'm close that I notice a stained-glass window on the wall, centered above the casket. If there's a window, why is it so dark inside?

I shine the light at the glass. No airy, joyful pastels here. Only deep rich colors, opaque, permitting no light. Many of the panes appear pure black.

I can't make out the entire scene, but a castle sits by a river. The river is unnatural, not signified by blue or green or white.

I move closer, hold my flashlight near the glass.

The river is red. Deep, rich red, the color of—

My hand shakes, and I drop the phone. It lands flashlight down. The chamber turns black, my phone a white rectangle on the floor.

Plunged into sudden darkness, I squat and grab my phone, shining the light to every corner.

No one is here. No rising spirits, no earthly creatures, no angry Marteau descendants.

And no vampires.

As my trembling subsides, I lower my gaze to the main attraction. A standalone tomb beneath the window.

I light up the name. GRÉGOIRE LÉON MARTEAU.

And below, a symbol etched in stone. The familiar V with the snake forming an S.

The letters must stand for a motto, some catchphrase that held great value for this man. The mysterious Grégoire Léon Marteau.

The name makes a spot between my shoulder blades tingle, a cold stab of awareness. Like an omen or premonition.

If I believed in such things.

I say his name and my voice wavers. So I say it again. Like a child playing Bloody Mary in the night. Taunting, daring, forcing myself to face the fear.

Suddenly, the atmosphere feels charged. I'm not a child. I don't believe in the undead. But that doesn't keep dread from seeping down my back. Thick and cold as oil.

Thunder rumbles outside, close enough to rattle the walls of the tomb.

In a matter of seconds, I'm out the door, through the metal gate, and back on the path, my steps clipping along at a hurried pace.

Above me, the sky churns, still threatens to rain. But my worry stays behind in the great stone tomb, my mind still stuck on symbols and puzzles.

Fixed on whispers of vampires.

And rivers of blood.

24

I'm on the east end of the park when the drops start to fall. Holding the garment bag close, I spot the peaks of the mansion spearing through the trees. I'm almost home. With barely enough time to beat the rain.

To save time, I head for the front gates of Maison Marteau, no time to cut around back through the gardens. Not unless I want to get soaked.

With my head tucked down, I don't see the figure until they leap from the bushes.

"Brooke!"

I stop short, jolted by the ambush. "Alice, what . . ." I look past her to the mansion, to the empty courtyard. "What are you doing here?"

"I messaged you last night and again today. Why haven't you answered?" Her tone is severe, her arms tense.

"I've been busy. I don't have anything else to tell you. Not yet."

She frowns at the garment bag. "Yet you had time for shopping."

I shift on my feet. "I had to get a costume."

"Costume?" Her brow wrinkles as she stares at the bag. Then her brows shoot up with excitement. "You're going to the monsters' dance?"

I nod.

"That's great. You'll be able to look around the main house."

"Alice, listen—"

"There will be lots of drinking, so whenever you can get away unnoticed, you can search for the journal. I bet one of them has it."

"No," I say bluntly. "I can't snoop around in their home. I told you I'd search my apartment, and I have." I remember the storage room with its maze of dusty boxes. "Well, most of it."

"Most of it?" Her face flickers to a frown again. "Can you go and finish now?" she asks, tone somewhere between suspicious and hopeful.

"I don't know, maybe. Maybe." The rain picks up, wetness soaking through to my skin. "I need to get inside, but I'll message you as soon as I can."

"When?" she demands.

"I know you're worried, and I promise I'm not giving up." I hike the bag up on my arm. "But I need to get out of the rain."

"I'll come with you." She walks ahead of me, toward the gate.

"Wait." I hurry to catch up. "You can't." I glance at the mansion. There's movement in the windows. *Shit, shit, shit.*

Grabbing her elbow, I pull her back down the sidewalk, praying no one has noticed us. "You can't storm your way inside. They won't allow that." I jut my chin toward the house.

Alice has already butted heads with the family and told me herself she's unwelcome.

"Besides," I continue, "the journal might not be in the apartment at all. Rose could have taken it with her."

Alice clenches her jaw. "She didn't take it, because she

didn't leave." The last two words grind through her teeth with anger.

"Alice, please." My weary tone draws her gaze sharply back to mine. "I saw Rose's Instagram."

"So?"

"Her last post talked about an adventure. And a new relationship. Some of her friends think she went away with someone."

Alice's laugh is a scornful bark. She invades my space and gets up close. "You have no idea what you're talking about!"

"Okay, okay." I back up, shocked by her sudden hostility. I'm seeing a new side of Alice. A domineering side.

Alice's eyes narrow to slits. "I know who you are."

I whip my head as if I've been slapped.

She moves in, crowding me. "I also know some bad things happened on your movie set. People are throwing around accusations, and I read charges might be filed soon."

Charges being filed.

Which could mean a trial.

And sworn testimonies.

"What's your point?" I say, trying to sound confident while my arms weaken and my stomach flutters.

Alice jabs a finger at me. "That's why you came to Paris, isn't it? Why you were afraid I was a reporter? You're hiding." Her mouth twists into a sneer. "And I bet you'd hate it if anyone found out where you were. *Especially* the press."

"I told you I would help you, and I am." I swallow against the rise of nausea. I need to calm her down and get her to leave.

"There are a lot of boxes in the storage room I haven't finished searching." I try to mollify Alice with an optimistic smile. "As soon as I've checked them all, I will contact you. Promise."

"Promise?" she mimics, glaring at me. "No. Uh-uh." She takes a deep breath and shakes her head. "Not good enough."

Angling across the sidewalk, she positions herself in front of the gate. "I'm going with you. I'll look for myself."

"No, I don't think—"

"Madam!" A man strides across the courtyard, his steps clipped and forceful. I've never seen him before, but he wears the black clothing labelling him as staff.

Beyond him, Victor stands in the open front door, his expression tight with annoyance.

"Alice, you need to go." I throw out my arm and point, making it clear I don't want her here. Trying to distance myself from her as much as possible.

I can't get involved in any more drama. Not now, right when everything in Los Angeles is blowing up.

The manservant is close enough to speak to us in French. Then, remembering himself, he switches to English. His stare bores into Alice. "You are not supposed to be here. I will call the authorities."

She moves down to face him, grabbing the bars with her hands and yelling at him through the gate. "I have every right to be here! I want my sister's belongings!"

I take the opportunity to tap in the code and slip inside the gate, shutting it quickly once I'm inside. I speak to the man. "I'm sorry, I—"

He holds up a hand to stop me. "Please, I will handle this."

"You bastards! Let me in!" Alice screams, jerking on the bars as if they'll budge.

Mortified by the spectacle, I hurry past him, wanting nothing more than to disappear. I toss a glance to the doors where Victor stands watching. Chantal and Lyam have joined him.

And Noah has stepped out of his apartment.

So much for not disturbing the family.

Turning away, I hurry to unlock my door. Once inside, I take one last look at Alice, still arguing with the man.

She's fixated straight ahead, shouting through the metal bars. "You're lying to me! I know you are!"

Her hateful stare is now for the Marteau family looking out from their mansion.

Slipping inside, I try to block out the chaos, because I can't bear the pain in Alice's voice.

Pain—and anger—as she screams for her sister.

My Hotel Peculiar

The sound of the woman's scream followed me down the tunnel. Terrified, I ran to the corner, making the turn and throwing myself against the wall.

Why did the woman scream like that? So high and sharp?

I'd never heard a person make that sound before.

My heart beat so hard, my whole body shook against the stone behind me.

I didn't know what to do, so I told myself to go back upstairs, to climb into bed and pull the covers over my head. If my father were to catch me down there, while he was . . .

While he was what? What was happening?

These were the questions holding me in place.

Then I heard my father's voice again. This time, he sounded calm.

Maybe they were playing a game? My family does like games.

I waited a little longer, listening for the rise and fall of my father's deep tone. In between, I listened for the woman, but she never spoke. Not that I could hear.

Feeling bolder, I sneaked closer, careful not to make a sound.

I walked slowly, trying to be quiet. A good thing, too, because when I got near, I saw the door wasn't locked. It wasn't even closed.

The door stood ajar, just a crack. Small enough to keep me hidden.

Wide enough to peek through.

When I looked, my body went cold. I didn't understand what I was seeing.

The woman was strapped to a wooden table, her sparkly shoes and dress in a pile on the floor.

"Please," she said in English. "Please, I want to go back up."

But my father ignored her. He put a knife to her neck before dragging it down the inside of her arm.

When he reached the tender skin inside her elbow, he made a sharp motion.

The woman screamed, louder this time. He took away the knife and put his mouth on her skin instead. Then he slipped his hand inside her underwear.

I held my breath, staring, strange feelings warming my stomach.

My father made a grunting noise, like an animal.

I watched for another minute or two, watched as he put the knife to another part of her body. Then to her bra strap.

Watched as he sliced at both.

When I grew light-headed, I knew I had to leave. I couldn't get caught down here. Not now.

I ran most of the way through the catacombs and back up the stairs. I took the servant stairway all the way up to my bedroom, stopping only to pick up the snack I'd wrapped in a napkin.

Once inside, I washed my feet, filthy from the steps and the dirt of the catacombs. Then I crawled into bed and pulled the covers up high.

My heart raced for several minutes, and my breaths felt cool and tingly in my chest.

Eventually, I settled down and closed my eyes.

But it was hours and hours before I slept.

25

I spend the rest of the afternoon reading articles online. The story is everywhere. Salacious headlines, speculation, accusations—all about things that happened on the set of *The Last Wave.*

Allegedly.

The articles might be little more than gossip, but I know the truth.

When it all began, I was a dedicated actress minding my own business, trying desperately to perform my best. I stayed focused and kept my head down.

When I heard about the weekend getaway on a local island, I didn't go with the others to blow off steam, and I never expected anything terrible would happen.

Though I should have.

Only the main players are mentioned in the articles—the accuser and accused. Their names leap from the screen, stirring up a storm of anger and regret.

Despite the unwelcome feelings, I read every article I can find. I'm in the middle of a blogger's conspiracy theory, when there's a knock on my door.

My first thought is of Alice, that she found a way inside the fence. My second guess is someone from the family, maybe Vincent or Chantal come to evict me.

Cautiously, I creep to the foyer. But it's not anyone from the main house.

It's Noah.

Relieved, I open the door. "Hey," I say, somewhat hesitant. "They haven't sent you to throw me out, have they?"

He grins but doesn't ask what I mean. He doesn't have to. He had front-row seats for the whole ugly scene.

"No. Don't worry about Alice. None of that is your fault."

He knows Alice? I don't know why this surprises me, but the feeling is swiftly overtaken by a kick of guilt.

Because today's drama *was* my fault. At least partly.

Noah glances over to the front gate. "Looked like you had a rough day, so I thought you might need some down time. Maybe come to my place for dinner and a movie?"

I lean on the door jamb with a heavy sigh. "You have no idea how good that sounds. I tried to work the television here, but everything's in French. The remote, the channels, everything."

"I have a solution to the TV problem, so there's only one question left." He pauses dramatically. "Pizza? Burgers? Vegan? I know the best places, and they all deliver."

"How good is the pizza?"

"Just like home." He steps back and holds out his hands. "You hungry now?"

I glance at the sky, realizing the storm has passed. "Starved," I say, slipping on my shoes and joining him outside.

I've been glued to my computer since I returned, so fixated on the articles I forgot to eat. And it would do me good to have some company, to get my mind off of Alice and the tabloids.

Noah and I make the short walk across the courtyard to his

apartment. Inside, he takes me to a living room, or what the French would call a *salon.* The modern aesthetic bleeds over from the rest of the rooms, but the American in Noah has left its mark. A big leather couch faces an even bigger television.

He steps to the coffee table and picks up a remote control. "I found a movie you might like." He hits a button, and the screen comes to life.

I don't need to read the title. All I need is a glimpse of the crisscrossed surfboards and the girl beside them.

A girl with my much-younger face.

Groaning, I put my hands on my cheeks. "Nooo. Where did you find that?" My very first movie. A coming-of-age teen comedy with more budget than directing talent.

"I looked you up on IMDB."

Nervous laughter escapes as I shake my head. "I was only seventeen. I'm sorry, but I can't let this be the first movie of mine that you watch."

"Who says it will be?" He lifts his brows, teasing me. "I saw another one years ago. It was listed in your projects, and I remembered the title. Then I remembered you." He steps closer, his voice warming. "You were good."

"Thank you," I say, almost a whisper. I've been an actress for years, dealing with all manner of insults and praise.

But one compliment from Noah, and I melt inside.

"Always nice to hear." Ignoring the flutter in my voice, I gesture to the screen and my teenage grin. "But this has got to go."

"No problem." He laughs good-naturedly. "I just wanted to see your reaction, but we can watch something else, something you haven't seen. Or acted in," he adds with a wink.

"I'd appreciate it."

"But I'm definitely going to your next movie when it hits

theaters. I've never known any actors and, honestly, it would be kind of cool to see your face on the big screen. I tried to read about it, but the description only said it was in production."

The first tendrils of unease wind through my stomach.

"What was it called?" Noah looks to the side before his gaze snaps back to mine. "Oh, right. *The Last Wave.*"

The last of my smile drops from my lips, and Noah notices.

He stops and frowns. He backs out of the streaming service, and my face disappears from the screen. "I didn't mean to upset you."

"No, no, it's not that." I reach out as if to touch him, but let my arm drop. "I love that you thought to have my first movie pulled up and ready to go."

"Well, something just happened," he says, taking my hand and guiding me to the couch. We sit, but he keeps hold of my fingers. "Is it Alice?"

"No," I say. "Not entirely."

Biting my lip, I decide to tell him about my last movie. And why I came to Paris. With articles shouting from every news site, he'll find out soon enough.

"The movie, *The Last Wave . . .*" I trail off, unsure what to say, how much to tell him. "It isn't going to happen," I say, trying to keep my voice and my nerves steady. "Production issues," I add.

Technically the truth.

"I'm not supposed to talk about what happened or why the film was shut down. I haven't spoken about it to anyone other than my agent, Lin. She's the one who set me up in the apartment. She sent me here to keep my head down."

I laugh at the absurdity of what I'm saying. "Basically, I'm hiding out."

Noah's face creases with concern. "Hiding out from who?"

"A scandal. The press. Paparazzi." I let go of his hand and lean back on the couch. "The movie fell apart after some accusations were made."

As soon as I say the words, I see Mackenzie's face, her shame as she confessed her secret.

And her fury when I confessed mine.

"Unfortunately, you can read all the details online," I tell him, hoping he'll understand I don't want to get into specifics. "Right now, all of us who worked on the film are keeping low profiles. No one wants their name attached to the film or to the negative publicity. Especially now there's talk of charges being filed, and there's the chance of being questioned. Maybe called to testify, if it goes to court."

"Will it come to that?" he asks.

"I don't know, but if it does, it could get ugly. Fast. These things are always messy, but when rich, powerful people are in the mix, careers can be destroyed. Lives can be ruined."

"I'm familiar with those kinds of people," Noah says.

I think of the Marteau family wealth and history. "Then you understand the risk of going against them."

"I do. It's why my mother took me to the States after my father died. She was afraid they would try to control her, have too much say in how I was raised, turn me into one of them." Noah puts his hands on his knees. "But I'm back now, claiming what's mine."

His shoulders are squared, his gaze is clear, not a hint of fear or intimidation.

"You're brave," I say. "But I'm not sure I am."

Or else I wouldn't be here, hiding in Paris.

"I agree with your agent," Noah says. "Stay here and let it die down. You don't have to worry about testifying if you don't know anything, right?"

"Right," I say, ignoring the small pang. Something aches inside, and I can't tell if it's fear or regret.

My phone rings in my pocket; I sit up straight. "Sorry," I say, pulling out my phone. I see the name filling the screen.

And my stomach drops to the floor.

26

Lin's calling me on video chat, and I'm afraid to find out why. "Sorry." I glance at Noah. "I need to take this."

He nods and gets up from the couch. "I'll go order the pizza."

When he's out of the room, I tap the screen to answer. "Lin," I say in greeting.

"Hey, I guess you've seen the news." She cuts straight to the point.

"I did. It's pretty hard to miss."

Lin sucks on her vape, then exhales before speaking again. "Took off faster than expected, that's for sure. No one connected to the film can go anywhere in this town without getting a microphone shoved in their face. Good thing you're not here."

She shakes her vape at me. "But listen, the story may have broken, but you still need to keep a low profile. And don't talk to *anyone* about what's happening. Not a word."

Cringing inside, I glance at the hallway where Noah just disappeared. "Right. I won't."

"Especially since I just heard from casting."

I whip my eyes back to the phone. "Casting?" My legs shake, making me glad I'm already sitting down. "About my audition?"

That was fast. Too fast.

"They passed on me," I say, finality deadening my voice.

"No, no, no." She gives me a smug look. "I called to let you know you made the final cut for consideration."

"Really?" Now my voice goes up an octave, floating on pure elation. "I can't believe it. I only sent in my audition last night." But six p.m. in France is nine a.m. in California. They had all of yesterday to review submissions.

"Yeah, you and three others are in the running."

"Do I know them?" I ask, already sizing up my unknown competition.

"They didn't share the names, but don't worry, your tape was good. Still, there are no guarantees. You know how these things go."

I do. I remember my mother once ranting about the unfairness of Hollywood, how she wasn't cast because she was too tall for the leading man.

"You doing okay over there?" Lin asks.

"Learning my way around."

"Good, good. Okay, I'll keep you updated. Just hang in there. Eventually, the vultures will grow tired of chasing interviews and quotes about *The Last Wave*. Plus, a high-profile couple just announced their divorce, so that's diverting some of the attention. Before long, the news cycle will have moved on, and you can come home."

She winks at me. "Hopefully to prepare for your new role."

My heart squeezes and flutters, excitement fizzing in my chest like Champagne about to burst. "Thanks, Lin. Thank you so much."

"You got it. Talk soon." And with that, she's gone.

I'm too thrilled to stay seated, so I hop up and trot to the kitchen. Grabbing the door jamb, I swing around, just in time to see Noah hang up.

"Pizza will be here in—" He breaks off when he sees me. "That must have been some phone call."

"It was." I ball my hands together and walk over to him. "That was Lin, my agent. She had some good news. Well, pretty good. Not the best. But still good." I hear myself babbling and press my lips together.

Taking two calming breaths, I gather myself, though I still feel like I'm coming out of my skin. "There's this part I auditioned for. Actually, I didn't even know about it until I got here, but Lin sneaked the script into my luggage. Anyway," I say, realizing I'm still prattling. "I've spent the last few days preparing to send in my video."

"And?" Noah steps closer, holds out his hands in anticipation.

"I made the final cut. It's down to me and three others."

"Congratulations." Noah moves in and hugs me, and for a split second, it's like we've known each other for years. Just two good friends sharing a joyful moment.

Then in an instant, things change. A shift in electricity, generating heat in every place where his skin touches mine.

I ease back, arms still looped over his shoulders. A current passes between us, and I swear I can feel his heart beating against mine. Hard, fast, insistent.

His fingers grip my waist, and he pulls me closer, dark eyes never leaving mine. His expression softens as he leans in, his lips inches from mine.

Then the kiss.

My blood warms as it travels through my body. I push closer. He slides his hand to my back.

A loud *ting!* sounds behind Noah's neck. We both freeze, then pull apart.

My phone is still in my hand from my call with Lin, so the push notification chimed right in his ear.

Noah gives me a kiss, but just a peck on the lips, as if he's putting a bookmark where we left off. "I'll pour us some wine."

He crosses the kitchen and opens a wine bottle, giving me time to check my phone. And space to consider what just passed between us.

While he takes two glasses from a cabinet, I open the app and tap the little red dot at the top of the screen. I have a new follower.

I read the notification.

All the heat from the kiss is replaced by shock.

Doucebête started following you.

It's French, but I remember that name. I remember because I typed it into my translator.

Douce bête.

Sweet beast.

The person Rose mentioned in her post, saying she would always treasure their time together. Time they spent here. *In Paris.*

"Do you like sangiovese?" Noah asks, holding up a bottle. "It pairs well with pepperoni."

"Sure," I say slowly, still focused on my phone.

Noah can tell I'm distracted. "Everything okay?"

"Yeah, sorry." I glance up at him. "Someone just followed me, but I don't know who they are." I try to pronounce the name but butcher it.

Noah repeats the words, working out what I'm trying to say.

His brows shoot up when he gets it. "Douce bête." His pronunciation sounding nothing like mine.

"Right," I say, tapping the generic photo. Not a face but a swirl of colors.

"Sweet beast." Noah comes over with the glasses of wine. He looks over my shoulder and says, "Yeah. That's Luci."

27

Back in my apartment, I shut my door and lean against the wood, a dreamy smile on my face as I think about Noah.

And the kiss.

Correction, the *kisses.* One a sweet peck on the lips, and the other more passionate, giving us a taste of what could be. But both equally tender.

I close my eyes and sigh at the memory, the residual thrill still buzzing in my veins. Not only did I have an amazing time with Noah, but my audition tape got me to the next level. I have reason to be optimistic, and reason to hope my career might survive.

But as I look at my phone, that buzz in my blood fades. Ruined by the truth I learned tonight.

The truth about Luci.

She is *douce bête.* Sweet beast. And she clearly knew Rose much better than she let on.

But why would Luci lie? Is she simply trying to stay out of the drama? Maybe. And after Alice's display this afternoon, I can't blame her.

I rub my temples where a headache is trying to bloom. All the back-and-forth is wearing me down. Seeing Rose's posts gave me hope that she'd left Paris on her own. That she was avoiding Alice and their personal issues.

Now I'm filled with questions again.

A scratch on the door tells me Clairee is outside. Peering out, I see her on the steps, so I open the door to let her slip inside.

"Waiting until I got home?" I say, following as she beelines for the kitchen.

She doesn't try to hide what she wants from me, her eagerness for dinner evident as she does her little dance while keeping hungry and hopeful eyes on me.

"Okay, okay. Give me a minute."

I sweet-talk her as I open the packet of food and put it in a bowl. Yes, she wants something from me, but she also gives back. Affection and trust. She lets me rub her belly at night. Two times. No more. Then she snuggles up next to me to purr herself to sleep.

Newly born trust can be such a fragile thing, yet she gives it freely.

I stare out the kitchen door and down the hall, my thoughts on the man across the courtyard. I haven't known Noah long, but it's nice to confide in someone, to have an ally while I'm here at Maison Marteau. Another outsider. Someone I can talk to. Maybe even trust.

Though I'm not ready to tell him the whole story.

When a yawn overtakes me, I leave Clairee to eat, turning out the kitchen light as I go. Exhaustion weighs on me as I pass the piano. Today has been an emotional rollercoaster, and all the drama has left me depleted.

Moonlight filters through the windows, the shining parquet floors lighting my way. My bare feet pad softly as I walk—the apartment still, the shadows silent.

Until I hear a thump.

Loud. Solid. Then followed by another noise.

Shrrrrr. Like something sliding across the floor.

Cold fingers poke their way up my spine.

Sounds carry strangely through the cavernous apartment, but the rasp has a sandpaper quality, light and crackling as it floats through the air.

And on the heels of the scrape, another sound.

A *thump-thump* from somewhere inside. Not the pipes. Not the settling of old wood. But something else.

Something human.

I reach for the first thing I see, a heavy brass candlestick on a nearby table. Removing the candle, I grip the metal weapon in my fist.

One shoulder grazing the wall, I creep up the winding stairs, eyes locked on the open air above.

Part of me expects to see a figure staring down from above.

But the view remains clear all the way to the top.

My heart swells in my chest, a muffled throb, sluggish with fear. I pause long enough to take a few deep breaths and clear my head. My imagination is running wild again.

No one is in my apartment. Why would they be?

But that scraping sound. Like a door being closed.

I take another tentative step, swallowing against a tight throat.

Gripping the candlestick, I ease my way up to the top of the steps and over to the light switch. I flip it on and suck in a breath, not sure what I expect to find.

I scan the landing, but no one is here.

Trying to slow my rapid pulse and ragged breaths, I lean against the dividing doors. Unmoving, I listen for the space of one breath.

Two.

Three.

Then I feel as much as hear the bumps on the other side. Low vibrations just beyond the wall.

In Luci's quarters.

I press my ear against the door and listen. A few soft knocks and a shuffling sound.

Is this what I heard? Someone moving around next door?

No. These sounds are stifled, lacking the crispness and clarity of what I heard before.

Nervous and on edge, I test the door handle. Still locked.

"Luci?" I say, my voice just above a whisper, part of me not sure if I want to be heard. "Are you there?"

The movement stills, but no one answers.

Backing away from the doors, I skirt around the railing toward my bedroom. An unfamiliar scent floats in the air. Like seeping perfume or lingering cologne. Could it be coming from next door?

It's nothing. Only Luci in her room. Probably perfume or a scented candle.

This is what I tell myself.

But when Clairee breezes past me, I follow her to my room.

Once inside, I lock the door, climbing under the covers with my clothes still on.

And the candlestick still in my hand.

28

When I open my eyes, I can tell it's late. Mid-morning sun warms the bedroom and casts the white wallpaper in a golden sheen.

Sitting up, I rub my face, feeling groggy and achy from over-sleeping. The result of a restless night. Tossing and turning, waking to every sound.

Both real and imagined.

The candlestick sits on the nightstand, my makeshift weapon. Like a movie on fast-forward, yesterday comes rushing back to me. Shopping for a costume, visiting a tomb, confronting Alice. Then the news breaking about charges filed.

With Mackenzie stuck in the middle of it all.

No wonder my nerves are frayed, my emotions bubbling just beneath the surface. Dinner with Noah was a nice distraction, but my problems haven't disappeared. They're still with me, still making me edgy and tense.

I pick up the candlestick and heave a heavy sigh. First, I was hiding from the prying eyes of the press. Now I'm hiding behind my own bedroom door.

I can't keep living like this.

Time to find a hotel.

Tossing off the duvet, I take a quick, hot shower and dress for the day. As I make my way downstairs, I go over my alternatives and things I need to consider before making the move.

My number one consideration is waiting at the front door, meowing to go outside. "Morning, Clairee." I don't know how hard it will be to find a hotel that allows pets.

And I don't know when the little stray cat officially became mine.

"Guess we better get you to the vet," I say, watching her race to the hedge and disappear.

Knowing she'll be coming straight back for breakfast, I stand in the open door and make a mental checklist of what I need to do to get her back to the States. Vaccines, a pet carrier, other kitty cat paraphernalia.

Soon, she bounds back across the grass, passing me in her flight for food. She gets to the kitchen first, circling her usual feeding spot like a feline shark. Yellow eyes wide, she makes pitiful sounds, as if she's on the verge of starvation.

"I'm hungry too, but we can both wait another minute." I get out coffee and spoon grounds into the filter. Filling the pot with water, I glance back at the cat. "Sorry, girl. Priorities."

The machine starts to hiss and spit as I make a bowl of Clairee's beloved wet food.

While I wait on the coffee, my gaze wanders to the garment bag hanging from a cabinet. My purse is beneath it on the floor, both left there yesterday when I scoured the internet for articles.

Crossing the room, I unzip the garment bag to let the dress fall free. I won't be leaving the mansion until tomorrow.

Because the dance is tonight.

I stroke the black satin and sigh. Despite my unsettling experiences at the mansion, I don't want to cancel on Noah.

I bend to pick up my purse, but it's heavier than usual.

Weighed down by the book I bought at the vampire store.

Setting my bag on the island, I retrieve the book and flip to the table of contents.

A voice inside warns me not to go down this rabbit hole. I don't need to read stories of the undead when I'll be spending the evening in the heart of this eerie mansion.

At an event called the monsters' dance.

But I have hours to kill, and my curiosity is piqued. I recall the glint in the shop owner's eyes as he slid the book across the counter to me. How he urged me to visit the cemetery and the mausoleum.

Is there something in the book I should read?

"I am starting to worry about my own sanity." Dropping the book on the marble, I round the island to the coffee maker and fill a cup.

But as I take my first sip, I'm already moving to pick up the book again. Leaving the kitchen, I cut through the entry hall toward the grand staircase. The portraits glare from the wall above. Especially the man in the center.

No matter where I go, I feel his eyes tracking me.

I enter the grand salon that faces the courtyard, a bright room good for reading. Careful with my drink, I settle into the midnight-blue *chaise longue* and stretch out my legs.

The title of the book may sound interesting, but the reading is dry. More long, fluid, and formal wording, similar to *Carmilla*.

Instead of boring myself with long-winded chapters, I skip through the pages, pausing to study the occasional drawing. The first sections detail human deformities, spiritualism, and how to recognize demonic activity.

When I come to a chapter on alchemy, I sit up straight and set aside my cup. The first pages list substances used in the defense against evil. But it's the chart of alchemic symbols that makes my heart kick at my ribs.

Under a category of "planetary metals," there's a drawing of the letter F nestled inside a larger V.

Similar to the late Grégoire Marteau's favorite symbol, though his had an S instead of an F.

I run my finger down the column, the ancient paper rough and fibrous. I stop on the words *vis ferrea,* followed by *force of iron* in parenthesis.

Vis ferrea. Latin. So, if the V stands for *vis* or force in the Marteau emblem as well, what does the S mean? I use the browser on my phone to search for Latin words starting with S.

There are more than two thousand.

Maybe I'm reaching. I can't be sure the Marteau symbol represents Latin. As far as I know, the letters could signify French.

Frustrated by the lack of clarity, I flip to the part I've been waiting for. The real reason I bought the book.

Vampires and related creatures.

The first reference dates back to the year 1047, to the Russian term *upir,* translating literally to "the thing at the feast or sacrifice."

Turning the yellowed pages, I read about a "madness" associated with vampire bites. How affected victims reportedly showed altered sleep patterns, increased aggression, and a sensitivity to light.

When it comes to the serious business—the killing of a vampire—desecration of the corpse is a repeated theme. Though the manner varies from country to country. A stake through the heart, burning the body, removing the head, a brick in the mouth.

I flip to the next illustration, the sketch I saw in the store. Then I recall the shop owner's words. *A brick to stop the bite.*

"So that's what he was talking about." Preventing the creature from rising and resuming its hunt for blood.

I'm so engrossed in the book, I barely register movement outside. A man in black is opening the metal gates. The servant from yesterday, the one who warned Alice to leave.

A white van drives into the courtyard, a French name on the side with a logo suggesting food and drink. Catering. Preparations are underway for *La Danse des Monstres*.

Reluctantly, I close the cover and check the time. I slept in this morning and now half the day is gone.

I need to wash and dry my hair before I get dressed, and the style I have in mind is complicated. A special twist I saw online, and one I can't put off until the last minute.

If I want to fit in with the affluent guests, I need to look and act the part. And tonight, that part requires me to chat, smile, mingle, and dance.

All while surrounded by monsters.

29

Noah arrives at my door at seven o'clock, bowing as I open the door. Punctual, polite, and deliciously handsome in his Van Helsing costume.

The trench coat, hat, and shirt buckles are unmistakable. "You're going as a vampire hunter?"

"Why not?" He tugs on the front of his coat. "I'm a monster to the monsters."

"But..." I start to ask him how Dora will feel about that, then I remember I haven't told him all I've learned. I haven't mentioned the talk of vampires, the mansion being a murder house, or that Alice has asked me to search for the journal.

Or that I snooped around his family's mausoleum.

The list of things I've kept from Noah is long, but correcting all that can wait. Tonight is not the time. "Where's your crossbow?"

"Too awkward to carry all night." As he speaks, his gaze tracks up and down, taking in my dress. "Nice," he says, reaching out to touch me, just a brush of one finger across the design on my stomach.

A red hourglass.

"Black widow?" He arches a brow. "Do I need to watch my back?"

Grabbing my beaded clutch, I ease past him and pull the door behind me. "Maybe," I tease, locking up as I leave the apartment.

The night is cloudless, no rain in sight, so we cut across the cobblestones. "The courtyard is beautiful at night," I say, feeling like a princess attending a ball in the castle. Even if I am a wicked princess.

Noah glances up at the moon. "It is, although this is technically the *cour d'honneur*, an entrance court."

"Okay. I will add that to my French lexicon." I grin at him as we walk up the stairs to the main entrance. Two doormen flank the entrance, pulling the doors wide before we reach the top step.

Just inside the foyer, the family stands in a line, welcoming their guests. Except Ric, who's glaringly absent. Chantal is busy speaking to others, but Vincent cuts a sharp look at me as I enter. Does he blame me for yesterday's scene with Alice?

"Brooke!" My name rings out, and Luci beams as Noah and I approach. At least one person seems happy to see us.

Dora is beside her granddaughter, and as matriarch of the house, she greets and welcomes us. "Brooke, you are *très belle*. Very beautiful," she clarifies, tilting her head and looking up from her chair. She is dressed in black, but I can't see enough of her clothes to guess her costume.

In contrast, Lyam and Luci both wear Victorian-style clothing, colorful and elegant, with no indication that either is a monster.

Dora shifts her attention to Noah and her smile fades. "Noah," she says, the slightest nod her only gesture of welcome.

"You look lovely, Aunt Musidora." He gives her a bow as he did for me, ignoring her obvious snub.

Luci breaks from the welcoming line, waving her hands for us to follow. "André's already here. Food and drink are being served in the blue salon."

I return her smile, but I'm still bothered by her lie. Why conceal her friendship with Rose? Why lie about such a simple thing?

Logic tells me I should be cautious, but there's a vulnerability about Luci that tugs at my heart. Even when she's happy, it feels like an act. As if a bruise of misery lives beneath the surface. Something anguished and sad, disguised by false cheer.

She leads us to a grand room with silk-papered walls in rich lapis blue. People mingle with cocktails in their hands, some holding plates, having served themselves from the banquet-style meal.

Champagne fountains sparkle, silver platters shine, and desserts create an ornamental display fit for royalty. Tables of food form a perimeter around the space, so much that if I tried a bite of everything, I'd be here all night.

I doubt I'll be eating at all, not with the nerves jangling in my stomach. At least a hundred people mill around the mansion, increasing the odds I'll be recognized. Since the scandal is all over the news cycle, I've come prepared. Ready with stock answers and cover stories, all slightly altered versions of the truth. That's what Lin would want.

No. Scratch that. Lin wouldn't want me at this party at all.

I stick to Noah's side as he introduces me to other guests. By first name only. He also helps by steering discussions to local events. Paris Fashion Week is coming up, a topic that keeps the group chatting about designers and trends.

Glancing around the room, I'm surprised by how relaxed the gathering feels. I thought a party of monsters might be intimidating, but even Hannibal Lecter seems tame with a pink drink in his hand.

Unfortunately, the same can't be said of Vincent. He's left the receiving line and now stands near the bar. He wears a robe with a black hood, an executioner from the gallows.

He swirls a glass of liquor in his hand but doesn't drink, his cold stare centered on me. He makes no attempt to hide his disdain, and I almost expect his lip to curl up in a snarl.

For the first time, I see how much Ric resembles his father.

I slip my arm through Noah's and rejoin the conversation. At some point, we split off from Luci and André, spending time with a man Noah knows through his work. People enter our circle, and others leave, a pattern that repeats until we've met half the room.

Every other person seems to bear an important title, but one in particular stands out. Noah introduces the Chief of Paris Judicial Police, describing the department as France's answer to the FBI.

I nod in his direction, keeping a pleasant expression plastered in place, but I can't help remembering the day I met Alice. How she approached me in the café, told me Rose went missing from the mansion, and claimed authorities did nothing to help.

Claimed the police were protecting the Marteau family.

And here stands a high-ranking official in Parisian law enforcement.

"I see someone you'll want to meet." Noah steps away from the group, and I'm happy to go with him, leaving the beady-eyed chief behind.

Time passes and drinks flow, turning conversations loud and boisterous. Even Lyam has grown more animated, joking and laughing and opening up. As if the weight of playing a role has fallen off his back, and he's able to be himself.

When he starts to expound on computer programming and

the joy of writing code, I tune Lyam out and scan the room. Luci leans on a chair nearby, focused on a phone.

Maybe it's the three Calvados and tonics I've had, the easy camaraderie, or the free-for-all party vibe. Whatever the reason, I jump at the chance to talk to Luci.

To ask her the question that's been burning in my brain.

I ease up beside her and jump right in. "I saw you followed me on Insta. I followed back."

"Oh, I know," she says, standing straight. "Now we can stay in touch when you're gone." She fakes a pout and wraps me in a hug. "Because I'm going to miss you." Her words hold a hint of a slur, telling me she's had a few drinks herself.

I hug her back, careful not to spill my pale-yellow cocktail. When she releases me, I say, "I found Rose's profile, too." I hold Luci's gaze. "She talked about you in a post."

Luci tenses. Glances aside. Gets fidgety. Looking down, she rolls the phone between her palms.

The mention of Rose makes her nervous.

And I want to know why.

"So, you hung out with her," I say. "The two of you were friends."

"Yeah, we... no." Luci shakes her head as if trying to remember what she's supposed to say. "I met her once but didn't know her very well."

The answer she gave me before. Verbatim.

I might not be a detective, but I know a rehearsed line when I hear one. She even hit the same beats as before.

"She tagged you in her caption and said she'd never forget the time you spent together." Suddenly annoyed, I press harder, trying to force the truth. "That sounds like you knew her. That you knew her *very* well."

Luci doesn't answer, just stares straight ahead and sips her drink.

"Did you say Rose?" Lyam leans sideways, his chin lifted in query.

He and a few others have migrated and are standing much closer than when I left them. How much did they overhear? Now I'm the deer in headlights, my mouth falling open but no words coming forth.

"André," Lyam says, pointing at the tall Frenchman. "Didn't you go out with Rose?"

He waves Lyam off. "No, I tried to date her, but she turned me down." André presses his lips together, as if searching for what to say. "She wasn't interested."

"I don't believe it," Noah teases. "Hope her rejection didn't bruise your ego." He and Lyam exchange a glance, laughing at their friend.

Luci rolls her eyes and walks off. I start to call after her but stop when André's hand falls on my arm. He glances after Luci. "Don't worry. Her moods can change quickly."

"Was it something I said?"

"No." He sips his drink and shrugs. "Maybe she's upset because I asked out Rose. I don't know. It's hard to tell. She's young, and, like I said, moody."

With Luci gone and André feeling chatty, I lean in and lower my voice. "So did *you* get to know Rose pretty well?"

"Not the way I wanted to." He looks stricken, shooting a worried look my way. But then he tilts his head. "I see no harm in telling you, since you never met Rose." He glances at the others. "But don't tell anyone else."

André shakes the ice in his glass and mirrors my posture, leaning in. "Rose wasn't interested in me," he says with a lift of a brow, "because she was gay."

30

Luci cuts through the crowd and leaves the blue salon. When she's gone, I tap Noah's shoulder. "I'll be back."

"The dancing has started," he says, glancing at my empty glass. "You want another drink?"

"Sure," I say without thinking. The way my head is buzzing tells me I'm already tipsy, but I blurt a response so I can follow Luci.

I want to get her alone for a minute. To speak to her. To apologize. Because I think I know why she denied knowing Rose.

By the time I exit to the hall, Luci is gone. I don't see her anywhere, so I follow the slow trickle of guests moving in one direction.

Music swells as we all flow into a ballroom. Chandeliers and sconces fill the space, reflecting off decorative gold molding and pearl-colored walls. A light parquet covers the floors, couples twirling smoothly across the herringbone pattern.

I glance around and spot Luci, tucked into a corner with a blank expression on her face. Ashamed of my suspicion, and my rudeness in the salon, I weave through the growing crowd to stand beside her.

Wearing what some might describe as a thousand-yard stare, she looks straight ahead, her mind somewhere else.

"Luci," I say, and her eyes snap to me. I ease closer, so I can keep my voice low. "I'm sorry."

"Why?" Her forehead wrinkles as she frowns.

"I shouldn't have asked you about Rose like that. Not in front of other people. I didn't know."

"Know what?" She lifts her chin, but sadness in her eyes give her away.

Rose's post about doucebête—who I now know is Luci—had the ring of romantic love. If she and Luci were involved, that explains why Luci didn't admit knowing her.

Appearances reign supreme with people in power, and the affair might have drawn disapproval from the Marteau family. Judgment. Anger. Possibly rejection.

"What didn't you know?" Luci demands, crossing her arms. She's trying to keep up a good front, but when her bottom lip quivers, I touch her arm.

"It's okay," I say gently. "I won't tell."

She blinks rapidly and sniffs, but her shoulders relax. "Thank you," she whispers.

I feel for Luci, and I won't betray her secret. But there's still the question of where Rose has gone.

"Is that why Rose is avoiding her sister?" I ask, hoping family drama is the answer to her disappearance. "Did Alice not approve?"

"No. Alice knew. What has she told—"

She cuts off and looks beyond me. I turn and spot Ric slinking around the dance floor, his gaze pinned on us.

A red-haired woman hangs on his arm. Judging by her hazy

eyes and uncoordinated gait, she's not holding on with affection. But for support.

As the pair draws near, I cringe, stepping closer to the wall to give them room to pass.

But Ric stops in front of us, wearing a lazy smirk. Towering over Luci and me, he blocks our view of the dancers.

"Brooke," he says, smacking his lips after my name.

His date sets an empty wine glass on a nearby table, her body swaying slightly as she reaches out. When she stands upright again, she breathes deeply and blinks several times.

"Isn't this place amazing?" She slurs in an American accent. She offers a smile, but it's droopy and unstable, as if her lips were painted by Picasso. She's highly intoxicated, by drink or drug or both.

"Like something out of a storybook," I say, hoping her presence will at least rein in Ric's lewd behavior.

She circles her fingers in the air, indicating the surroundings but barely able to keep her eyes open. "I've lived in Paris for . . . long time, but I never thought I'd get to come to this famous ball."

"We're happy to have you," Luci says. She wears a charming expression, but a hint of irritation lies in her tone. Is she irritated by Ric's presence? Or the condition of his date?

"Sorry we missed dinner," the redhead says. "Ric was showing me a room upstairs." She gives an exaggerated wink. "Showing me the ceiling." She laughs at her own joke.

Scoffing, Ric jerks his arm, consequently pulling her off balance.

"Hey," she protests as she loses her footing.

Ric clenches his jaw until the muscles bulge. He leans close to her face. "What did I tell you?" he says, voice sharp and cruel as a razor.

The exchange is uncomfortable to witness, and next to me, Luci clears her throat.

Huffing, Ric lifts his arm to dislodge his date. His upper lip curls in disgust. "Go clean yourself up."

Eyes downcast, the redhead speaks to Luci. "Can you show me the restroom?"

Luci glances at me, as if she doesn't want to leave me with Ric, but she's a member of the esteemed Marteau family. She can't let a guest who's clearly upset wander around lost.

Too bad Ric doesn't show the same courtesy.

His stare still burns with temper as he grabs my elbow. "Let's dance," he says. Not a request, but an order.

"No, thanks." His fingers tighten painfully, but I wrench free. "I'll wait for Noah."

As if on cue, I glance over his shoulder to see Noah approaching. "There you are," I say, making sure Ric knows we have an audience.

Noah comes to my side and hands me a drink. "Ric," he says, facing his cousin.

Ric tips his head in response, his lips pressed into a thin line.

Sensing a mutual dislike between the men, I lift my drink. "The apple brandy is delicious, but I think this is my last one. I'm getting a little light-headed."

"We can leave whenever you're ready," Noah says.

Ric narrows his eyes. "But we saved the best part for last, and we don't want Brooke to miss out, do we?" He bumps his glass against Noah's chest. "Why don't you leave? And I'll take care of Brooke."

Noah gently pushes the drink back toward his cousin. "Don't be an ass." He speaks under his breath, but the low tone can't disguise his anger.

"Ric, stop." Lyam materializes beside me. "Father will be furious if you cause a scene."

Ric sneers at his younger brother. "Good little Lyam, always doing what's *expected* of you." He tosses back what's left of his drink and turns back to Noah. "And you. Why are you even here?"

Noah goes rigid. "Because I'm family."

"Oh, *now* you're family." Ric sniffs with disdain. "That didn't stop you from leaving. You ran away with your mommy, like a coward." He glances at me and smirks. "After his girlfriend's little sister died in our tunnels."

"That's enough," Noah says, stepping up to Ric as I gasp.

Is Ric talking about the little girl who went missing? The one who was later found in the catacombs?

In *their* tunnels? Below Maison Marteau?

Fury sparks between them, an unspoken challenge straining the air.

But then Ric laughs and backs down. He pats Noah's chest, as if to calm him. As if he doesn't want to make Noah angry. "Okay, Cousin. Okay."

Ric lifts his glass in a gesture of peace and speaks to Noah in *French*. Taking a drink, he turns to go, walking to the door where Luci and his date exited.

I stare at Noah. He stares back, but I can't decipher his mood. If he's still angry, he hides it well.

The music changes to a slower song. Before I can say a word, Lyam extends his hand. "May I have this dance?"

I glance between him and Noah, but manners win out. I don't want to be rude to Lyam. He's done nothing wrong.

I hand my drink to Noah. He smiles but his eyes show strain, the only evidence of his lingering ire.

Happy as a schoolboy, Lyam lifts my hand to kiss my fingers, then slowly pulls me out to dance. Without objection, I glide onto the floor, his arms still encircling me as we dance.

"Sorry about Ric," Lyam says. "He always wants what he can't have."

"It's fine." I shrug and pretend to let it go. Trying to salvage what's left of the night, I wink at Noah as I twirl by.

He gives me a smile, but I can tell his mood has changed. Tension rests on Noah's forehead, a reminder of Ric's callousness.

He didn't explain his cousin's cryptic words. And I won't tell him it's a story I've already heard.

But as I sway with Lyam beneath the chandeliers, I know two things.

The little friend Ric mentioned was the missing girl.

And Noah was here when she died.

My Hotel Peculiar

The next few days after the party, everything returned to normal. Normal for everyone else. But not for me.

Nothing felt the same for me, not in my mind and not in my body.

Because I had changed.

All I could think about was my father, about the sounds he'd made in his special room. And how the woman screamed.

I didn't understand what I was feeling then, when I saw my father cut her skin. The blood. I never knew it could be so dark, but seeing it trickle over her white skin . . . it made me feel funny. It made me ache in a way I couldn't explain. A good ache, like I was hungry and hurting all at once.

Every night I lay in bed, remembering her screams, the twisted look on her face.

I wondered why my father did that to her. And yet, somehow, I already knew.

He did it because it was fun.

I thought about the woman a lot, even more than my father. I remembered the slow roll of blood across her throat. It was beautiful. Like a painting brought to life.

Every time I pictured it, my breath got caught in my throat, and I knew I wanted to see it again. I wanted to know how my father felt.

Thinking about what he did to the woman always made my stomach get that funny ache.

And if a memory could make me feel that way . . .

How good would it feel to do it myself?

31

Two hours later, we've returned to the blue salon. I'm eating again to fill my stomach, convinced bread will diminish the effects of alcohol. Or at least prevent a hangover. I'm not drunk—not exactly—but my movements are sluggish, and I've stifled more than one yawn.

The partygoers have started to thin out, with Dora and Chantal posted at the doors to bid farewells. Noah and I sit with Luci, André, and another two couples. Most of the people remaining are either family or their personal guests.

When Noah breaks from conversation, I give him a small nudge. "Should we go?"

"You can't leave yet," Luci says. She must have overheard me. "The fun part is just getting started."

"The fun part?" I glance around the table, and it's clear the others all know what's coming next.

"You'll see." Luci dances in her seat, clearly excited. "Ah-ah." She points at Noah when he opens his mouth to explain.

He tosses up his hands and sits back, just as Dora enters the salon. She wheels herself over to us. "I hope you've all enjoyed yourselves," she says, paying special attention to me. Her manners confirm I'm the last of the true guests. Everyone else here is friend or family.

"Everything was wonderful," I say. "Thank you again."

She speaks to the others in French before patting my hand and rolling back from the table. "You young people have a good time and be safe. I'm afraid I must excuse myself from the next portion of the evening's revelries."

It's as if everyone here is speaking in code, intentionally spiking curiosity. I let a young man in black remove my plate, barely paying attention.

What's the big secret, and why is it planned for so late at night?

Dora exits the room, passing Lyam as he enters with Ric, his date trailing behind. The red-haired woman sways on her feet but manages to stay upright.

Noah stands when Lyam comes over to our table. "It's time?"

"It's time," Lyam says with a grin. "All right. Everyone up."

"Okay, what are we doing?" I ask Noah, but he only puts a finger to his mouth.

We all follow Lyam through the corridors, twisting and turning until we end up in a game room. A bar lines one wall, liquor bottles backlit and glowing against dark wood. There's a pool table with crimson felt, a dart board, various playing tables, and a sitting area with sofas.

Lyam holds a black bag, then he lifts his arm and gives the bag a shake. Something rattles inside. "A long-standing tradition at *La Danse des Monstres* is the final and most exciting part of the event." He scans the room, brown eyes lingering on each of us, the dramatic pause meant to heighten suspense.

"It's time," he finally says, "for the dark hunt."

A cold pit opens up in the bottom of my gut, a pit that absorbs what little enthusiasm I'd started to build.

The dark hunt? My mind conjures terrible images.

What kind of games do these people play?

I shuffle my feet and glance at Noah. He doesn't look worried, so I breathe deep and try to keep an open mind.

Lyam reaches into the bag and pulls something out, keeping it tight in his palm so none of us can see. Then he makes his way from person to person, allowing each to slip a hand into the bag.

When he comes to me, I do the same. Flat, round objects rest inside the silk. Cool, hard, and rough. Like stone. I take mine and keep it curled in my palm.

When the last person takes their turn, Lyam tosses the bag aside. "For those of you who are new to the *La Danse des Monstres*, let me explain the rules. We will all look at our stones at the same time. Not yet, Luci," he teases his cousin.

"Your stone will be either white or black. If it's white, you are a victim. If it's black, well, let's just say you'll be doing the hunting." His laugh is a sadistic rumble, and now I turn to Noah in surprise.

"So, my costume doesn't make a difference?"

"Not for the game."

"We will have two winners," Lyam continues. "The monster who catches the most victims, and the last victim standing. The one who survives."

"A final girl," Luci calls, sending me a look when she uses the American term.

I try to return her enthusiasm, but the reference doesn't make me feel better.

"Or we might have a final boy," André says, giving Luci a playful elbow. "Because I'm going home the winner this year."

From across the room, Ric groans. "Can we get on with it?" He and his date lean against the pool table. His arm hooks around her neck, and her hand rests on his stomach, just above his belt.

Their body language reeks of foreplay and sends sticky shivers over my skin. Thoroughly revolted, I refocus on Lyam.

"Right," he says, extending his hand, fingers up. "Everyone, on three. Ready?"

The rest of us lift our arms.

"One, two, three!"

I uncurl my fingers and stare at my stone. It's white.

"Oh, bad luck." Noah winks and holds up a black disc between two fingers.

Around the room, people squeal or laugh, several hurrying from the room.

"What's happening?" I ask. "What do I do?"

Noah doesn't answer, but André grabs my hand. "Come on," he says, dragging me through the room.

Our path takes us by the pool table. Ric looks far too pleased with the lottery, and as I pass, he leans forward. "You better start running."

Out in the corridor, I lift my dress as I zigzag through the mansion with André. The *click-clack* of heels has me glancing back to find Luci right behind us. "This way," she says, passing us and turning into an empty room. The three of us race through, ending up in a rear hallway.

"Where are we going?" I ask, slowing and pulling my hand from André's.

"We only have a minute's head start, and like I said, I plan to win." He nods to Luci who's several paces ahead of us. She leads us into a ridiculously large kitchen and down a short passage to a white metal door.

When she punches a button, I draw back. "We are going up, right?"

"No," André answers. "The house might be more comfortable, but the ones who hide inside are the first ones found."

"Other people ran upstairs."

André lifts his huge shoulders. "Maybe they don't want to get their clothes dirty. Or maybe they're too scared."

"Scared of what?" I ask, but the doors have opened and he's already pulling me into the tiny elevator.

Luci taps a button to close the doors. She and André look at each other, laughing between frantic breaths.

I want to share their excitement, but I'm more concerned with the drop in my stomach. The elevator is going down. Far down.

I twist my hands together, hoping we're headed to a basement or wine cellar. But when the door opens, light spills from the cab into a dark tunnel. The first thing I see is a wall of skulls.

A hundred hollow sockets stare at us, black holes where eyes used to be. "What are those doing here?"

"It's the catacombs," André says, giving me a look as if I shouldn't have to ask.

"I know, but skulls? Here? Beneath a house?"

Luci steps out for a moment, and a single light turns on, its dome creating a sickly, yellow illumination. "Legally," she says, "the owners of a residence have the right to access the property below, including the famous catacombs. But you'll never see this section on a commercialized tour."

André chuckles. "Especially when the property is one like Maison Marteau."

"Great," I say, peering out in both directions. Spaced ten or fifteen feet apart, more lights cast the tunnel in an eerie glow.

Luci leads us to the right, walking with confidence in the gravel, despite her high heels.

As we move deeper underground, a strange smell assaults my nose. I don't want to think about the source of the musty scent or how long it's been down here.

As we creep through the shadows, Luci stops on occasion, looking one way and then the other way before deciding where to go. At one point, we come face-to-face with a large headstone. Situated on a mound of dirt, the tablet sits in front of a wall of femurs, French text engraved on the stone.

I make out the words "*combat*" and "*éternité*" with a date inscribed below. Some kind of memorial.

Luci and André stop and speak rapidly in French. As they plot our next move, I wander toward a side tunnel.

Luci grabs my arm. "Not that way." Her eyes are wide, almost afraid. "Please, stay close. The tunnels flood when we have too much rain."

I think of the girl found down here years before. A child, lost and alone in the cold, damp, dark. Is it possible she drowned? Or developed hypothermia? Trapped in an endless maze filled with bones.

A cold shudder shakes my body.

What a horrible way to die.

A scraping sound echoes in the tunnel behind us.

"Shh," Luci hisses, guiding us to a small alcove. "Wait here."

"Where are you..." I trail off, because she's already gone.

André peeks around the corner, concerned with being caught and losing the game. After a few minutes of silence from the tunnels, I cross my arms and lean against the wall.

I catch myself at the last second, jerking upright. I don't want to touch whatever corpse residue may have accumulated over time.

"I'm surprised the family takes the joke this far."

André turns his head but stays in position by the door. "What do you mean?"

"The monsters' dance is about making light of the gossip. Odd, but acceptable." I pause and consider my next words. "But playing a game like this? In the place a child got lost and died? I don't know." I lift a shoulder. "It's a bit too morbid for me."

He stands straight, studies my face for a moment. "Yes, but

the dance and the hunt began before . . . before what happened to the girl. It's a terrible thing, but life goes on, *oui*?"

"That's true." I try to sound agreeable. He and Luci obviously enjoy the tradition. I give a little laugh. "But the vampire rumors. How wild is that?"

André bobs his head. "Where Maison Marteau is concerned? Not so much."

"What? André, don't tell me you believe in vampires." I tilt my head, encouraging him to keep talking.

"No." He looks over his shoulder and walks closer. "But one of them thought he was. Grégoire Marteau, the man who built the mansion."

I nod in the dark, and André spills.

"It's not really a secret, but that man was *fou*." André drops his voice to a whisper. "Bat. Shit. Crazy."

He looks back again, as if afraid someone will sneak up and catch us talking about the revered Grégoire Marteau. "The family pretends. They want people to think they don't care. Because if they can laugh off their history, so will everyone else. But trust me, it's a sore subject. A *dark* family secret."

André pauses and licks his lips.

"What's the secret?" My muscles are rigid as I lean forward.

"He had Renfield Syndrome," André says.

"Renfield." I roll the name on my tongue, the taste familiar. "Isn't that Dracula's helper?"

"Yes. He was enthralled by the vampire and developed a craving for blood. Grégoire Marteau liked to drink blood, too." André rolls his eyes. "He thought it would give him powers or something. Make him immortal."

"That is . . . different," I say, landing on a neutral description.

"But listen, don't bring it up to the family. Not even Lyam or Luci."

"Of course," I mutter, rubbing the chill bumps on my arms.

André returns to his post, watching the tunnel. Then we hear Luci call his name. Her whisper-shout carries a long way in the empty tunnel.

"*Merde.* She's going to give us away." André hurries outside to find Luci, leaving me alone to consider this new information.

Renfield Syndrome. I read about it once, when a friend auditioned for the movie inspired by the Renfield character. The disease is also known as clinical vampirism and involves an obsession with drinking blood. Sometimes, people with the syndrome suffer delusions of immortality or superhuman abilities.

A strange illness and one I can see inspiring gossip. The route from Renfield to vampire is a short, straight line. It's a logical explanation, and much better than the horrors I'd had in mind.

But as I stare out at the yellowed-tinted light, a question remains. It scrapes around the back of my brain.

Where did Grégoire Marteau get the blood?

32

Where are they?

I'm still waiting in the alcove for Luci and André. It feels like they've been gone forever, but I'm not sure if five minutes have passed or fifteen. Time is shifty down here in the dark. And minute by minute, I grow more claustrophobic. I can almost feel the weight of the earth above my head.

Sixty to eighty feet. That's how deep some of the catacombs run. A possible eight stories of stone between me and the fresh night air.

I have no idea what time it is, not with my phone still upstairs in my purse. When André and I made a mad dash from the salon, I left my clutch sitting on the table. Inside, my phone and its charged battery. With a clock. And a flashlight.

I peer up at the light in the tunnel, shedding weak illumination the color of watery mustard.

Maybe I can find my way back. I know which tunnel we last exited, and we only took three turns to get here. Or was it four?

As I stare down the dim shaft, a terrible thought occurs to me.

What if Luci and André got caught?

Have they been taken somewhere by the monsters of the game? Are they back upstairs in the mansion? Have they forgotten about me?

No. Of course not. I rub my chest and take a breath.

Stay calm. Don't panic. One breath in.

And back out.

Hand still on my chest, I focus on the rise and fall as I breathe. No one's forgotten me. I just have to stay put. Wait here like Luci—

A scream echoes through the tunnels, and my skin tightens on my scalp. Who was that?

Easing out of the small recess, I take a few steps back the way we came, listening, straining to hear voices.

Low rumbles carry to my ears. Maybe a man's voice? I wait to hear more, but the passage falls quiet again.

I debate whether to keep creeping forward or stay where I am. I don't know what happens when a victim is caught, but it can't be worse than being down here.

My mind is muddled, and I can't think straight. The cold underground sobered me up, but the effects of apple brandy remain, clouding my thoughts like cotton in my head.

"Luci? André?" My voice is a dull echo.

I walk forward, stopping only when I come to a branch in the passageway. We came from the left. I'm *positive* we did.

"Hello? Is anyone there?" I cry out louder this time, hoping someone—anyone—will call back.

At this point, I don't care if I'm caught. I *want* to be caught. Especially if that's a one-way ticket back up to the house and other people. *Living* people.

Keeping my distance from the wall of bones, I study the curve of the tunnel. A brass plaque hangs up ahead. I remember passing it earlier.

Confident I'm headed back to the elevator, I rush down the tunnel to the next junction. It's a three-way split, the one where Luci paused to think about where she was going.

But staring into each of the shafts, I can't tell which one to take. This area feels colder, damper, the foul scent of dust and mildew giving me a headache.

"Hello?"

I listen, but my own voice is all I hear.

Panic builds in my chest again, a tightening of my lungs that spreads to my throat. I swallow and press a hand to my heart.

I can't get lost down here. These tunnels go on for miles.

Fighting the urge to run blindly, I trail my fingers along the wall and try to think what to do. Maintaining contact with the stone, I travel to the next area where the route diverges and take the first tunnel to the right.

I come upon a design made out of long bones, a circle of skulls creating a pattern in the middle. None of this feels familiar. I would remember this. Wouldn't I?

The longer I'm down here, the less certain I am of anything.

I'm about to turn around and go back when I see a door farther down. The weight in my chest lifts.

A door means a room, possibly access to stairs. An exit. If there are steps, I don't know where they'll take me. But as long as I come out above ground, I'll be happy.

Taking my hand off the wall, I cross the shaft and make my way to the door. The first thing I notice is the color. At one time, the door was painted red, but time has altered the color. The wood has dried, and the paint has peeled.

But when I draw close enough to look squarely at the front, my stomach drops, falling down to the dirt and gravel floor.

A symbol is carved into the wood. A symbol I've come to recognize. A large Gothic-style V with a snake in its center.

Why is this here? Grégoire Marteau valued this emblem, enough to wear it on his clothing and engrave it on his tomb.

Grégoire Marteau.

A man who liked drinking blood.

The handle of the door is old and rusted, but I find myself reaching for the lever. The metal is rough against my palm, the decay of time scratching my skin.

I press down and push.

But the door is locked.

Air rushes from my lungs, a release of tension. As much as I need to know what's behind this door, I'm not sure I'm prepared. Not sure I can handle the shock of whatever a sick, disturbed man might keep hidden down here.

Shaken and afraid, I turn and walk swiftly toward the niche where Luci left me. She'll come back for me. Noah will come back for me.

Someone will. They have to.

But what if they don't?

I come to the three-way split and look in each direction, uncertainty making me light-headed.

Then the lights go off.

I cry out in the dark, the sound raw and primal, curdled by fear.

Finding the wall, I lean against it, trying to anchor myself in the sea of black. My breaths come too rapidly, and I start to feel dizzy. Pressing my back to the wall, I slide down, squatting with my hands on my face.

My calm unravels and my sanity frays. I need to hear my mother's voice. I need her to tell me what to do, even if her words are only a memory.

But I can't hear her through the static in my head.

I'm on the verge of crying when male laughter floats in the air.

I shoot to my feet. "André!"

No one answers, but scuffling sounds ricochet in the dark. Footsteps on the gravel.

Not caring who I find, I slink along the wall, straining to follow the sounds. The only sign of life in the pitch black.

Another laugh, female this time. Coming from my left.

"Please, turn on the lights. I'm ready to go back up." My voice is a rasp, barely audible over the roar in my ears. My heart, pulsing hard enough to rattle my veins.

More low sounds from ahead.

A growl, then a grunt, followed by whimpering.

"Who's there?"

The lights come on, shockingly bright after the deep, pure darkness.

Ric stands in the tunnel, staring at me. His red-haired date leans on the wall. No, she's held there by him, a black band wrapped around her throat.

I can't make sense of what I'm seeing until she pulls at his arm. "More," she whines. "Squeeze harder."

But Ric ignores her, his unfeeling eyes focused on me. A predator spotting its prey.

"Was that you crying in the dark, Brooke?" He moves away from the woman and steps toward me. "Did you get lost, little lamb?"

I blink as my eyes adjust, taking in the space behind him. I know that wall, the depression in the stone. The elevator is right behind him.

"Yes," I say, working up a watery smile. I can be sweet to Ric if it will get me out of this dank, dark hell.

"Don't be scared," he says, taking another step in my direction. "We were just getting started."

"I'm on my way up," I say with a light laugh. "I'll just go and give you some privacy."

Ric is close enough now that I have to step around him. But when I try, he blocks my way. "Three is always more fun," he says, sliding his hand beneath my jaw and into the hollow of my collarbone.

My skin crawls beneath his touch, and I lean away.

"Come on, now." He skims his eyes down my body then back to my face. "I know you didn't wear this dress for Noah."

Before I can speak, he snakes an arm around my waist, jerking me hard against his chest.

"No." I slam my palms against his shoulder and push back. "Don't touch me. I want to leave."

His upper lip curls but he doesn't release me. "Don't. Stop. Wait." His fingers dig into my hip. Forceful. Painful. "Women like you know exactly what you're doing. What you're asking for."

He presses close, his warm breath on my face when he speaks. "Then, when they get it, they bitch and moan and lie about what happened."

Still holding me, he slides a hand down my side, then rubs a circle on my stomach, on the red hourglass. "This costume is perfect for a woman like you. Luring men in, only to strike after you get what you want."

He leans in and licks my cheek, his hoarse whisper in my ear. "Like your friend in Hollywood."

Shock travels through my body, a surge of disgust. He knows who I am. He's heard the story. And he's using my trauma like a knife.

Worse. He's using Mackenzie.

"Let me go," I say, but my voice is timid.

"I bet she fucked that man." Ric reaches around, his hands fumbling at my lower back, searching for the zipper. "I bet you fucked him, too."

I close my eyes, traveling back in time. To another party, another dark space.

And another man who thought he could take whatever he wanted.

The flashback stabs my brain, slicing through the freeze and signaling the fight. "Stop." A rush of adrenaline gives me strength.

"Stop!" Rearing back my arm, I drive a fist into his throat. He stumbles back, coughing and cursing.

Seizing my chance, I rush past him, lunging for the elevator where I hit the call button again and again.

Out of the corner of my eye, I watch Ric. He stands straight, rubbing his throat. "Bitch," he rasps, striding towards me.

He's a few short steps away when the door opens, and I fall inside. Crushing into the corner, I punch the top button and face the door, waiting for Ric to appear, to reach in and grab me again.

But seconds pass and he never does.

The door slides shut with a *hiss*.

In a trance, I stare wide-eyed at the panel on the wall. The numbers tick off as the elevator climbs. Not fast enough. Finally, I reach the top and spill into the hallway near the kitchen.

Instead of going back to the blue salon, I turn toward the front of the mansion, running down the hall until I know where I am. Another turn, and I see the foyer. A group of monsters stand in a cluster.

Ignoring them, I rush to the front doors, focused only on escape. Escape from the tunnels, from Ric, from this cruel world of wealth and its twisted rules.

"Brooke."

Noah's voice. But I don't stop to answer.

I'm at the doors, fling one side open before I race into the night.

Noah calls my name again, but I keep going.

I don't stop, I don't slow down, and I don't look back.

33

I'm sobbing by the time I reach the gate. Instead of going to my apartment, I run straight across the cobblestones, instinctively pulled to the nearest exit.

Gripping the black bars, I close my eyes and press my forehead to the cool metal. I open them again when I sense a presence, the alarming sound of someone behind me.

I whirl, my chest tight as it builds a scream.

But it's only Noah, worry stamped into the lines of his face. "Brooke." He says my name softly, like he's speaking to a fawn who might bolt any second. "Are you okay?"

Collapsing against the gate, I cross my hands over my heart. "I . . . I thought you were him."

Noah goes rigid. "Who?" His expression rolls from concern to fury. "Ric?"

"Yes." I shake my head. "No. I don't know." I picture Ric, but his image blurs with another's. A sob rises in my throat, but I trap it inside with a strangled sound.

My lips tremble, my tears stream, and I know I'm in the midst of a breakdown. One that won't be stopped.

I tug at the fabric of my dress, then the red spider's mark on my stomach, before hooking my fingers in the high collar. Suddenly suffocating, I pull and tug. "I have to get this off. I have to get this off."

Is this a panic attack? The squeezing chest and shallow breaths?

"Okay." Noah's hands fall on top of mine, grip gently. "We'll get you out of that dress. Come on. I've got you."

Arm around my shoulders, he leads me toward his apartment instead of mine. I don't object or refuse. Folded into Noah, I already feel safer.

And I can't be alone in my apartment right now.

One bump or creak or flickering light might shove me right over the edge.

He guides me inside and to a downstairs bathroom. "I'll be right back," he says, holding up a hand in a halting motion, as if I'll try to leave.

As if I could.

My whole body is shaking now. The adrenaline from before drains from my system, leaving me a cold and quivering mess.

Hands on the sink, I look in the mirror. And see a madwoman staring back. Hair disheveled, eyes wide.

The first thing I do is unhook the dress clasp at the base of my skull, then I pull the zipper down a few inches. The tiny relief lets me take a deep breath.

Next, I pull out the clip and shiny pins from my hair, rubbing my fingers on my scalp before splashing my face with cool water. I have a hand towel pressed to my cheeks when Noah returns.

"Here. These will be too big, but they're soft and stretchy." He hands me a navy-blue sweatsuit.

"Thank you," I say, too embarrassed to meet his eyes. "I'll be out in a minute."

I close the door and strip out of the dress. The sweats swallow me whole, but the soft fabric is soothing.

When I'm clothed again, I step out to find Noah waiting. He leans casually against the wall, but his expression is strained.

"I have water and paracetamol in the living room."

He doesn't say anything else, letting me be the one to decide where I want to go, what I want to do.

I amble down the hall, not speaking until I'm nestled securely in the corner of his big, cushy couch. True to form, the first words out of my mouth are an apology. "I'm sorry about that." I lick my lips and keep my head down.

"You have nothing to be sorry about," he says. "But I do. I should never have taken you into that nest of vipers."

His hands are balled together, his knuckles turning white as he squeezes. "Will you tell me what happened?"

Fatigue and alcohol swamp me at once, and I don't have the energy to keep my secrets. I don't want to. Because they're killing me.

So, I tell him everything. Starting with Luci and André disappearing from our hiding place in the catacombs, and me trying to find my way out. The door with the symbol.

And Ric with his date, engaged in foreplay.

I don't tell him how Ric put his hands on me. That he might have done far worse if I hadn't fought back.

A vein already pulses in Noah's temple, so I minimize what happened. "Ric grabbed my arm, and he invited me to join him and the woman he brought tonight." I glance aside. "If you know what I mean."

"That asshole." Nostrils flaring, Noah grinds the heels of his hands together.

"Yes. He is an asshole, but . . ." I pause, hesitant to say any more. Afraid to let go of the biggest secret. The one I've held inside for three years.

Only two other people know what happened.

Only Mackenzie.

And *him*.

"Tonight isn't the first time Ric's touched me," I begin, "and what he did tonight was awful." I double-swallow. "But what he said was worse."

Noah waits in silence, his eyes never leaving mine.

"He mentioned a friend of mine," I say. "Her name is Mackenzie."

Noah doesn't nod or speak or even move, but the shift in his eyes tells me he's heard her name before.

"So you know she's part of what's happening in LA."

He lifts a shoulder, explaining with a single word. "Yahoo."

The last image I have of Mackenzie appears in my mind. It hits me like a blow, a one-two punch of guilt and pain. My eyes burn and tears start again.

I picture one of the savage headlines. "She isn't lying. She's telling the truth." I put a hand to my stomach where nausea coils.

"And I should know."

34

Grief and regret are a flood, pouring out of me as I confide in Noah. "I knew what he was like. The producer." I take the box of tissues Noah offers. "I met him a few years ago, at a party."

Memories flash—the empty bedroom, the locked door, the sound of his breathing.

"He tried with me, thought that he could get away with it like he probably has a hundred other times. But I was raised in Hollywood, and I knew what to do. Mention a few other names, heavy hitters, people I claimed were close family friends."

I look at Noah and shrug. "Most of it was a lie, but I know how these men operate and what will scare them. And that's anyone who wields more power."

"You stood up for yourself," Noah says.

"I protected myself, but after I got out of that party, after I was out of harm's way, I never said anything. Not a word to anyone."

If you want to get ahead, you have to get along.

I shut my eyes and shake off the sound of my mother's voice.

"But keeping my mouth shut was the wrong thing to do. It made me complicit."

"No, it—"

"Yes." I cut Noah off. "I should have warned other women. They call it the whisper network, letting people know who to watch out for. At the very least, I should have warned Mackenzie. I grew up in that world, but she didn't. She thought she was safe. With the *Me Too* movement and so many people speaking out, she thought things were different from before. But they're not."

My words flow in a stream, quick and emergent. As if I'm purging toxins and have to get them out as fast as possible. "Things haven't changed. Not really. The monsters are still there." I grind my teeth. "They just got smarter."

Noah tries again. "None of what happened to your friend is your fault. You didn't do anything wrong."

I stare at the wall, unable to look at him or accept his absolution.

"But I did." A tear rolls down my face. "All I had to do was tell her to be careful, to watch out for him. But I was afraid. I was worried she'd tell someone else and word would get around. I bluffed the producer once, at that party, but if he found out I'd bad-mouthed him, he would destroy my career."

A scornful laugh bubbles out of me. "My *career*. I put my own self-interests over Mackenzie's safety. Now she's the one who might be ruined. She's the one who was *hurt*. Because of me."

"Because of him," Noah insists. "You kept quiet because of fear. He did what he did, because he's evil." For the first time, Noah touches me, his fingers grazing my hand. "There is no comparison."

"She's not talking to me now." Sniffing, I dab my face and

continue the purge. Sharing my truth with Noah is cathartic, and now I can't stop. I want to tell him the rest.

I want to tell him everything.

"She confided in me, and I told her I wasn't surprised. That made her furious. She wanted to know how I could have let her go away for the weekend, to an island, with all of the cast and crew. When I knew what he was like. That he might try to coerce her into bed. Find her alone and tell her she'd be smart to keep him happy."

Nausea licks at my stomach and I cringe. "Just like he did me."

"You told her what he did to you?"

"No." My voice is soft, full of shame. "I never got the chance. She left the set that day, then all hell broke loose." I release a long sigh. "Two days later, I was standing at the gates of Maison Marteau."

Feeling wrung out and empty, I lean my head on the soft couch. "I've been a ticking time bomb ever since. Getting the audition helped for a while. It was a nice distraction, but with Alice and Ric, the talk of murder and vampires—"

"Wait." Noah doesn't try to hide his shock. "You know about the vampire thing?"

"I never believed it, and now that I know about your ancestor, that he had Renfield's Syndrome, it makes a lot more sense."

"Okay." He nods. "Sounds like you've heard a lot."

"I heard some things. Others I found out for myself," I admit. "And I've snooped around the apartment looking for a journal that I'm not sure even exists."

When he looks confused, I say, "Alice told me Rose had found a journal when she was here. Supposedly, she'd read some awful things in it and was really scared. I told Alice I would look for it, but over time, I started to question whether or not she was telling me the truth. I think Rose might have left on her own and just didn't tell her sister."

I don't mention a possible love interest, and I *won't* bring up Luci.

That's not my secret to tell.

"Did you find it?" Noah asks.

"What?" I yawn as the night's drama takes its physical toll. "Oh, the journal? No." I give him a half-hearted smile. "Have you seen the state of that storage room?"

"Right," he says, but his voice is distant, his tone troubled.

The sound of the front door opening carries through the apartment right before André calls, "Noah? You here?"

Aware of my red and swollen eyes, I rise from the couch. "I should go to my place." But the chill of the catacombs still prickles my skin, and Ric's wicked leer still haunts my mind.

Noah sees my hesitation and takes the decision out of my hands. "I have a guest room. The sheets are clean, and the bed is made." He hands me the water and pills I still haven't touched. "André can sleep in another room. He'll be fine," he says quickly, heading off my argument.

With a reluctant nod, I let him show me the way upstairs. After making sure I have all I need, Noah wishes me a good night's sleep and leaves me alone.

My eyes are already closing as I crawl into bed. Still a little drunk and emotionally spent, I curl onto my side in the fetal position. Feeling safer than I have in days, I finally give in to exhaustion.

And sleep pulls me down like a cool, black lake.

35

I wake up to silence in Noah's apartment. Still wearing the sweatsuit he gave me, I make up the bed, grab my discarded dress, and tiptoe downstairs.

There's no sign of Noah. Or André, either. But I find a note on the kitchen island next to my purse.

Had to leave town for a couple of days. Family needs me to handle a business emergency.

Make yourself at home.

Noah.

Frowning, I stare at the note. I'd hoped to talk to him this morning, to apologize for getting so emotional last night.

But *the family* interferes again.

Like some curse I can't get rid of.

Keeping the paper with me, I turn in a circle and scan the kitchen. Noah's offer to stay was what I needed in the moment, but now I want a long, hot shower. In my rental, with my own shampoo, and my own clothes.

Plus, Clairee is probably waiting at the door, ready for her morning bathroom and breakfast ritual.

I check the time as I cross the courtyard. It's after eleven, but the day is gloomy, distant clouds bruised and swollen. A sign that another storm is coming.

The perfect kind of day to stay inside, curled up with some snacks and a blanket and my cat and a book. But no lusty vampires this time. Only feel-good romances allowed. Maybe one with a puppy.

After last night, I need an emotional cleanse.

As soon as I turn the key and crack the door, Clairee slips out. She throws an unhappy mewl my way for leaving her alone all night.

"Sorry, girl. Couldn't be helped."

She does her business and is back in a flash.

A half hour later, I'm showered and downstairs, whipping up cheese toast and tomato soup. Comfort food. Finding a tray in the pantry, I carry it all up to the study. My laptop sits where I left it on the desk, so I have a seat and open the browser.

Unburdening myself to Noah was a good start, and my dark secret looks different laid bare to the light.

Still, whatever revelations I make in my personal life, the mansion isn't good for my state of mind. I need to leave. Which means finding a pet-friendly hotel and moving out. That's the plan. A solid plan.

But when the homepage loads, that solid plan crumbles.

The leading story is still about the protests, but the accompanying photo is from a bird's-eye view. Likely taken from a helicopter, the picture shows thousands of people filling the streets. Thousands of people *blocking* the streets.

Taxis won't be running. Not when they can't drive anywhere.

Copying the French text, I open up a translation site. I read the English version, and the news is bad. What started as a transportation strike is now also a labor strike involving all manner of businesses. Including hotels.

Plopping back in the chair, I swivel in a circle and consider my prospects. How long can a protest of this magnitude really last? Surely, it's close to a breaking point.

I spin for a minute and then finally accept the reality. I'm not going anywhere, at least not today.

Huffing out my frustration, I take the laptop and tray over to the sofa. The first drops of rain hit the window, and I consider building a nice, warm fire.

After a bite of cheese toast, I log in to check my email. The usual correspondence fills my inbox—newsletters, blogs, ads, junk. I'm halfway through the list when a subject line jumps out at me.

Approval to join the *Tour the Dark* forum.

My fingers freeze on the touchpad. The dark tourism site. I completely forgot.

Closing my eyes, I try to return to the state of mind from five minutes ago. When I had decided on a new perspective.

One that doesn't include the gruesome events surrounding this mansion.

I look again at the screen. What will it hurt? Most of the questions I had about Maison Marteau have been answered. A murder-suicide happened here many years ago, and a child died in a tragic accident. I know why Luci lied. The vampire talk is based on a man's mental illness. And Rose likely left of her own free will.

Yes, I'm stuck here for a little while longer, but all the bumps in the night won't be as scary. Now that my previous worries have been laid to rest.

And I make sure never to be alone with Ric.

Then why the itch of curiosity in the base of my brain? What more can I discover?

The green skull from a T-shirt floats behind my eyes. Like a creepy, neon harbinger of doom.

But what was done to her body.

Forging ahead, I click the link and confirm my account. I enter the username and password I previously submitted, then the screen blinks, and I'm in the forum.

I scan the page and find my name. A small triangle points to the words *My posts*. I click and am shocked to see paragraphs of discussion, a back-and-forth chat about my original question.

Scrolling to the bottom, I read what I wrote first and then the responses. The initial comments are about *La Danse des Monstres*, because that's the reason I found this site in the first place. I skim most of this topic, because I'm now familiar with Grégoire Marteau and his Renfield Syndrome, but one topic bleeds into another.

I slow down when I find dialogue about death and murder.

As expected, the man who killed his wife and then himself is mentioned. One user extolls the history of the mansion, praising the building for its many sordid tragedies. Practically gushing over the myriad deaths linked to Maison Marteau.

A dark tourism super-fan.

A green light glows next to his username. He's online.

I click on his name, GraveDanger, and a pop-up gives me the option of sending a message.

My first question is short. I want to grab his attention before he logs off.

Can we talk Maison Marteau?

I wait less than thirty seconds before I get a reply.

Always.

Flexing my fingers, I think of what to write.

Hoping you can answer a question. I met a guy outside MM. He mentioned a woman being killed there. Any idea what he meant?

I hit "send" on the message and wait.

More than one woman I know of. One from the 1920s was the first. Killed by her husband. Left behind a couple of kids.

I do the math in my head. The children left as orphans then would have been the right age for one of them to have been Dora's parent. I'd guess she's around seventy years old.

But none of this answers the burning question.

Anything weird done to her body?

She was stabbed thirteen times.

I widen my eyes and blink. This guy really does know the mansion's history.

Nothing else?

He's gone for longer this time, and I understand why when I see the length of his response.

There are two categories when it comes to deaths associated with Maison Marteau. First, the ones that definitely happened inside the mansion. Other than the murder-suicide, most of those are people who died of natural causes.

Then you have the "associated deaths." The ones that happened somewhere in the vicinity of Maison Marteau but for one reason or another were blamed on the mansion. Like the place is cursed or something.

This guy really is a font of information. My fingers fly over the keyboard.

Tell me about the associated deaths. Any of them women with something weird done to their bodies?

Another short pause.

There was a girl found in the catacombs. Scrapes and bruises attributed to banging around in the dark. But I think you're asking about the party girl.

The words "party girl" jab from the screen and send a shiver down my spine. I haven't heard anything about this one. What party? When?

I start to type, but GraveDanger beats me to it.

Happened in 1985. Her body was found in Bois De Boulogne, a forest on the west side of Paris. Covered in leaves and dirt but not buried deep. Sloppy and amateur, like someone didn't know what they were doing or didn't care if she was found.

I read his response again. Confused, I ask a follow-up question.

Why linked to Maison Marteau?

He takes a long time, and I nibble on my thumbnail. Watching the screen, my muscles tense, clenched with sickening dread.

At last, he comes through.

She went to a party there on the night she disappeared. Info about her last activities is hard to come by, but the police issued a statement saying she had last been seen crossing Pont d'Iéna, the bridge near the Eiffel Tower. Online sleuths don't buy that story. The witness was never named, and the investigation dried up.

Another investigation into the Marteau family stalled out. Because of police corruption? The money and influence of the family? I lean in and continue reading.

There were other reasons people think party girl died at the mansion. Did you read the earlier comments about the guy who built the place? How his habits started talk of vampires?

Dropping my hand to the computer, I type two words.

Yes. Why?

I hold my breath and watch the screen.

His answer pops up and my stomach drops.

Because party girl's body had been drained of blood.

My Hotel Peculiar

I knew from the first moment I saw her.

She's the one. The one I want.

She was walking through the park behind our home, wearing a pink dress and matching ribbon in her hair. Shiny blonde hair, almost white. My own little angel.

It was a Sunday, almost lunch time. I guessed she was walking home after church. She carried a sack, maybe picking up something for her mother. Milk or butter for family dinner.

I glanced around, torn between my longing to touch her and fear that someone would see.

But she was following the pebbled path, and soon she would pass by a thatch of high shrubs. Hurrying up the path from the rear gate, I positioned myself behind the bushes.

I swallowed my nerves and looked back and forth. I couldn't see any people.

So that meant they couldn't see me.

Heart throbbing in my throat, I waited. Soon I heard her footsteps, quick and light.

When she came into view, I stepped forward. "Hi," I said, my smile bright and my voice playful. "Going shopping?" It was the first thing I could think of to ask.

She shook her head. "I'm finished shopping."

"Did you buy chocolate?" I ask, crossing my fingers behind my leg, hoping she hadn't.

"No. Only eggs." She made a curious face. "I don't know you."

I told her my name and gestured to the towering roof of Maison Marteau. "That's where I live," I told her.

Her eyes widened. "You live there? It's like a castle."

Inside, I felt proud, but I only shrugged. "My family makes Marteau chocolate. We have so much of it, we sometimes have to give it away."

She looks down at her grocery bag then back to me. "You give it away."

"Yes, but only to people who like chocolate." I nodded but said nothing more. Let her ask. Please, let her ask. Let her think it was her idea.

She pressed her lips together as if thinking. Then, in a small, soft voice, she said, "I like chocolate."

"I can give you some. It's just inside." She looks down the path, uncertain. "It won't take a minute, then you can take home a surprise for your mother."

Then it was her turn to shrug. "Okay. But I have to hurry."

I tossed another glance around the park. Only an old man with his dog were in my line of sight, and he was looking at the ground.

"Follow me," I said, hurrying down the path. I glanced over my shoulder. "Don't want you to be late," I told her, though that wasn't the real reason I was in such a rush.

I was actually doing it. I was taking her inside.

And I couldn't let anyone see us together.

We slipped through the back gate and then into a door near the kitchen. My whole head pounded as we walked to the elevator, as if my heart had moved to the inside of my brain.

"Where are we going?" she asked.

"We keep the chocolate cool in the cellar. It lasts longer that way."

She nodded, but her forehead pulled into a wrinkle. The door opened, and she looked both ways down the hall.

I did, too.

No one was there.

Another moment. I held my breath, and then she stepped inside.

Down, down, down, we rode, the tiny wrinkle fixed firmly between her pale eyebrows.

When the elevator door opened again, cold, musty air rushed inside. The tunnel before us was dark, only the interior light from the small cab shining on the stone walls.

"This is your cellar?" she asked, backing up in the elevator. She started shaking her head. "I don't want to go in there. It's too dark."

"Don't you want the chocolate?" I asked, my gaze moving between the girl and the tunnel. We were almost there.

"No. I want to go back up."

The door started to close again, but I jabbed the button. "Come on. It won't take long."

"No." Her eyes were wide and frightened. She wasn't going to budge.

That's when I fell on her, grabbing her arms and pulling her out.

She yelled and dragged her feet, but her Sunday shoes slid easily on the floor.

Another jerk, and she flew from the elevator, landing in a pile on the dirty ground.

Stunned, she stared up at me. And then she started to wail—high, piercing cries that echoed through the catacombs.

"Be quiet," I shouted, angry that my plan was failing. I wanted to take her to the room. I wanted her to lie still. I wanted her to smile at me.

Everything was going wrong.

"Let me out!" She tried to stand, but one arm was caught up in the handle of her shopping bag. I lunged at her, throwing myself on top of her. I pressed my hand over her mouth, but she wouldn't stop screaming.

I lifted her head. Rammed her back down. Again. Again.

Her eyes closed and her cries fell quiet.

I was breathing hard and suddenly so tired. So drained.

As I stared down at the lovely blonde girl, a shadow fell across us both. Before I could look up, my father spoke.

"What have you done?"

36

This can't be real.

Pacing back and forth behind the couch, I chew on my thumbnail as my mind whirls. Too many questions bombard me at once, but I can't grab hold of a single one. Because I'm stuck on a panicked auto-repeat.

This is crazy. This is crazy. This is crazy.

I try to convince myself that GraveDanger is wrong, that he's misinformed or a sensationalist. He's a dark-tourism junkie I met online. I don't know him. Why would I trust anything he says? Much less the wild claim made in his last message?

I stop and stare at the rain-lashed window, streams of water distorting my view of the park.

Because despite the absurdity of what he wrote, it fits the pattern of Maison Marteau. Just one more dark puzzle piece sliding perfectly into place.

But what was done to her body

Because her body was drained of blood.

Two similar stories from two different sources.

"But they're dark tourists," I say to myself, walking toward the desk before pivoting to walk back, Clairee's golden eyes tracking my every step.

The rational, left-lobe part of my brain argues against acceptance. Because it's crazy.

It's crazy. It's crazy. It's crazy.

But the other side, the one governed by instinct and intuition, the one prickling hairs on my neck and stabbing pins in my heart . . .

That side is horrified.

That side has no doubt at all.

"Okay, let's think this through." I glance at Clairee, my feline sounding board. "Let's look at all the events individually." I nod to myself, eager to examine the data and dispel the panic.

The first thing I consider is the murder-suicide. Something more common than most of us would like to admit, and certainly no reason to be afraid of the mansion.

Then there's the girl found in the catacombs. A tragedy for sure, a horrific accident. But in all probability, that's all it was. A terrible accident.

Hands on my hips, I stare into space, still pacing but with less agitation.

Thinking rationally is helping. It's calming me down. Instead of the tourist with the skull T-shirt, I think of his girlfriend and what she said. That a house as old as Maison Marteau is going to have history. And it's going to have seen some death.

"So, what's bothering me the most?" I look to Clairee, but she's closed her eyes.

"I guess that's your advice," I say, leaning over the sofa to rub her back, her silky hair a balm to my nerves. "Don't worry and just go to sleep."

But it's the middle of the day, and I can't stop worrying. Not with blood humming through my veins and in my ears.

Blood.

Bloodlines.

Missing women.

Dead women.

Why did GraveDanger's message unsettle me? Because it's another claim that bad things have happened here.

But more concerning, they've happened in recent years.

I need to talk to someone else. Someone who has questions like I do, who doesn't trust the Marteau family, and won't tell me I've come unhinged.

The only person who checks all those boxes is Alice.

My phone lies atop the desk, so I snatch it from the wood surface and open the photo-sharing app. I haven't heard from her in two days. Not since she screamed at the manservant and the mansion in general.

I keep the message short and simple, telling her we need to talk. As soon as I hit send, I'm back to pacing. This time, I keep hold of my phone, fully expecting an instant reply.

But the more minutes pass, the more my frustration grows.

I consider trying to leave again, just packing up and putting this place in my past. But the strikes are still in effect. I won't be able to get a cab or check into a hotel. That paints an ugly but realistic picture—me out in the rain, struggling with two pieces of luggage and one small cat.

I don't even have a pet carrier. Leaving is impossible.

Nibbling my thumbnail, I jitter my leg. I need to stay where I am. I might be on edge, jumping at every sound, but I'll do what I did the last time I got scared. The night I read *Carmilla* and felt like I was being watched. I'll bar the doors and check the windows, then lock myself into the bedroom to sleep.

Maybe I'm overreacting. Maybe I'm paranoid. Maybe my distress over Mackenzie has messed with my head.

But I've learned too much to take any chances.

Lunging for my laptop, I check to see if GraveDanger is still online. When I see the little green light beside his name, I shoot off one more question.

Do you know the name of the girl from the party?

I don't have to wait long.

Lina Ivarrson

Ivarrson. Sounds Nordic. Maybe Swedish?

As in a tourist who might have been in Paris alone. With no one to miss her.

Like Rose.

Thanks for your help.

I quickly send the message to GraveDanger before jumping over to a search engine. I type the name Lina Ivarrson and Bois De Boulogne, the park where she was found. Then I add Paris for good measure.

There aren't many links to online publications, because the murder occurred before the invention of the internet, but I do find a true-crime blog.

Clicking on the link, I pull up the post and copy the text. Then I paste the words into a translation site. The English makes it easier to skim the paragraphs, and I don't need to read far before the words I'm looking for leap from the screen.

The victim was identified as Swedish tourist Lina Ivarrson, a source close to the case revealed.

A sensation of crawling skitters down my back.

I was right. A tourist.

I read on, paying closer attention and looking for any specifics that might corroborate GraveDanger's information.

Why was the body exsanguinated before being abandoned in one of Paris's busiest parks?

"Holy shit." I slap a hand to my mouth, still scanning the text. The blogger writes that Lina Ivarrson was last seen on the bridge, that the witness's name is undisclosed, and the case was never solved.

But then that's all. The post ends on a cliffhanger. No mention of suspects, or a party, or Maison Marteau.

Is this evidence of corrupt law enforcement being bought off by the Marteaus?

Or is it nothing more than an online conspiracy theory?

Rubbing my forehead, I drop the laptop on the couch cushions and pick up my phone. Still no word from Alice.

I'm too disturbed to sit still, my body and brain both buzzing with alarm. Trying to figure out my next move, I cross my arms and stare at the fireplace. The hearth is an empty hull, blackened and coated with soot.

Then my eyes travel to a small round table, the *Carmilla* book resting on the shiny wood. The book I found on the red chair downstairs. The one I convinced myself had been there all along.

But it hadn't.

Someone came into the apartment and left it for me to find.

But why?

I've known something was off about this mansion for a while, but I didn't want to believe it. Now all the stories and hearsay are coming together, like photos and strings on a murder board.

But the center is missing an essential piece.

As I stare at the book and its worn and yellowed pages, the answer clicks in my head like the strike of a match. There's still one place left I might find some answers.

I lift my gaze to the ceiling.

And I know what I have to do.

37

The journal must be in here.

I stare into the dusty storage room and feel a certainty in the marrow of my bones.

I've searched the rest of the house, hitting every pillow and testing every floorboard. Looking under beds and the bottom of drawers. No police search team could do a better job.

So there's only one place Rose could have hidden the journal.

The storage room and its thirty-odd, taped-up boxes.

If she left the journal here at all.

I shake my head and slip off the negativity. I can't afford to think like that. No second-guessing or backing off. It's raining a torrent outside, and I have nowhere else to go. I might as well use this opportunity.

Stepping in the room, I flip the switch and turn on the weak single bulb. This time, though, I came prepared. With a flashlight I found under the kitchen sink, a knife to slice tape, and a box of tissues for when I start sneezing.

The musty smell assaults my nose, and I almost reconsider.

But then I recommit and move toward the right-hand corner. With the flashlight propped up and pointing down, I slice through the top of the first box I come to.

Linens sit inside, neatly folded and stacked. My first instinct is to set them aside and move on, but I stop myself from closing the lid. I can't afford to be lazy.

I sift through the material, lifting out sheets and lace and napkins before squeezing each bundle and checking the bottom of the empty box. Nothing. Not in this one.

Exhaling, I glance around the room. At this rate, I'll be here for hours.

But I need to know what Rose found out. What did she read in the journal?

Leaving the door standing open, I take the first box out into the hall. As soon as I clear a spot inside the room, I can shift the boxes around, stacking the ones I've checked in the empty corner.

The process is laborious, but checking off containers makes me feel productive. I go through toys, art projects, vinyl records. All the personal detritus we all collect in a lifetime. Again and again, like a well-oiled robot. Open, sift, clear, restack. Open, sift, clear, restack.

Many of the containers aren't taped at all, simply held closed by overlapping flaps. Changing my plan, I focus on these boxes first. After an hour, I'm a quarter of the way finished and considering a bathroom break.

When I step back to survey my work, I kick into something hard.

The old steamer trunk.

But there's no way the journal is hidden inside. I tried opening it last time, and the latches were locked. Weren't they?

My memory from before plays in my mind like a film. I remember the navy-blue leather turned gray by dust. I see my hands reaching for the lock. And then I remember jumping when I saw the black spider.

But I tried to open the trunk. Didn't I?

Uncertain, I kneel down. The two latches on the end are open, but when I pull the one in the middle, it's locked tight, my fingertips scraping over rusted brass. Rusted. Could it simply be seized by the rust and stuck in place?

Pressing the fingers of both hands in from each side, I pull with all my might. The latch doesn't give.

I need oil from the kitchen, or a pump of hand soap. Or maybe a few good knocks will loosen the rust.

My sinuses are swollen from dust and my eyes filled with grit, so I *want* the journal to be inside the trunk. I want to have an excuse to get out of this room.

Annoyed and exasperated, I give the trunk a swift kick.

Something makes a soft *thud.*

That sound didn't come from inside the trunk. Something fell and hit the floor. *Behind* the trunk.

Stepping closer, I shine the light into the space between the trunk and the wall. There, in the corner.

My head rushes and I blink three times, almost afraid to believe what I'm seeing.

A book.

The journal.

It has to be. This is Rose's hiding place. Why else would a book be lodged behind an old steamer trunk? A trunk shoved into the corner of a storage room?

I can tell the gap is too narrow for my hand, so I spend another minute muscling the heavy trunk away from the wall. When I think I have enough room, I reach for the crack—freezing up when I picture the spider's tickly black legs.

Clenching my eyes almost shut, I shove my hand down and

pull the book free. Even before I shine the light on the cover, I know it's dark blue. Just as Alice said it would be.

Light-headed, I wipe my palm down the cover. I'm desperate to see what's inside, but also afraid of failure. What if it's just a misplaced copy of a classic tale? Or an address book that outlived its usefulness?

Holding the flashlight steady, I balance the book on top of the trunk. I take a deep breath. And blow it out. Then I turn to the first page.

Today, Father told me a family secret.

38

I need a break.

Closing the journal, I stare at the dancing flames in the study fireplace—stunned, shaken, sick. Horrified by what I've read, I curl into myself and try to block the images.

A man committing murder. Here. At Maison Marteau.

And a child following in his bloody footsteps.

I glance over at the door, willing myself to remain seated. I don't need to check again. I know it's locked.

Though I feel the monster right here beside me, crawling from the pages of a killer's diary.

But whose? What child wrote the journal? What father led them down the path of depravity?

I pick up the journal again. Even touching the book makes me feel filthy, makes me want to wash my hands. But I'm desperate to know whose story I'm reading.

The paper gives me no real clue. A singe mark darkens one page, as if someone once tried to burn the book. Whether they changed their mind or were stopped by another, exposure to flame yellowed the paper. It's hard to tell how old the journal actually is.

The handwriting is no help either, the lettering plain and simple, neither masculine nor feminine. And the quality of the writer's voice, plain and direct. The only thing I'm sure of is that they were young when they wrote the journal. Too young to attend an adult party.

My stomach rolls as I picture a child watching their father do such terrible things.

And being thrilled by the sadism.

A long, torturous moment passes before I'm able to open to the last page I read.

Swallowing against nausea, I focus on the identity of the child. Proficiency in English is point of pride in the Marteau family. Any one of them could have written this journal.

Except Chantal. She married into the family, so she couldn't be the author.

That leaves Vincent, Ric, and Lyam.

No. I can't let my emotions or feelings for anyone affect my judgment. This journal could belong to Luci or even Dora. Almost everyone at this mansion had a father who was born a Marteau.

Even Noah.

I read the word *strapped* and a shudder wracks my body.

"*Nooo.*" I tuck my chin to my chest and reach out for Clairee. The little cat is my only source of comfort on this cold, cruel day.

The rain has only worsened, blurring the windows and blackening the sky.

Turning the page, I prepare myself for whatever shock comes next. One hand still on Clairee, I lift the journal, the front half pinched between my fingers.

A folded paper falls from the back and drops into my lap.

Setting the book on the end table, I open the paper. Handwritten notes on front and back. The first line is a nail hammered in my spine.

Someone is coming into the apartment.

My eyes quickly skim the rest of the page. There's mention of the journal being left in the kitchen, Ric's creepy and inappropriate behavior, and near the bottom a question.

Should I tell Luci?

There's no doubt in my mind. Rose wrote these notes. She must have stuck the paper in the journal before hiding it behind the trunk.

I flip the paper over to keep reading.

But a sound comes from above my head. A single high-pitched groan that cuts off in an instant.

The creak of floorboards.

My heart climbs in my throat.

Seconds pass in heavy silence. And then I hear it again—two soft thuds and another creak.

Someone is walking across the floor.

Upstairs.

A droning hum fills my ears, panic and blood pressure straining my veins. Immobilized, I stare at the ceiling, tracking the movement. Not directly above, but out in the corridor.

Another step. Two. Whoever it is, they're moving toward the stairs.

I lunge for the fireplace tools. Every piece made of iron. Black and heavy. I rip the poker free but end up knocking the stand over, tools clattering on the marble hearth.

Clairee startles awake.

Fire poker in hand, I look upward. My lungs heave with terrified breaths and my heart is an urgent gallop in my chest.

The footsteps land faster and with less caution, moving down the hallway. Back the way they came.

I listen until I can no longer hear anything, then I break from the daze. I grab my phone and dial 911 before I remember I'm in France.

What's the emergency number here? What is it? What is it?

The numbers pop into my head, so I stab 112 on the screen. A robotic voice answers in French. I hear words that sound like *excuse* and *minutes*.

I hold out my phone and stare wide-eyed. "What the hell?" This is supposed to be instant assistance.

Then I remember the strikes. And the protests.

The emergency call center must be overwhelmed.

"What do I do?" I talk out loud as if someone will hear me. A self-comforting act as I stand in the study, waiting to hear footsteps running down the stairs, coming for me.

Eventually, fear turns to something else. Closing my phone, I slip it in my pocket as a burning sense of self-preservation drives me from the study. I walk across the landing and pause by the balustrade.

I look up, waiting to see or hear activity. I wait another minute, and then slowly sneak up the steps. Remembering the sounds, I visualize the route the intruder took. Across the center area and down the hallway. But to where?

Using the poker, I ease open the doors to the third-floor rooms. All of them are empty. To be safe, I check under beds and in bathrooms. No one. Whoever was here is gone.

But how did they get out? How are they accessing the apartment? Coming and going at will?

Coming back out to the landing, I glance around, wondering how many times they've entered my space. To leave a copy of *Carmilla*. To stand in the shadows. To watch me sleep.

The idea rattles me to the core, and I know I can't sit down or relax. I can't spend another minute—let alone another night—in this apartment. Not until I figure out how they're getting in.

Whoever *they* are.

Glancing around the top level, I notice another door. One that didn't occur to me right away, because it's concealed, hidden in the paneling.

Of course.

The door to the hidden staircase.

Clenching my elbows tight to my sides, I use both hands and readjust my grip on the poker, the iron slick from my sweaty palm. Crossing to the panel, I push in and let it pop back out.

The panel brushes over the floor, soft as a sigh.

I let out a gasp, because I recognize the sound. Like a whispered, "*Hush.*"

I heard it my first night in the apartment, when I was coming down the stairs.

They've been coming inside since the very first night.

Ignoring the prickle of unease, I study the plain, wooden steps before me. I've only used these stairs once before, the day the cobwebs and spider ran me out. I never made it to the basement. I never checked the door.

But the sounds came from up here. From the top floor. That would mean . . .

Leaning into the darkness, I tilt my head and look up. Stairs to the attic. When Luci gave me a tour, she told me the basement door was double-locked.

But she never mentioned the attic.

Pulling out my phone, I turn on the flashlight and creep upward, cringing each time I take a step. Expecting a creak to give me away. I feel cold and hot at the same time, as if every nerve ending is out of whack.

Dread fills my gut like curdled milk, but I need to push on. I need to know.

Once I reach the door, I stay quiet, certain the intruder is on the other side. Listening, waiting to ambush me. When I can stand it no longer, I grip the old brass knob. Turn. And push.

The door moans as it opens, swinging freely into the shadows. Not barred by a lock from either side.

Anyone from the main house can walk right in.

My phone pings in my hand. I startle so hard I almost drop it but manage to clench it in my fingers before it falls.

Pulling the attic door shut, I hurry down to my apartment, close the panel, and lean against the wall.

I check my phone. Another push notification. Opening the app, I find a message waiting for me. From Alice.

But when I read her message, the world bottoms out. And everything I know is turned upside down.

39

I feel whiplashed as I stare at my phone

I found Rose!!

Alice's message. She knows where her sister is.

But on the heels of surprise, a sense of release. A warm fluidity relaxing every fiber.

Rose is safe. She isn't missing.

Sliding down the wall, I set down the poker and type a response.

Alice, that's wonderful! I know you're relieved.

And so am I. If Rose didn't disappear from Maison Marteau, then there was never any danger. Not for her. Or me.

Hope tries to rise, but reality rushes in.

No. Someone was here. In my apartment.

And if the *Carmilla* book is any proof, they've been here before.

Fear is creeping back in when a trail of bubbles pops up. Alice is typing.

Sorry I didn't write back sooner. But it's good news! Rose just posted, and we've been messaging. She's fine! Met someone and took off for a new adventure.

Rose posted? Needing to see for myself, I type Rose's username into the search bar and go to her profile. A new photo sits at the top, a view of a sandy beach and crystal-blue water. Palm trees swoop in from both sides, completing the generic tropical scene.

The picture is location tagged as Bali, Indonesia.

Something niggles at the back of my mind. Mulling over what Alice has told me, I send a reply.

I'm so glad Rose is safe. Have you talked to her?

A single photo isn't much proof, especially when Rose isn't pictured. Then it strikes me. The wording of the caption is what's bothering me. *A new adventure.* Similar to Rose's previous post. But is it too similar?

Alice responds.

Yes, we've spoken. I'm leaving tonight to go and meet her.

She's leaving tonight? I rise from the floor, thinking about what I want to say. I can't shake suspicion, the growing feeling that something isn't right.

Wow, Bali! What an amazing place. And you'll get to meet Rose's new boyfriend.

I hit send, bite my lip, and wait. Time passes, but I don't dare take my eyes off the screen. The bubbles appear. Stop again. Reappear.

I need Alice to respond.

I need her to say the right thing.

Another minute, and I let my head fall back against the wood panel. Then my phone pings again.

Yes! He really makes her happy. Seems like a great guy.

A groan escapes my lips. Grabbing the poker, I dart a terrified glance down the hall.

André said to keep it secret, that nobody else knew Rose was gay.

But her sister did.

I drop my phone to the floor, shuffling away as if it's dangerous.

And in a way, it is.

I don't know who I've been messaging with.

But it isn't Alice.

My Hotel Peculiar

My father lifted the little girl in his arms. "Follow me."

He led me through the winding shafts until we came to a stop beside a door. I recognized it from the night I came down by myself.

The night I saw him with the woman from the party.

But I paid more attention this time. A symbol was painted on the wood, one I'd seen many times before. "Grégoire's symbol," I said, pointing.

My father only grunted, struggling to unlock and open the door with the girl in his arms.

A coil of blonde hair fell over his elbow. I reached out to stroke the silky length.

"Wait," my father barked at me.

Guiding me inside, he turned on a light. Not the same yellow bulbs as the tunnels, but a round fixture with a bright white glow.

Mesmerized, I stared at the items in the room. Ancient walls, like the rest of the catacombs, but shiny steel tables along one wall, covered in instruments. I didn't know what they were, but they made me tremble, made me feel oily inside.

In a good way.

The space smelled wet like the tunnels, but also different. Metallic.

A long table sat in the center of the room, and my father laid the girl there. Then he strapped her hands down with some sort of leather cuffs. They were attached lower on the table as well, but her legs didn't reach.

"Come." My father motioned for me to join him at the table. His dark eyes seared into mine, so I looked down. He put his hand on my shoulder and smiled. "I knew it would be you."

My chest felt puffed up, fizzy and tight. I looked up at him again. "What do you mean?"

The girl whimpered then, a small sound, like a mouse in a trap.

My father turned to her but spoke to me. "Today, you will learn of our legacy." He stroked a finger down her thin, white throat. "Our family secret."

40

I sit for another moment, clutching the fire poker. Then I launch into action. Whoever's been coming into the apartment has been using the hidden stairway, so I need to barricade every door. And then, when I'm done, when I feel more protected . . .

I have to finish the journal.

It takes me fifteen minutes to wrestle large pieces of furniture in front of all three doors, and then another twenty to check every single wall panel in the place.

I can't afford to miss any other secret entrances.

Satisfied I'm safe for the moment, I make sure Clairee is still asleep on the sofa before locking us both in the study.

I no longer chastise myself for overreacting. I no longer wonder if I'm being paranoid. The truth still sounds crazy, but I can't ignore facts the details recorded in the journal.

One of the family members is a sadistic killer.

Maybe more than one.

Again, I pick up my phone and dial the emergency number. And again, I get a recorded message.

With no other recourse, I curl up on the couch and pick up

the journal. Locating the page where I left off, I breathe deeply, swallow the fear lodged firmly in my throat, and resume reading.

The next entries are a nightmare, a transformation from curious youth to depraved monster.

I read several pages in a blurry rush, as if speeding through the words will lessen the horror. By this point, the author of the journal has found a young girl that they're . . . *interested in* and has lured her to the mansion.

The following descriptions leave me sick to my stomach, and I can't help imagining this happening right now, beneath this very mansion.

And happening to Alice.

I've got to get help.

I'm dialing 112 again when I'm struck by what I've just read. I have the last piece, and all the clues line up. They make sense.

Dropping the phone in shock, I keep my ears attuned to the robotic message as my mind spins. As I connect a timeline to the murder described in the journal.

It's the young girl found in the catacombs.

She didn't drown. That's not how she died.

She was murdered.

And it all happened when Noah lived here.

Noah and Ric. Both young men at the time, possibly teenagers. I think back to the confrontation they had at the dance. Ric called Noah a coward and accused him of running away after the girl was found. The little sister of Noah's girlfriend.

A vise clenches my chest. I can't draw a breath. It's as if the air has been sucked from my lungs.

Was Noah involved?

I turn and stare at the wall, but what I'm really seeing is Noah. The kiss we shared. The safety of his apartment. The note he left me this morning.

Is he really out of town? Or was that a lie? A cover story for why he can't be reached?

Because he's busy doing other things.

I feel like I'm losing my mind, but right now, everyone is a suspect. I'm only reading about one murder, but I know there were others.

Like the journal said, it's a family secret.

Lina Ivarrson was killed in 1985. Noah and Ric hadn't even been born yet.

Four decades later, Rose disappears. Now Alice.

But how many others in the years between?

I remember dancing amongst all the monsters, and I fold my arms over my stomach. The deaths are a joke to them. *The family.* And I was there with them. Dancing, laughing, playing, eating.

I've known too many wealthy and powerful people, the elite who believe they're superior. Believe they're entitled to do whatever they want. Take anything. Hurt anyone. And they continue to get away with their crimes.

Unless someone speaks out.

I pick up the journal. Pages and pages describing murders.

I have proof. Evidence.

And the emergency lines won't be busy forever.

The folded paper with Rose's notes lies on the sofa. I flip it over, to the side I haven't read yet. She lists a few more strange things she experienced in the apartment, but what grabs my attention are the words at the bottom.

Where every other note is written in neat, steady script, the last entry is scrawled diagonally across the page. Large, messy letters, as if written in a hurry.

Photos behind his eyes.

At first, the words make no sense. What photos? Is she being literal or figurative? And whose eyes?

Leaning back on the sofa, I try to figure out what she meant.

Then it hits me. *His eyes.* The most conspicuous eyes in this apartment.

And a great place to hide pictures.

I'm off the sofa in a heartbeat, grabbing my phone and the poker to take with me. Because this is a real horror movie, and I want to make it to the final scene.

And get the hell out of this murder house.

Glancing outside, I check to see the chest of drawers still blocking the hidden door. Then I dash to the main staircase. Halfway down, I stop to study the oil paintings. All of the Marteau ancestors glare at me, all sharp-nosed and aloof.

But the man in the middle, the largest portrait, his eyes are the meanest. Standing to the side in case it falls, I pull the bottom of the frame away from the wall. The shadow from the painting is too dark for me to see anything.

I pull it farther from the wall for more light. There. An envelope. One end is stuck between the canvas and the frame. The other flops away, weighted by something inside.

Standing on my tiptoes, I grab the envelope and the let portrait fall back against the wall. I open the envelope and tip it to the side.

Photos spill into my hand. Polaroids. Black squares surrounded by white.

I flip them over to see the front.

My brain burns and my psyche rebels.

No. No. No. No. I don't want to see this.

I shut my eyes and try to block the images. The sheer volume of evil in this house makes me physically ill.

Light-headed and dizzy, I lean on the wall. Try to center myself.

And finally, I open my eyes again. Because I have to look.

I need to know.

The pictures are of a young girl. About twelve years old, that fragile cusp between childhood and adolescence.

Wearing only panties and a T-shirt, she poses for the pictures. Positions and gestures too evocative for her age.

At first, I only glance at each photo, too disturbed to take in details.

But then I look at her face. An eerie distance fills her eyes, as if she's removed herself from what's happening.

Sadness settles in the pit of my heart, and I study the background of the shots. Dark, rich wood, the corner of an embroidered chair, shelves of books.

My skin prickles with recognition.

I know this room. I've been there. The pictures were taken in the library, here at Maison Marteau.

Homing in on the little's girl's face, I slap a hand to my mouth to smother my cry. *Oh, no. Oh, no.*

The young girl in the polaroids.

It's Luci.

41

I slide the journal into the space behind the steamer trunk and let it drop. It's been hidden in the storage room for months, so it should be safe for another few hours.

Enough time for me to enact my plan.

I return the envelope of polaroids to the portrait, seeing the wisdom of Rose's decision. Two hiding spots. Spread out the evidence. In case some of it's discovered.

Since I found the photos, I've been going over all I've learned. Seeing my experiences here from a new perspective. I think there's only one viable conclusion.

Luci's been coming into the apartment. I believe she crept into the apartment when Rose lived here, leaving the journal and photos for Rose.

Just as she left the *Carmilla* book for me.

The handwriting, the photographs, the handwritten accounts of homicide. All of them can be used as evidence to prosecute a killer, and providing them was Luci's way of trying to help.

Or crying for help.

She's still so young. Not even old enough to buy a drink in the States.

And now that I understand, I don't want to let her down.

Easing between stacks of boxes, I leave the storage room and hurry downstairs. Clairee has relocated to the crimson chair. Right where I found *Carmilla*.

Going to her, I give her a few rubs and a kiss on the head. "I'll be back soon. Stay safe."

Leaving Clairee where she is, I take the only chance I've got left. I put on my jacket, take the apartment keys, and step out into the cold rain.

Wind whips the rain into my face, stinging my cheeks until I lower my head. The heavy downpour is a constant drone, and after only a few steps, my hair is soaked to my scalp.

Staying close to the building, I creep to the corner and peek around. I doubt any of the family are out in this weather, but I scan the courtyard anyway. All clear.

Careful on the slippery cobblestones, I run to the front gate and punch in the code.

Nothing happens. I don't hear the usual buzz and click of the system opening the lock.

Maybe I entered the wrong numbers, my wet fingers slipping on the buttons. Carefully, I try again, punching in the same code I've used every other time.

Still nothing.

Shock courses through me, a cold realization chilling my bones. Panicked, I type in the code again. And again. "This can't be right." My voice breaks as anguish tightens my throat.

They've changed the code. Or disabled the system. Either way, it amounts to the same thing.

I'm locked inside.

Whirling around, I glance at the main house, expecting to see Ric or Vincent running toward me. When I don't, I make a dash back toward my door. Instead of going in, I keep moving, heading toward the gardens and the back gate.

As I run through the prickly holly and rain-soaked leaves, I look for any weak spot in the fence, any place I might be able to climb out. But the tall black bars are impenetrable, built to keep people out.

Or to keep them in.

I pass an area with a space between the shrubs and hurry over to look out. The weather is terrible, but there might be people in the park. Someone cutting through the grass as a shortcut home, or maybe someone walking a dog. People have umbrellas. They go out in storms.

Pushing through the tall bushes, I grip the bars and push my face close to the black metal. Leaning one way and then the other, I search the park. Rainfall turns the air gray, but even in the low visibility, I see no one else.

Only heavy gusts thrashing the trees, and brown water streaming from the pebbled paths.

Slapping my hand on the bars, I curse and pull out my phone to dial the emergency number. This time, I don't get the recorded message in French. I don't get anything at all.

I check the screen, and the signal is gone, a circle with a slash through it where the bars should be. The same symbol covers the WiFi symbol, too. I have no service.

"No, no, no." I try texting Lin, to let someone know I'm in trouble. But it doesn't go through.

No service. A different code.

Not a coincidence.

Squeezing my phone, I continue through the gardens, telling myself I can climb the back gate. If I put one foot on the handle, I can throw myself over the bars. I can get out and go straight to the police.

But when I finally make it down the rear path, I see my

memory has deceived me. There is no knob on the door, only a curved handle with a thumb latch. Too flat for me to stand on.

I step to the side, to the box beside the gate. Even though I know what's happening, even though I know what to expect, I raise a shaking hand and type in the code. When nothing happens, I try again.

Four beeps. And nothing more.

I can't get out. And I can't call for help.

Defeated, soaked, and icy cold, I turn slowly to look up at the building. With no other option, I walk back along the path.

I return to Maison Marteau.

42

Back inside the apartment, I lock the door and peel off my wet jacket. Then check the lock one more time.

But they have keys.

The Marteau family is now a collective in my mind, one great and looming *they* that includes every one of them. Except Luci.

Were *they* watching me race around in the rain, laughing as I tried to escape? And while one of *them* kept an eye on my progress, did someone else sneak into my apartment?

Standing stock still, because I don't know what to do, I survey every dark corner of the entry hall. Any one of them could be hiding, just waiting for me to come close.

This is what they do. The thrill of the chase—spying on me, stalking me in my own apartment. A fancy Paris rental where they knew I'd feel safe.

I run to the kitchen and the knife block on the counter. My hands and arms shake, so I topple the wooden block on its side. In my terror, I grab one knife in each hand and back into a corner. Weapons up. Eyes wide.

Seconds pass. Maybe minutes.

Fear is a fire in my brain, smoking out rational thought. My basic instinct is to stand here, ready to fight. Or to hide, to crawl into a small, dark space, close my eyes and wait to be rescued.

Except no one knows I need help.

I can't call or text. I can't climb the fence or scream through the storm. And if Noah was telling me the truth, he won't be returning for a couple of days.

That leaves me. The only person who can help Alice.

Me.

And Luci.

But if those photos are any indication, Luci might be in danger, too.

Before I can help them or myself, I have to calm down.

My mother's voice comes to me, a memory from one of my first auditions.

Control your fear, or it will control you.

I picture her face, and I almost crumple.

Refusing to give in to the terror, I close my eyes. I ground myself and focus on my body. The countertop edge pressing into my waist, the handles of the knives in my hands, the white marble glaring at me.

I'm aware of my body's natural response to fear—rapid heartbeat, quick shallow breaths, overwhelming images making it hard to think straight.

I studied this in an acting class, trying to mimic the natural panic reaction. Understanding the response is different from experiencing the real thing, but at least I have step-by-step knowledge of what's happening in my body.

I know how to work myself into a panicked state, so I should be able to reverse the process. To calm my over-agitated system.

At first, it's hard to take deep breaths, but I keep trying. In through the nose, out through the mouth. Filling my belly and lungs, I inhale, hold for two seconds, and exhale for eight.

Through sheer force of will, I take control. When my pulse slows and my mind clears, I remember the next step. Focus on the primary goal, the thing that needs to be accomplished first. When that's done, the next goal. And the next.

A heaviness still crowds my vision from the edges, but I keep breathing until it's gone. Until the static fades and the tremors diminish.

I'm still not sure what to do, but I know one thing for sure. The Marteau family has the upper hand. They have the advantage. I'm on their territory, and this isn't the first time one or more of them has killed.

The only thing working in my favor is the element of surprise. I can't allow myself to lose control again, to race headlong into peril with a scattered mind and two kitchen knives.

After another long exhale, I set aside the larger blade, keeping a narrow one of medium length. One I can slip into my back pocket.

With the knife sitting at an angle and partially exposed, I pull my sweater down to cover the handle.

What is the last thing they'd expect me to do?

And as soon as I ask the question, the answer is clear.

I need to go deeper into the mansion.

As a plan materializes, I take slow, steady steps, exiting the kitchen and heading to the stairs. The fireplace poker still sits in the study, and I need it with me in case things go wrong.

As I climb the wide, curving steps, I grow more confident and more convinced. I can do this. I can get out of this alive, hopefully with Alice and Luci.

Because I have a plan, one I can thank the Marteau family for. Or at least whoever's been sneaking into the apartment.

They've given me an idea.
And I'm going to use their own tricks against them.

43

This is a terrible idea.

I stand at the top of the servants' staircase, my hand gripping the knob of the attic door. Now that I'm here, all my previous certainty starts to crumble.

Fear-based questions rise up in my mind, scary and timid, like the faces of lost ghosts.

Should I go back to the study and lock the door?

Maybe, but I can't stay in there for two days. I can't creep around the apartment waiting for Ric or Vincent to leap from the shadows.

Can I go to the front gates and scream?

The storm is still raging, and odds are, one of the family will get to me before a neighbor happens to glance outside. Even if I'm noticed, they might not understand what I'm doing.

Is there a better way to get inside? To get to Luci?

No. The only other option is to knock on the connecting doors near her quarters and hope she's the only one who hears me.

I picture Noah's smile and remember how kind he was after

the dance. When I basically broke down in his arms. My heart caves in a little, but I stomp on sentimentality and refocus on the goal. The big goal. The only goal that matters.

Surviving this night.

All of us. Luci, me, and Alice.

I imagine Alice being hurt, being drained of blood as I stand here, wavering.

And I picture the little girl Luci used to be. Young, innocent, trusting. Abused.

Like Mackenzie.

My conviction floods back in, and I turn the handle. I won't be that person again. I won't be selfish. Or a coward.

Luci's room is on the second floor, and I feel better about sneaking down from the attic than up from the basement. But there will still be a short trip to Luci's room. And I have no choice but to sneak through the house.

Hopefully, I won't run into any family members. Or servants. I don't know if I can trust them either. Money is a powerful motivator, and I remember the expression on the manservant's face when he confronted Alice. No compassion. No mercy. Only blind loyalty to the Marteaus.

I have to risk it. This is my only path to Luci.

And maybe a way to reach the police.

The door opens with a plaintive groan, as if it knows what I'm about to do and is wailing for me to stop.

Even the rain seems to tap out a pattern. Drops hit the round windows and beat a refrain, a chorus of voices warning me to run. *Go back. Go back. Go back.*

The attic spreads out before me, only dim light on the stormy day, leaving the far end swallowed in darkness. The air smells stale and unused, a thin layer of dust on every surface.

As I peer at the wooden planks, I can make out a trail. The coating disturbed by someone else's footprints.

A shiver of unease wracks my upper body. I already suspected someone had been entering the apartment, but the undeniable evidence shakes me to my core.

Panic makes a bid for return, so I take a deep breath. In through the nose, out through the mouth. I'm swamped by the smell of dust and neglect, but I repeat the exercise two more times.

Taking light, easy steps, I follow the footprints, doing my best not to make any noise. When the floor creaks beneath me, I freeze. My heart swells against my ribs as if it wants to escape.

Tense and afraid, I wait and I listen. But I don't hear any movement.

With my feet still in the same spots, I look back to see how far I've come. By my estimate, I'm still over my apartment.

I haven't even reached the danger zone yet.

A door waits farther down, an entrance to the mansion. I'm so close.

Lightning streaks across the sky and lights up the attic. When thunder follows, I use the sound as cover and cross the remaining stretch.

At the door, I press my ear to the wood. Hearing no noise of any kind, I test the knob.

A chill grips me, crawls down my back, and no amount of deep breathing can calm my racing heart.

This is it. I'm crossing the threshold.

There's a greater chance now that someone will find me.

Someone who might not be Luci.

I look back down the length of the attic, judging the distance. I try to picture what part of the mansion I'm about to enter. I've come farther than I expected, and I'm unfamiliar with the upper levels.

I have no idea what's on the other side.

Giving myself no time to second-guess, I slowly turn the knob.

Unlocked, the door silently swings open.

Another servant's staircase drops below me, though this one is in much better shape. Clean, cobweb-free, with a cut-glass globe covering the light.

I don't dare turn it on. Instead, I use the phone's flashlight to show me the way.

A board creaks beneath my foot. I go still and listen. Hoping no one heard me. A minute passes before I'm ready to try again.

Except I move to the side, placing my foot on the edge of the tread. No squeak, so I keep close to the wall, taking one heart-stopping step at a time until I come to the first exit.

The cut in the wall is familiar, one of the panels. It should push outward, the same as those in my apartment. But I don't know what room I'm about to enter.

Or who might be waiting.

Steeling myself, I put my phone in my pocket and hold tight to the poker. Counting to three, I ready myself.

One. Two. Three.

With a small push, the panel opens, and I find myself in a salon. Green and brown tones fill the space, with velvet-covered sofas and a large TV. The room screams of masculinity. I'm afraid I've gone too far and overshot Luci's quarters.

The panel I've opened is in the middle of the wall, leaving me exposed and in full view. If anyone comes inside or even passes by, they'll spot me instantly.

Slipping inside, I shut the panel, then hurry to the windows overlooking the gardens. I haven't traveled as far as I thought, so a slight backtrack should take me to Luci's rooms. Right next door.

If she's not there, I can hide and wait until she returns.

Maybe her room has a landline. I can call for help. Worst-case scenario, if things go very wrong, I'll have to make a break for the attic and bar myself inside my apartment.

Skin prickling, I walk quickly but quietly to the wide doorway. I check the hall in one direction. Then the other. The hallway is empty.

To my left, the adjoining doors mark the end of the corridor.

I'm almost there. Just a little farther.

I step out, but a male voice rises from below. Jerking back, I press against the wall. The voice is distant, only a murmur really, so I can't tell who is speaking. After a moment, the sound subsides.

I dart down the hallway to the next open door. A quick look inside reveals a more feminine chamber, white bookshelves and vases filled with fresh flowers. But Luci isn't here.

I run to the next door. It's closed, but I'm certain I'm in the right place. Pushing inside, I slip through the crack and quickly close the door behind me.

Luci is lying on her bed, a book in her hands. She sits up, and I expect surprise or a smile of greeting.

Instead, her mouth firms and her expression falls flat. Rising from the bed, she puts the book on a nightstand and levels me with an empty stare.

"You shouldn't have come here."

44

I can't read Luci's expression, so I keep my approach slow and my voice calm. "What do you mean? Why should I not have come?"

"I don't know. It doesn't matter." She furrows her brow and stares at the floor.

I believe Luci can be trusted, that she wouldn't cause me any harm, but I'm not sure how much she knows about her family's dark history. I can't rely on her empathy. Can't be sure I won't lose out to family loyalty.

"Luci, do you know what's happening?"

She shakes her head, still refusing to look at me.

"I came here because I need your help." I blow out a breath and cut to the heart. "I think I'm in danger."

Her head whips up. "What? Why?"

I can't tell her everything. Not yet. "Did you come into my apartment? Did you leave the book for me to find?"

She tilts her head, confusion plain on her face. "No, I never—what book?"

"*Carmilla*. It's an older story about—"

"I know the story." Her skin turns white as I watch. "No. It wasn't me." Wringing her hands, she turns away and then back to me again. "Oh, no. I was afraid of this."

"Afraid of what?" I ask, trying to catch her eye as she starts pacing back and forth.

"I had a feeling something was wrong. He acted the same way when . . ." She stops moving and stares, her next words chilling me to the bone. "You have to leave. You need to get away from Maison Marteau."

"I can't."

"You have to. I wasn't sure before, about Rose. But now I am." She shuts her lips, clenches her fists. "Come. I'll take you out."

She pushes past me, but I grab her arm. "No, listen to me. I want to leave, but I *can't*. The gates are locked, and my phone isn't working, either. I think someone's using a jammer."

I don't want to spook her, but I have to make her understand the urgency. "Someone is trying to keep me here. And I need your help."

Releasing my hold on her, I glance around the bedroom. "Is there a landline in the house? A way to call for help? I tried before, but the emergency lines were busy. But maybe you can call someone else. Someone you trust."

"No."

Fear twists in my gut, and I face her again. "You won't help me?"

She moves to the bed and sits on the edge. "I mean, there's no one to call. No one will stand up to my family."

So she does know something. But how much?

Her bottom lip trembles, and her shoulders have folded in. She seems so fragile, but I can't let her disappear into herself. I need to reach her somehow.

Easing closer, I choose my words with care. "Did Rose try to stand up to them?"

Luci bites her lip and clenches her eyes. "I don't know. But she was asking me a lot of questions before she left."

I draw a deep breath and say out loud what she already suspects. "Are you sure she left? Or did something bad happen?"

She claps her hands over her ears and shakes her head. "No, no. Please, don't make me think about it. I hate him. I hate him. He knew how I felt about her, and he . . . he . . ."

I don't press her, but she continues anyway, as if she needs to tell the truth as badly as I need to hear it. "I knew something was wrong. I knew it. The way he looked at her."

Luci swallows and rubs her mouth. "I told her to stop, to not make trouble." A sob breaks free, and tears trickle down her cheeks. "But she must have, and I think something happened to her."

Luci's teary eyes meet mine. "Because she wouldn't leave me behind."

Lowering my voice, I speak gently, worried the words could shatter her. "Her sister thinks someone in your family hurt Rose."

I don't know what reaction I expect, but I'm surprised when Luci nods. "I do, too."

"Do you know why?"

She buries her face in her hands and cries great, heaving sobs. Finally, she gulps in a breath and says, "Because I loved her. But he would never allow that. He would never allow anyone else to get close."

"Who?" I touch her knee. "Luci, who wouldn't?"

She shakes her head and licks her lips. "No. I can't."

"Luci, tell me."

"I can't. I'll be punished. And so will you." She lunges at me and starts dragging me toward the door. "Please, get out now. While you can. I can get the gates open."

"Good, good." I take her hand. "Then we can run and get help."

She pulls her hand free. "I can't go with you."

"Yes, you can." I wrap my arms around her in a gentle hug. She shakes in my arms like a baby bird. "You have to come with me, Luci, because I'm not leaving you alone."

The way I left Mackenzie.

Clearing my throat, I tell her the rest. About the journal, the dark tourist forum, Lina Ivarrson. And someone using Rose's phone to post on her account.

"I think Alice is in trouble now, and we can't abandon her."

"Alice?" She stumbles back, her mouth open in shock. "Rose's sister?"

"Yes. Someone messaged me pretending to be her." When she doesn't speak, I try to sway her emotions. "Rose would want you to help Alice, and she would want you to be safe."

"But I am safe."

"No, you're not." I take her hands in mine. "I don't know who you're afraid of, Luci, but you don't have to stay here. Not with him."

She's not budging, so I have to push harder. "Luci, I saw the polaroids. The pictures taken in the library."

She backs up and tries to pull away, but I won't let go. "Luci, I know what happened to you."

45

Luci's face flames pink, and she drops her head.

"I'm sorry. I know it's painful to talk about, but Luci, you know it wasn't your fault."

"It doesn't matter." She jerks free. "Nothing matters! Not me. Not the truth. Nothing but the Marteau name with all its money and influence."

"Of course you matter. We all do."

"My family isn't perfect, but my grandmother has always tried to protect me, to keep me out of the family business. And other things. The whispers and the talk of monsters." Her face goes dark. "But she never knew about him, what he did. He's sick and twisted."

"Who? Tell me."

But as she looks at me, her eyes go blank again. It's as if an automaton has slipped inside her skin. "You should go." She steps back.

She's clearly terrified of someone, whoever took the polaroids. Whoever abused her. She's been under his control since she was a child.

"I need you. I can't find Alice by myself. You and I have to get out of this place, and then we can come back with help. We can save Alice."

"The police won't do anything." Her voice is small and distant, as if she's been drugged. The reality of her life numbing any chance of hope. "There's no fighting them. They have too much power."

"We're powerful, too." I cup her face in my palms. "But only if we stick together."

Luci draws a breath as if to speak, but then her gaze shifts. She stares over my shoulder.

At something behind me.

Her brown eyes widen. "No, don't!"

I start to turn, but an arm wraps around my neck. A man's arm, his elbow bending. Squeezing, choking, until black spots fill my vision.

He holds me against his chest, so I can't see him.

His arm cinches tighter, and my lungs start to burn. My chest feels like it's going to explode. I pull at his arm, but my vision blurs.

In an instant, the world goes dark.

46

I wake in increments, first aware of the cold on my arms, then the smell of dank, sour air. When my eyes open, I think I'm still asleep, seeing nothing around me but darkness. Pure dark. Total black.

"What happened?" My throat feels sore when I speak, and clarity is lost in the haze. My mind can't translate the signals I'm receiving. I blink as if that will clear my vision, but the blindness remains.

I try to wipe my eyes, but my hand is fixed. I can't lift my arm. Am I strapped down?

The image triggers an avalanche of memories, starting with my stealthy trip through the attic, to Luci crying, to her eyes widening. And finally, a man's arm around my neck.

Despite the dark, I'm fully awake now, terror ripping through my body and setting off alarms.

The dark, the cold, the smell.

I'm in the catacombs.

And I'm strapped down.

The hard material at my back is wood, like the table described in the journal.

I know exactly where I am. A hundred feet below ground, behind the door with the Marteau symbol.

In the room where people are drained of blood.

Terror pumps in my bloodstream like poison. My vision changes colors, turning a deep crimson. I yank my arms and kick my legs, but I only rub my skin raw beneath the straps.

Eventually, I tire and release a keening cry. Desperate. Terrified.

Who brought me here? When will they return? What will they do?

I know the answer to the last, but my subconscious blocks the reality. The truth is buried deep in my psyche, lost, hidden—beneath a terror like I've never known.

My chest rises with each frantic breath, a harsh sound echoing in the chamber. The frenzied rasps of an animal caught in a trap.

As I lie in the dark, the table seems to open up beneath me. Like I'm sinking into a void, being swallowed by a hollow space in the earth.

Searching for anything to ground me in the here and now, I flail my hand around the wood. Rough, weathered, splintered. Made of one solid slab, not planks.

My fingers slip into a groove, and my stomach lurches. *That can't be what I think it is. Please, please.*

Stretching my hand as far as I can, I follow the indentation until it curves toward the edge of the table. And a sob is wrenched from my chest.

A channel, scored into the wood.

A trench to direct the flow of blood.

I feel my mind crack, and I slide to the edge of insanity.

Then I hear a sound, a clanking of metal. Like a key in a lock.

I snap to alertness.

A low scraping sound follows, and dim light fills the room. I'm blinking at the change when a bulb flashes to life in the ceiling above.

Blinded, I turn my head to the side.

"Brooke," he says, still standing in the door.

I don't want to believe it's him.

I don't want to be here.

I don't want to die.

As I tug against the restraints, I remember my first thought upon seeing the mansion.

I came here to disappear.

And when I see the emptiness in his eyes, I know I will.

47

Lyam stares down at me, no trace of the playful young man left to be seen. His brown eyes burrow into me—flat and lifeless, as if he doesn't see me, only what I can give him. Only what he wants to take.

"You?" I say, too shocked and afraid to make sense of his presence. Logically I understand why he's here, but the pieces of the puzzle didn't add up to him. Not *him*. Young Lyam, with the sweet smiles and helpful disposition.

He's so young. Too young. If he killed the little girl when Ric and Noah were teenagers, then how old was Lyam? He can't be thirty yet, not that much older than Luci.

Luci.

I remember the day in the courtyard, how Lyam reacted to Luci's flirtation with Andre. He wasn't being protective.

But *possessive.*

The polaroids flicker in my mind, like cards being shuffled. I close my eyes and swallow, afraid I'm going to be sick.

I take deep breaths. Over and over. Finally, I roll my head and shoot him a look of pure disgust. "I know what you've done."

"Yes." He lifts a shoulder. "That's why you're here."

"I'm not just talking about Rose and the girl and the other kills recorded in your journal." I clench my jaw, anger and fear blending to make me reckless. "I know what you did to Luci." I pull at my straps. "When she was just a child!"

The thought of Luci chills me again. "Where is she? What have you done to her? And to Alice?"

"Hmm. Do you really want to know? Won't it be more fun to find out for yourself?" He twists his mouth to the side, playing with me. Because he likes the game.

"You can't do this. My agent knows I'm here. How will you cover up two missing women? Two women who lived in the same apartment?"

"Who said you'd go missing?" He goes to the head of the table and leans in. He looks down on me, eye to eye, but his grin is upside down. "You'll be found in the bathtub with your wrists slit. It will all be very sad. So, so tragic. Maybe you were afraid you wouldn't get that movie role. That your career was over."

He clicks his mouth, making a *that's-too-bad* kind of sound. "All of the failure combined with the drama surrounding your last movie, well, you just didn't see a future for yourself. And, of course, you're still grieving your dead mother."

How does he know so much? Everything about me. My private life and private thoughts, as if he's crawled inside of me.

I tear my gaze away, refusing to look at him.

My eyes land on a table against the wall. Tools splay across the top: knives, straps, strange black masks. And metal implements I've never seen before. Some spiked or curved. But all of them sharp.

Someone whimpers.

It's me.

Lyam trails a finger down my cheek. I cringe away, but he

keeps talking. "Then there will be the text to your agent, telling her how deeply sorry you are."

I blink back tears. "That's what you did to Rose. You took her phone and faked the social media posts."

He moves into my line of sight and nods. "I've had a lot of practice, so I know how to cover my trail. But to tell the truth, it is sad. Truly. I liked you, Brooke, from the very start. I watched, but I might not have ever touched."

His voice turns sweet, like the Lyam I knew before. As adept at slipping into character as any actor I've known. "But you just couldn't stop digging into our family's past. Asking questions, searching online—"

My muscles clench. "How could you possibly know that? My laptop is password- protected."

He tosses back his head and laughs. "Brooke, Brooke, Brooke. Not very tech savvy, are you? As soon as you connected to our WiFi, I had access to everything." He winks at me. "I'm a skilled hacker. Started learning at a young age."

I shake my head. "But why?"

He puts his mouth next to my ear and licks the lobe before whispering, "Control. Why else?" He stands up. "Money brings power and power brings money. And people like us, we never let go of either."

As he pulls away, I glare at him. "People like you. You mean sick, depraved people. The kind who write down the evil things they do, so they can relive them again and again."

One side of his mouth lifts in a confused half-grin. "What are you talking about?"

"Your journal. Someone left it for me." As he continues to stare blankly, I say, "You know. *My Hotel Peculiar*."

Lyam only shakes his head, his smile wilting, as if he's confused.

Behind him, a rustle, then a new voice carries from the doorway.

"That's my journal," Dora says, sitting in her wheelchair. "And I want it back."

48

I watch Dora roll herself into the underground chamber. "I don't understand," I say. "The journal was written by someone young, practically a child." The numbers flit through my head, but they don't add up. "The little girl in the catacombs, that was what—nine or ten years ago?"

Dora edges up to the table, right beside my face. "She wasn't mine, I'm afraid. But the first one was."

Baffled, I wait for her to explain.

She sends a smile to her grandson. "I revealed the truth to Lyam years ago. I knew he was the one. And he wanted to impress me, to pay homage. You see, I made my first kill all on my own, without my father's knowledge or permission. And he was so proud."

She beams as if talking about winning a blue ribbon at a fair. Instead of murdering a child. "When I told Lyam, he wanted to do the same. Tradition is very important in our family."

"I wanted to be like you," Lyam says, his tone soft and obsequious, one meant to ingratiate himself to Dora.

"Unfortunately, both times were mistakes, and we both had to learn the first rule." Dora laughs. "Don't hunt at home."

My mind whirls. Two little girls. Dora's first murder, the one in her journal.

And later, Lyam. When he was in his teens.

I want to cover my face but can't move my hands. "What about the girl from the party in 1985?"

Dora frowns and almost looks embarrassed. "Another mistake. And the first and last time I ever tried ecstasy." She smiles and looks upward. "Oh, but the kill was divine. I never felt anything like it, before or since. Not even my first."

Nausea grips my gut again, but I push it back down. "That's not tradition. That's sadism."

Dora tilts her head. "No, dear. It's a necessity. An obligation."

She licks her lips and speaks in a warbly voice, almost whispered, as if in reverence. "*Vis sanguinis.*"

At first, I don't understand, the words foreign to my ears and slurred together. Then I make sense of what she's said.

Vis sanguinis. VS.

"That's what the symbol stands for," I say. "The one Grégoire Marteau always wore. The one on his tomb."

Dora nods. "Latin. It means the power of blood. You see, my great-grandfather understood the properties of human blood. He understood the power, the advantages he could gain with its consumption. It is the essence of life, the spirit of all that we are. Blood strengthens the body and the mind."

"That's insane." A breath of shock explodes from my lungs. "You murder people, because you think their blood makes you powerful?"

"Not murder, dear. Sacrifice."

She says it with such conviction, and I can see by the softness of her smile that she's trying to convince me.

"No. You don't kill people to take some mystical, made-up power. You kill people because you enjoy it."

"Oh my, dear. Such a simplistic view." Dora speaks in a pleasant voice, but her smile slips, and I can see the hate. The condescension. "My family has known this truth for generations, and the ones living at Maison Marteau accept this reality. They understand that we do what we do because we are special. We are chosen.

"Sadly," Dora continues, "the occasional family member refuses to go along. And anyone who threatens our bloodline must be removed."

"Bloodline?" I think of Luci's parents, their bodies rotting in the family crypt. Shock spreads through me like a fungus. "Did you kill your own son?"

Dora's expression flickers, a flash of sadness in her eyes, but only for a moment. "His death was quick. He and his wife were in a plane crash. Those tiny, private planes." She lifts a shoulder. "So many things that can go wrong."

Her gaze drifts back to me. "Not everyone believes in the power. Not everyone is suited for the gift. Grégoire Marteau was the first. Then his son, then my father, then me." She smiles up at her grandson. "And now my sweet Lyam."

With a shrug, she speaks to me again. "Not everyone can be special. Sometimes the gift skips a generation."

That's when it hits. "You said something similar to me before, about how some things run in families. When we spoke about Luci."

Now I'm the one to laugh, but the sound is harsh and scornful. "I thought you were talking about mental illness, that you were telling me Luci was depressed or, or . . . bipolar. But you meant she wasn't like you. Luci is the one who *got skipped*."

I glare at Dora. "You and Lyam, you're the sick ones. You're both *psychopaths*."

For the first time, her mask slips. Her top lip curls and her face twists with anger, giving me a glimpse of the real Dora. "Psychopath," she all but spits at me. "An ugly word for ignorant peasants. What would you know of the power we have?"

She waves an arm around, indicating everything above us. "Just because you were briefly *allowed* to occupy our space, don't think you understand our world."

"And what about Luci? Does she understand?" I flick my gaze to Lyam and back to Dora. "Or is she in danger? Will she have to be removed from the family line?"

"No," Lyam says quickly, stepping forward, drawing his grandmother's sharp gaze. He notices and looks at the ground.

"Luci is precious to me," Dora says, her tone softer, mediated by the apparent love she has for her only granddaughter. "One day, I will tell her the secret, and she will understand. She's smart, she's strong—"

"She's damaged."

Dora recoils, but then she carries on, ignoring what I said. "Luci will come to accept the truth of our family. She's like me in so many ways. I had hoped her father would carry on the bloodline, but he was weak."

She glances fondly at Lyam. "No matter. I have my heir. One who values the Marteau legacy."

"You made him your heir?" I can't hide my revulsion. "After what he did to Luci?"

Now I have her attention. Dora rolls close again, her mouth pinched. "What are you talking about? Lyam has always guided and protected Luci, like an older brother."

"What kind of brother—"

"Enough." Lyam grabs my hair, pulling hard enough to stretch my neck. "We know what you're trying to do. You think others haven't tried to lie their way out of this room?"

He yanks again, and I feel pinpoints of pain, hairs ripping from my scalp.

But even as I grimace, an idea flashes. I see a light at the end of this tunnel of death. And, as Lyam said, a possible way out.

I might be restrained, but I can still fight.

"Tell her what you did." I force the words through gritted teeth.

Dora looks confused. "You mean killing Luci's lover? I approved that. I was not going to lose my granddaughter to Rose. That British *goudou*."

"No. Not that. I mean the pictures. Of Luci." My gaze locks with Dora's. "The ones Lyam took."

49

Lyam shoves a knife under my chin. The point slices, and a warm trickle runs down my skin.

He knows what I'm about to tell Dora, so he presses the blade harder. As if he can cut the words from my throat.

"What pictures?" Dora slaps at his arm. "Stop now. I want to hear."

With a snarl, Lyam releases me. He retreats a few feet to stand behind Dora. But his eyes hold mine, furious, filled with warning.

I refuse to be scared into silence. "When she was a child, just a young girl. Lyam—" I jerk when he lunges forward, but then rattle out the words. "Lyam abused her."

Dora gapes at me, saying nothing.

I draw a deep, painful breath. "He abused her. Sexually."

Dora's eyes go wide, and she slams her hands on the arms of her wheelchair. "Lies!"

"No, I swear."

Lyam reaches for me.

"I have proof," I say quickly, trying to sway Dora before Lyam can get his hands on me.

Choke me or bleed me. Silence me forever.

Dora lifts a hand, and Lyam stops in his tracks. But his jaw grinds, and his veins bulge. Barely contained fury.

"There are photos," I tell Dora, my words spilling out in an urgent rush. "Polaroids. But I hid them. Somewhere you'll never find them. Not without my help."

Expression blank, Dora watches me.

Time stretches, the only sound the throb of my pulse in my ears. One heartbeat. Two. Three. F—

"Untie her." She doesn't make a move, but her tone holds authority.

"Grandmother," Lyam says, "she's obviously lying. Trying to pit us against each other."

I shake my head. "I'm not lying." But I am trying to manipulate them. If I can get out of these straps, at least I'll have a chance.

"Do it, Lyam." Dora whips her chair toward him. "Do it now. If you want to inherit, you'll do as I say."

Lyam moves to the table and unties my feet. "I don't know why you're listening to her. You know how desperate they become once they're on the table."

"Because this is my Luci, and if you've . . ." She can't finish, her hands and eyes clenching at the same time. "I told you to stop, what you did with those girls. It's improper. A disgrace to the legacy. A dishonor to our heritage."

"I did stop." Lyam whips the strap free from my right wrist, leaving a friction burn.

Dora shakes her head. "If you've hurt Luci that way, then I was clearly wrong about you. If you don't value family, you don't value tradition or our legacy."

This from the woman who murdered her own child. But I

say nothing. I only wait, biting my lip as Lyam circles to my other arm.

Dora rolls around, forming a sloppy figure eight. She thumps a fist on her armrest, overcome by her growing rage. "She isn't lying. I know it. I feel it."

Stopping, she thrusts a finger at her grandson. "I will choose another!"

Lyam pauses, the strap on my wrist unbuckled but not removed. His face drains of color. "You can't."

"Of course I can. I am the ruler here."

Lyam steps toward her. "And who would you choose? My father, the drunk? My brother, Ric, who only cares about chasing women?"

With my free hand, I reach for the remaining strap, but I keep an eye on Lyam.

He towers over Dora now, casting a shadow on her face. "Or maybe Noah, the spineless American. He's not even of your blood!"

"Luci!" Dora shouts back.

Lyam laughs darkly. "She's a weakling."

"She's only young. She can still be taught."

"No." Lyam lowers his voice, his body going still, as if his anger has drained away. To be replaced by something else.

He has his back to me, so I can't see his face.

But Dora can, and her reaction makes me work faster to free my hand.

"I won't let you. The inheritance is mine." Lyam bends over. He wraps his hands around Dora's neck. "It always has been."

Focused on the strap, I pull at the knot, trying to ignore the gurgles coming from Dora. At last, my hand pulls free and jerks upward.

Lyam doesn't notice, too consumed by killing his grandmother. Preserving his birthright, and all that power. He shoves her back into the corner, holding her up when her chair falls over. She dangles beneath the hands clenched around her throat.

Eyes bulging, turning red, she claws at his arms.

For the smallest slice of a second, I feel an urge to help her. But then I think of the girl in the tunnels, the party girl, Rose. I think of Alice.

And as Lyam chokes Dora on the cold, dirty floor, I burst through the doors into the tunnel. And I run.

50

Run. That's all I can do. Run and don't look back. Run and hide so Lyam can't find me.

My heart crushes against my ribs, but I don't dare stop—terrified, frantic, feeling Lyam reaching for me, expecting his hands to grab my shoulders.

The winding tunnel stretches before me, old bones blurring in my peripheral vision.

My feet pound on the ground, but I hear something else, a jumble of heavy sounds behind me.

Lyam.

He's on the move.

Instinct rules my body, the drive to live pushing me forward. I follow the tunnel to the three-way split. Without thinking, I dart down a shaft and keep running.

It's only when I pass the brass plaque on the wall that I know where I am. And I remember Luci. I picture her leading André and me through the catacombs. What did she tell me?

Panic fractures my mind, and my thoughts. I can't think. I just keep going.

My only chance is to evade Lyam. To lose him in the underground passageways. He probably knows the catacombs as if he was born to them.

And in some ways, he was.

My breaths burst from my burning lungs, ragged and loud. Giving me away. When I come to another split, I stop long enough to glance both ways.

As I stare, the tunnels seem to shrink around me.

And then I hear it.

A steady, rhythmic sound. Soft but firm, growing louder every second. The sound of footsteps on gravel. Lyam is close.

Veering to the right, I sprint until I come to another division. I choose a shaft, but it ends abruptly, with an arched doorway blocked by iron bars. A bright light shines on the other side. Some sort of utility room? A place where I can find a weapon?

Running to the bars, I push and pull. A padlock hanging down.

And something else. Inside on the floor.

A body, curved in fetal position, blonde hair falling across the lower half of her face.

It's Alice. And she's not moving.

I gasp. "Alice. Alice, can you hear me?" No response, so I take a closer look. She's curled inward, one arm extended. Beneath the curve of her elbow, a dark stain spreads on the floor.

Blood. Fresh. Seeping.

"Alice." I try rousing her again, but there's something about her motionless form. So quiet and still. Too still. I'm not sure she's breathing.

My hands grip the cold bars—old, rusty, and rough on my palms. "I'm sorry," I say, my voice splintering. "I'm so sorry." I let my forehead fall against the metal, staring at Alice.

That's when the lights go out.

Nothingness surrounds me. Everything is dark. My heart

pumps in my ears, the beats so fast they blend to a single sound. *Gadunkgadunkgadunkgadunkgadunk.*

Blood pounding in my head, I turn and press my back to the bars. But still, there's nothing, only a fluid gray filling my vision.

I lose track of time. Pressed to the door, my brain stalling out in the absence of light. I'm almost grateful for the cold on my skin, and the shuffle of my feet on dirt. Physical stimuli keeping me grounded.

I'm still alive.

But I can't stay here, trapped in a dead end.

Groping for the wall, I keep one hand on the rough stone and follow it to the corner. I edge forward, going in the same direction as before, keeping contact with the wall as I walk blindly down the tunnel.

Adrenaline hyper-focuses my mind. I have one clear goal.

Stay away from Lyam.

The scrape of feet sounds far too loud, but I keep moving, following the wall. Maybe I'll find another door. A way out of this subterranean hell.

My bare foot lands in water, and I bite back a scream. The cold liquid stuns me, and I lift my foot. A thousand grotesque images flicker in my brain.

Fungus. Rot. Blood.

Even in the dark, I clench my eyes shut. *Stop it. It's none of those things. Only runoff from the rain.*

Another few breaths and I calm down. I take another step.

Water covers the sole of my foot, and silt squishes between my toes.

Hardening myself, I take another step.

The water rises higher, almost to my ankle. A tremble overtakes me, but not from cold. I remember the night with Luci and André. I remember her warning.

Not that way. The tunnels flood when we have too much rain.

And it's been raining.

A lot.

Moving cautiously, I ignore the freezing water, even as it rises to my calves. Even when I shiver and my toes go numb.

The water sloshes and gurgles with every step, the sound brutally loud in the dark.

"Brooooke." Lyam's voice echoes through the catacombs, his sing-song voice close behind. Too close.

I have no choice. I need to keep going.

Hand scraping the wall for guidance, I move faster. Putting space between myself and the sadistic glee in Lyam's voice.

My leg suddenly drops from under me, and I fall, plunging into a pool of black.

51

The dark water swallows me whole.

I hold my breath, even as terror jolts through me like lightning in my veins. I can't tell up from down, only blackness pouring into my eyes, my ears, my nose. My soaked clothes drag on me like weights, pulling me down into the abyss.

Just when I'm certain I'll disappear, my feet bump against the bottom, and I thrust myself to the surface. My head breaks the water, and I gulp for air.

My gasp is loud, ricocheting off water and stone, echoing in what sounds like a hollowed-out space.

I flail my arms and reach for a wall, but my limbs feel like rubber. Cold. So cold. My heart is a constant flutter in my chest, not only from panic but the sudden drop in temperature.

I have to get out.

For seconds, my fear of drowning in the murk overrides my fear of Lyam.

Kicking gently, I propel myself forward. I've lost my bearings and don't know where I'm going. If I can find a wall, maybe I can feel my way to a tunnel.

I can't see, but somehow the space doesn't *feel* big. Something about the way sound travels, my ragged breaths bouncing back at me.

Easing through the water, I try not to think about how cold I am or how deep it is. Or what might lie below.

Serious shivers have set in, signs of hypothermia, so when my hand finally slaps against rock, I don't mind the painful scrape on my skin. The stone is jagged, but it's solid. Reassuring.

As I'm tracing my hand upward, searching for anywhere to climb out, a slight shuffle fills the hollow space. Then a scrape.

"Brooke. I know you're there."

Lyam's voice in the dark, floating from somewhere above me.

I need to move away from Lyam, but I'm still operating blind. And scared of getting lost in the flooded tunnels.

Lungs burning, I break the surface, gasp for air, then go back under. The rocky wall scrapes my palm raw, but at least I know I'm moving in one direction.

The next time I come up, I keep my head above water, drawing deep, filling breaths. I need a moment. I need oxygen.

Gently moving my arms and legs, I glide through the water. Silent. Stealthy. Straining for any sound that might give Lyam away.

When I first see the light, I blink and blink, certain I'm imagining things. I've gotten used to the dark, and it takes my brain a few seconds to comprehend.

A pearl-like color splashes on a wall. Dim. Pale. But definitely light.

Be an exit. Please, be an exit.

A loud splash carries through the cavern, followed by the sound of limbs chopping through water.

Lyam's in the water.

And he's moving fast.

Letting go of the wall, I kick off the stone, following the light instead. I find a burst of energy and swim at full speed.

When I round a corner, the light brightens, so I bullet forward. I can see around me now, the gloomy water and craggy walls. And there, beneath the glow, what looks like steps carved from the stone.

I can get out. I can get out.

When I reach the steps, my hand slides in a layer of slime. Drawing my knees forward, I start a slow, cautious climb. Water streams down from above, but finally, slippery algae becomes coarse rock.

I run up the steps, feet slapping against stone. The stairs wind in a spiral, climbing higher and higher. My thigh muscles scream from overuse.

"Don't waste your time, Brooke." Lyam's gleeful voice rises from below. "You can't get out that way."

My heart clenches at his words, the loss of hope crushing my ribs.

He's lying. Trying to trick me. I convince myself to keep going. Light is pouring in from somewhere, and if I can reach the surface, I can find help.

Near the top, I stumble when a stone shifts beneath my foot. But my forward motion carries me up the last few steps. I stumble into a chamber.

Solid walls enclose the small space, illuminated by light coming in through a hole.

No. A window. A window in a door.

I know this place.

Throwing myself against the door, I press my face to the slit in the metal. Falling rain hazes the world outside, but I know what I'm looking at. The alley behind the gardens.

I'm locked behind the mysterious door.

I drag my hands up and down the metal, hoping to find a

lever, some way to open the door. All I find is a hole where a handle might have been. And I remember the padlock on the other side.

I'm not getting out.

Terror bubbles up, and I shove my arm out the hole. "Help!" Waving my hand, I scream into the gray. "Please, I'm here. Help me!"

"Broooooke." Lyam is taunting me again, letting me know he's coming. I hear the smile in his voice and realize he had the advantage all along.

As I listen to him climbing the steps behind me, I press my face to the bars. I scream again. And again and again.

But no one answers. No one hears me. No one will help.

And now I'm trapped.

52

The downpour drowns my screams, cutting me off from the world outside. But I can't quit. Can't give up. I press my face to the window and try again.

Nothing but the constant drone of water. Even if my voice carried to the park, no one is out there, not in this weather.

I glance around the space. Small. Cramped. Dark. Several feet between the metal door and the stairway leading down. Down to the catacombs. And straight to Lyam.

With my eyes shut, I press my back to the door. The ground shifts beneath my feet—a sudden shudder and tilt. Only it's me who's quaking.

Because there's nowhere to run.

Nowhere to hide.

I'm all by myself. Alone with a killer.

My jaw chatters from cold and fear. Drenched clothes. The verge of hypothermia. Bare feet and empty hands. But wait . . . *the knife*.

I slap my hand on my back pocket, feeling for the blade I'd hidden there. But of course, it's gone. Taken when I was unconscious. Or lost. When I fled through the tunnels or fell in the water.

Sound rises from the stairwell, and my heart shreds itself.

Slow, steady footsteps. Coming closer.

Lyam is here.

Turning in a circle, I scour the ground, the walls, searching for anything I can use to defend myself. Maybe a rock, or piece of stone if I can free it from the mortar.

Wait. On the stairs. The broken step.

I drop to my knees at the top of the stairs, dragging my hand along the edge of each step. I lost my footing when something shifted beneath my foot. If it's cracked, maybe, just maybe—

A sharp point gouges my palm.

My hand jerks in reflex, but then I grab onto the piece that jabbed me. Part of the step slants down, probably cracked long ago, damaged further when I stepped on it.

Gripping the broken section, I pull up and then push down, lending the weight of my body to the effort.

"I don't usually have to work this hard." Lyam's voice. He stands below me on the steps, a lazy grin on his face.

My throat tightens and my skin chills. My nervous system is at full tilt, yet he stands there, smiling.

How is he so calm? Why isn't he angry?

Because he's done this before. Hunted women like prey, mice in a maze scurrying for escape.

This is the part he enjoys the most.

"Come here," he says, his tone confident. Commanding. As if after all this, I'll simply obey.

I keep my eyes on his but slide my legs down. Sitting, I angle to block my hand from his view and continue to work the broken stone.

He climbs a step. Then another. He scrapes something along the wall. A long, metal tool. With a hook.

I remember the table in the bleeding room. Covered in torture devices.

"Get up." He snaps at me, testy and impatient, used to people following his orders.

"Or what?" I ask, trying to keep him talking as I continue to move the fragment back and forth. "You'll strap me back on that table like you did Alice? And Rose? And how many others before?"

The chunk shifts beneath my hands with a sandpaper scrape.

Lyam takes the final step, looming above me in the tight stairwell.

Only the space of a breath separates us now.

"All of you thought you were so special. Beautiful, or accomplished, or famous." He drags his eyes up and down my body and licks his lips. "Exactly the kind of girls I like to bring down a peg or two."

He leans over and strokes my neck. "But you were the most fun, Brooke. I loved watching you rehearse your lines. So serious. So dedicated. There's more to you than just sparkle. I wanted to let you live. I really did." He tilts his head. "So I could keep watching."

Arm stretched behind me, I push and pull on the hunk of stone. The ragged edge slices my palm. But I ignore the pain, squeezing tight as I try to keep Lyam from noticing.

"You're a monster," I say, filling my voice with contempt. I want him to hear how disgusted I am. I want to keep his focus on my words.

And not what I'm doing behind my back.

"Killing them was never about power in the blood. Not for you." I curl my lip in revulsion. Even now, as he stands over me. Bigger, stronger, and experienced in the ways of murder. "You're nothing special. Just an everyday psycho, a common pervert who was born into privilege and had the luxury of living out his sick fantasies."

Lyam's face twists, anger narrowing his empty eyes. "There's nothing common about me." The slap comes out of nowhere. An explosion in my cheek before I slump against the wall.

Lyam drops down, straddling my body. He wraps one hand around my throat. And with the other, he lifts the hook.

He presses the sharp point to my breast. Then gives one, quick pull.

I scream when the metal cuts my flesh.

Lyam tightens his grip on my throat, squeezing until I start to wheeze.

"Don't worry. You'll be back," he says. "I'll watch your sparkle fade many times before I'm through."

As he chokes me, my free hand shoots out, pressing against his chest. But his arms are longer, and my attempts to block him are like a child's—weak and ineffective.

My lungs seize up. My head feels swollen. And beneath the pain, the horrible knowledge of what comes next.

Because Lyam told me.

He'll choke me until I black out, then revive me again. He'll bring me back just to kill me. Over and over and over, watching me die until he gets bored. Until the last time.

The last time for me.

But there will always be another girl.

The thought sparks a fury in my belly. And fury becomes a fire, a blaze of energy burning from my center. I lift my arms up through his, then drive my elbows back down.

His arms buckle, breaking his grip, and he slides to one side.

Air flows down my throat like cool water, giving me a small boost, just enough to kick out. My foot hits Lyam on his hip, and he loses his balance. Gaining his feet, he leans against the wall to steady himself. Which buys me a few crucial seconds.

I roll over and smash my hand on the broken chunk. A loud *crack!* fills the stairwell as the piece breaks free. I grab it and stand up, facing the monster.

It's not a brick. And Lyam's not a vampire.

But close enough.

Lyam lunges for me, and I slice out, leaving a gash in his forearm.

"Fucking bitch!" He curses me, his eyes narrowed and teeth bared.

I scramble to my feet and into the chamber, backing up to the metal door.

Lyam rushes after me, too angry to care about the weapon in my hand.

With a roar, I smash the rock into his jaw.

He grunts and lists to one side, eyes widening as blood trickles from his mouth.

Taking advantage, I hit him again. Hard. Something small and sharp pings off of my cheek.

A shard of tooth.

Groaning, Lyam clasps both hands to his face. He sways on his feet. Seconds pass as he stands in shock, cradling his jaw. Then his expression hardens, and the anger is back.

He steps toward me.

I raise the bloody chunk of rock.

Lyam tries to speak, but the sound is a gurgling mumble. After one last glare, he retreats, backing away with unsteady steps.

He backs toward the stairwell, teeters on the top step.

Gravity overtakes him, his upper body bending back until one leg flails in the air. Then he's gone.

Thuds and grunts echo as he tumbles, but at last, he's silent.

I wrap my arms around myself and lean against the door.

Emotion builds in my gut before climbing out in tearless sobs. Every breath hurts, whistling through my swollen throat.

Still desperate to be outside and away from this place, I grasp for the rim of the window.

A hand wraps around mine, and I scream.

"Brooke. It's okay. It's okay." Wet fingers squeeze mine. André. "Help is coming." He reaches through and puts a hand on my shoulder.

"How did you know?" I ask, my voice scraping through bruised tissue.

"Luci called me. She called everybody." He pats my shoulder. "I'm here now, and I won't leave you. Just hold on."

His assuring gaze fixes on me, and I sink with relief. With it come the tears. Tears of pain and fear, anger and loss. A flood of emotion that chokes my words. With my head resting on the door and my hand in André's, all I can do is nod.

And hold on.

53

The foyer is filled with people. I sit on a bench in Maison Marteau, a blanket around my shoulders and Luci at my side.

It's been an hour since André found me, and he, too, remains close by. After Luci called him and told him what was happening, he went out into the storm, checking the nearest entrances to the catacombs.

When he found me, he stayed with me, his hand locked with mine. Not long after, a neighbor came with tools to open the door.

I'll never forget that moment. The metallic snap of the bolt cutter, padlock clanking to the cobblestones. I pushed out for my first breath of freedom, never happier to see the sky. Even as it poured rain on my face.

Across the room, Ric stands huddled with his parents. Chantal and Vincent wear tense expressions, but neither of them looks like they've shed a tear.

Though their son's body lies below us in the dark.

Lyam didn't tumble far, but the fall was fatal. André and the neighbor went down long enough to find him and confirm his death.

His body will be recovered, but not before Alice's. Luci made sure of this when the first police officers arrived. She sent them down with a hand-drawn map after I described the room.

The room where I found Alice.

I picture the dark, red stain beneath her, and shivers course through me.

"You're freezing," Luci says, wrapping her arm around me as if to share her warmth.

I meet Luci's gaze and squeeze her hand. "I'm okay," I tell her, a hitch of emotion in my voice. "Thanks to you."

Her eyes water, and she nods. "I'm just sorry I didn't—"

Sirens wail outside, growing louder as they approach. A chaotic racket from multiple vehicles.

André opens the doors to reveal a police car and two ambulances pulling into the courtyard, the imposing black gates now open wide.

A uniformed officer gets out from behind the wheel as two plainclothes men exit from the passenger-side doors. One of them is Armand Phillipe, the Chief of Judicial Police. A man I met at the monsters' dance.

And a close friend to the Marteau family.

He enters the foyer, his jaw firm and his chest puffed out, arrogance surrounding him like bad cologne. He spares me a glance before speaking to another man in a suit. Then he makes a beeline for Vincent, Chantal, and Ric.

The four of them share a heated exchange, their harsh whispers a low, unintelligible scrape.

Watching them takes me back to the catacombs, to the room with Lyam and Dora. What had Dora told me? The ones living at Maison Marteau accept the reality.

The reality of murder.

Now the remaining family members huddle together, anxiety and angst lining their faces.

Chief Phillipe pushes his hands at them in a halting motion, and they all fall silent. Turning back to Luci and me, he gestures to the other man and they both come over to me.

"Ms. Summers." Chief Phillipe bows his head. "Such terrible circumstances in which we meet again. I'm sure you're tired, so Captain Armand will be brief. A few questions before you are transported to the hospital."

He gestures to the medics filing inside. Two of them carry a stretcher and call out something in French.

André answers and guides them toward the back of the house.

"They will go down," Luci tells me. "They will bring Alice . . ." She bites her bottom lip and looks away.

But I don't need to hear the rest.

I know what she means.

"Perhaps we could go somewhere private?" the captain says, dragging my attention back to him.

I glance between him and Chief Phillipe, feeling exposed beneath their piercing stares. I tug the blanket, pulling it tighter as worry knots in my chest. I don't trust this man. "I'd rather stay with Luci and André."

"I'm afraid that won't be possible." The captain smiles. Too congenial. Too smooth. "I should speak to you alone."

"*Non.*" A new man walks through the doors, his steps quick and his expression hard. His stare directed at the captain and Chief Phillipe, he barrages them with French.

Stepping in front of Luci and me, the new arrival blocks us from the chief. "Ms. Summers, Mademoiselle Marteau. My name is Luc Denis, and I will be handling this investigation."

Chief Phillipe's face turns white. "I did not send for you."

Mr. Denis turns slowly to face the chief. "The Paris prosecutor's office sent me."

"Why? On whose authority do, do—" he stutters and takes a deep breath before switching to French again.

"You will not be involved in this case, sir." Mr. Denis cuts him off, answering in English, presumably for my benefit. "You and Captain Armand should leave now."

I understand what's happening, and the knot releases.

Denis turns his back on the officers and speaks to Luci. "Our office has received a call from Noah Marteau. He insists we ensure the integrity of this investigation."

Luci stands and stares across the room, her eyes locked on Chantal, Vincent, and Ric. "Yes, I know." She speaks again to Mr. Denis. "Because I'm the one who asked Noah to call you."

She holds herself tall and straight, but her arms tremble.

So I stand with her and take her hand.

"Very good." Mr. Denis nods at us before moving to the open doors. He signals someone outside, and two more men in suits appear. One of them walks to me and the other crosses to the three Marteaus across the room.

I can't hear what the investigator says to them, but Ric surges forward and speaks rapidly in French.

Vincent stands and grabs Ric's arm, but his son breaks free. Ignoring his parents, Ric follows the investigator outside.

Before any of us can say anything, voices carry from the hallway. The paramedics return with their stretcher, and one of them says something in French.

Luci's hand clenches mine.

"What is it?" I ask. "What did they say?"

Her eyes are wide when she looks at me. "He said . . . *she's alive.*"

Three Months Later

"You're going to do great." Noah smiles at me from the screen of my phone. "You've got this."

I'm in LA, and he's in Paris, but our friendship remains intact. A friendship forged by trauma, and something more.

It's the something more that keeps me hoping I'll get back to France one day.

"Thanks. I can't believe how nervous I am." I run a hand down the front of my shirt, then stop to sit on a wooden bench. "How are things there? Is it settling down yet?"

"For the most part, although we still have a handful of reporters and paparazzi that won't give up."

"A new story will take them away soon." As I say the words, a sense of déjà vu whispers over the nape of my neck. It's hard to believe how things have changed. Once I was the one hiding from scandal and the dogged press.

Now it's Noah and Luci.

The events at Maison Marteau changed the family forever, leaving Noah and his young cousin in charge. Now it's their duty to guard the gates, and try to pick up the pieces of a shattered dynasty.

Lyam didn't kill Dora that day, at least not down in the catacombs. First responders found her on the floor, barely drawing breath. Despite receiving the best medical care, she died two days later in the hospital.

But not before making Luci her heir. Heir to the mansion, the chocolate company, and every dime of the Marteau fortune.

And in a move that shocked everyone, she designated Noah as trustee.

On top of dealing with the press and the authorities, Noah is not only supporting Luci emotionally, but he's guiding her, training her in the ways of business and money management.

A door opens and footsteps clatter, bringing me back to the present. I glance down the hallway to see who's entered. A woman in a pencil skirt and heels clips her way across the marble floor. Briefcase hanging from one hand, she turns and disappears through a doorway.

"Luci doesn't seem to mind the press," Noah says, continuing our conversation. "Or if she does, she's not letting it show." A cloud passes behind his gaze. "She's different now, after what happened. But she's finally starting to smile again. She's strong. She'll get through."

"She will," I say firmly. Because I believe it.

Dora could have chosen Ric or Vincent, yet she picked the one person who would put an end to the twisted history of the Marteaus. No more missing women. No more abuse of power.

And no more *vis sanguinis*.

Luci and Noah have their own power. A strength they'll need in the coming months.

I don't know what changed in Dora at the end. Maybe it was the loss of Lyam or his betrayal of her family values.

Or maybe she simply loved her granddaughter. A child she'd failed to protect from the monster she created.

Despite it all, Luci has a good heart. Damaged and bruised, maybe, but in the process of healing. Through therapy, freedom, and Noah's steady hand.

As it turns out, Luci didn't know the family secret. To her, Dora was a loving grandmother and stern matriarch. Not a serial killer with a thirst for blood.

Still, she'd become suspicious, sensing something was wrong after Rose disappeared.

Dora sheltered her from most of the horror, and Luci's ignorance is why she's not being investigated. Vincent and Chantal are another matter. They've been charged with a slew of crimes, including the French equivalents of accessory to murder and obstruction of justice.

And Ric? A growing number of women have alleged sexual assault, so he struck a deal with the prosecutor. He's spilling all he knows about the family murders, trying to reduce his time in prison. He admits he and Lyam both came into my apartment.

Lyam to stalk me.

But Ric for different reasons.

He's the one who left the *Carmilla* book for me to find, just as he left Dora's journal and the photos for Rose. He wanted someone to go to the police, to report Dora and Lyam.

His plan was to blow everything open. With Dora and Lyam out of the picture, he assumed he would be the next chosen heir.

But he never counted on Luci.

Lots of people didn't count on Luci. But I did, and she saved my life.

"How's André doing?" I ask, smiling as I think of the presumed playboy turned hero.

"He's good. He's good." Noah lifts his brows. "He's been spending a lot of time with Alice."

I can't stop myself from laughing. Even in our darkest hours, life can surprise us with a happy twist.

Dora wasn't the only one brought up alive. When paramedics rushed a barely breathing Alice straight to the hospital, André went to sit with her. He didn't want her to be alone when she woke up.

Her parents arrived later that night.

But André still stayed with her.

My laughter dies as I picture Alice, her body crumpled on the cold, hard ground. She knows too well what her sister suffered, and now so do her and Rose's parents.

I don't know the specifics of what Lyam did to the bodies, but eventually they became part of the ossuary in the catacombs. Bones of murdered women. Hidden in plain sight.

I was almost one of them.

But I made it out, and the Marteaus are the ones behind bars. Though they aren't the only ones in trouble. The Prosecutor's Office in Paris is pursuing charges against Chief Phillipe and Captain Armand, along with any other corrupt officers. Those bought and controlled by the Marteau fortune.

They all need to be held accountable.

"So." Noah walks through his apartment and sits. I see the sofa in the background and long to be there with him. "When do you start shooting?"

"Three weeks." I got the role of Claudia in *The Whisper House* shortly after my return to the States, but I still get a warm thrill in my chest every time I talk about the movie.

If I'd been worried about being attached to scandal before Paris, the horrors of Maison Marteau amped up those concerns even more. But when I met Joyce Sandman, she looked me in the eye, said I was right for the part, and nothing else mattered.

I raise my brows at Noah. "You're not going to believe who's playing—"

"Brooke Summers." The woman in the pencil skirt leans out of the door and looks at me.

"Sorry," I tell Noah. "I have to go in now."

"Good luck," he says, then, "oh, and give Clairee a rub on the belly for me."

"I will." The last time I saw my cat was this morning, splayed on the floor and soaking up the California sun. "She's such a sweetie. Now Lin is saying she wants a cat."

With one last grin, Noah waves and wishes me good luck again.

Once the call ends, I stand, smooth down my hair, and walk to the woman. I rub my hands on my thighs. *This is it.*

"Ms. Summers?" she clarifies.

At my nod, she directs me to the lone chair on one side of a conference table.

Several other people sit in the room, all of them on the other side of the table or seated along the wall. I spare a brief glance for two people in the corner.

I don't need to look long.

I know who's there.

Still moving at an efficient pace, the woman in the pencil skirt sets a glass of water in front of me.

At one end of the table, a man sits with a laptop in front of him and headphones covering his ears. Files and notepads cover the glossy wood along with what I presume is some sort of recording equipment.

Taking off the headphones, the man stands and speaks to the others at the table. "All set." Then to me. "Ms. Summers, let's begin. Please, raise your right hand."

I do as instructed.

"Do you affirm that the evidence you shall give to the court in this matter shall be the truth, the whole truth, and nothing but the truth, and that this is your solemn affirmation?"

Now I do look at the corner. I take a deep breath, sit up taller, and meet Mackenzie's eyes.

I answer her grateful smile with one of my own and say, "I do."

Afterword

Did you enjoy reading *The Paris Rental*?

If so, please consider leaving a review on Amazon! Check out my website where you can sign up for my newsletter and be the first to get updates on my books.

http://www.rachelkeerey.com

You can also follow me on Amazon, or join the Reader Hangout on Facebook.

See you there!

Acknowledgments

Like many thriller readers, I also love true crime documentaries. I already had the idea for this book whirling in my head when I watched a particular three-part series on HBO about a man who had done horrible things, but more than that, he came from a line of men who'd done horrible things. The idea that cruelty and evil could be taught—and literally passed down through generations—stuck with me and became the final piece of The Paris Rental story. And as my fellow thriller readers know, there's nothing more terrifying than things that happen in real life.

I owe a great debt to many people for their advice, support, and hard work in taking this story from a documentary-inspired note on a sticky pad to an actual book. I want to thank my brilliant editing team, Kristen Weber for her invaluable feedback on the story and also for her unending patience, Halley Sutton for her brilliant suggestions on making the story shine, and Rosie Walker for her keen eye for detail.

I am grateful to my first readers for their help in making this book the best version it could be. Maja Sickert, Dorothey Beecher, Kelly Baucum, Cynthia Rubino, Shelley Manner, Cheryl Buckham, Sheri Korker, and Monica Wilson, you have my gratitude! And of course, my friends in the Reader Hangout. You have all been so supportive, encouraging and, above all, patient as you waited for this book to find its way into the world. And to the Psychological Thrillers Readers group, I've been watching and learning from all of you over the last few years. Your opinions have not gone unnoticed!

Lastly, but never least of all, to David I give my endless love and appreciation for never giving up on the dream of this new genre. And for always magically knowing when I needed a pizza night. I couldn't do it without you.

About the Author

Rachel Keerey writes psychological thriller novels. She currently lives in Germany with her husband and can usually be found reading, watching scary movies, or taking walks with her cats. When not writing, she also enjoys exploring castles and abandoned buildings. *The Paris Rental* is her debut novel.

www.ingramcontent.com/pod-product-compliance
Lightning Source LLC
LaVergne TN
LVHW091106080826
845145LV00008B/1828

* 9 7 8 1 9 4 2 3 1 8 5 8 3 *